B.T. ANNETT

The Perfect Blood Series
BOOK 1

This is a work of fiction. Names, characters, places and incidents either are the product of the author's imagination or are used fictitiously. Any resemblance to actual persons, living or dead, events, or locales is entirely coincidental.

Copyright © 2022 by B. T. Annett

All rights reserved. No part of this book may be reproduced or used in any manner without written permission of the copyright owner except for the use of quotations in the book review.

First paperback edition March 2022

Book cover design – Coverdungeon

ISBN 978-1-7397888-0-3 (Paperback)
ISBN 978-1-7397888-1-0 (ebook)

Published by B.T.Annett

www.btannett.com

To all the fourteen-year-olds out there with an idea, believe in yourself because I did.

To my first reader and best friend, Thank You.

The Darkol, Bible of Mayhemic Magic.

The fifth Perfect Blood shall change the world...

Prologue

It was a rare, humid and sticky night in the small town of Oakdale, England. The roads were calm and the surrounding forests were still. Everyone was at home and everything was as it should be. However, deep within the moonlit forest stood a tall, lithe man wearing a large trench coat. The tall man with cold, hard features held his mouth cautiously against the neck of a young woman, aware of his surroundings through his impeccable hearing.

He held her upright effortlessly, pinning her against the rough bark of a large oak tree. She had succumbed to his strength, having stopped fighting some time ago. She gazed upon the moon, frail, now visibly close to death.

The looming figure cracked his head back from her neck, taking a deep breath. Under the faint light gifted by the moon, two visible, elongated white fangs dazzled in the light. The man's mouth was smothered with crimson liquid; blood dribbled from the tips of his fangs. A bloody mess had been left around the girl's neck where two puncture holes continued to ooze blood. His two fangs slowly retracted back into his gums, vanishing in between his teeth.

"Tasty, but not tasty enough," he said haughtily. He had fed the roaring and immediate hunger within his body. Eventually, the sweet scent of this woman had lost its appeal. Her breathing was now shallow and barely discernible; she was deeply unconscious. He bent once again and licked the neck of the woman, savouring the last few ounces of blood. He flicked his long tongue around his lips to check for any last drops of blood as he turned away, walking gracefully and noiselessly through the trees without so much as a glance behind him. A satisfied smirk played around the cruel corners of his mouth.

The trees thinned, and the edge of the forest grew closer; the figure could clearly see cars rushing by on the Oakdale bypass beyond. He exited the forest opposite Oakdale Athletic Club, the warm and welcoming clubhouse fully illuminated. The girl he had almost just murdered had been wearing the distinctive athletic club uniform, and he quickly glanced away without pity or remorse, secure in his own invincibility.

Heading towards the town centre, following the road along the edge of the forest with a smooth, confident walk, pulling his hood closely around his face, he felt the temperature suddenly start to drop. What was previously a clear starlit sky had now been quickly obscured by thick, dark clouds. Feeling a prickle of unease as the stars were disappearing from view, the man allowed himself a quick glance behind to see if he was alone, and he was.

Walking into a biting wind, he gazed up the road and noticed it had entered an untimely peaceful stretch. With certain unease, a pristine layer of white fog exited the neighbouring forest. The fog moved across the ground like an agile ballerina, consuming the road.

"What the..." But before he finished, the fog slapped the man backwards through the air, and it was when he slammed against the ground he realised this was no ordinary fog.

The invincibility he once felt was now dwindling away. Jumping to his feet, the bright lights that had so recently been visible from the athletics club had now been consumed by the substantial fog. Creatures such as he didn't panic, top of the predator list, but even they were hunted…

"Is that you, Zouku? If this is your idea of a joke, it isn't funny." He shouted into the wild fog which swallowed the sound. Eagerly awaiting a laughing reply from his friend, he was instead met by reedy laugher.

A sudden thought crossed his mind, *Was the woman whom he was just with a creature of the supernatural world?* He questioned himself but quickly dismissed the thought, remembering her distinctive sweet scent, still even being able to taste her. Supernatural creatures always had a different scent, and he shook his head, certain now that whatever this was, it was unrelated to his recent meal.

"Okay, Zouku," he shouted. "That's enough now." But the utter silence which followed was disorientating. Desperation started to etch into the man's body; he was ready to hear his friend's ridiculous laugh and more than ready to forgive him.

Unexpectedly, something like a hand brushed against the face of the man. Startled, he backtracked, falling to the ground. The fog separated as a layer of grass comforted his fall. Massaging his hands into the ground, trying to think what was happening, the man was snapped out of his trance when he became aware of the footsteps walking towards him. Forcing himself back to his feet, he whirled around screaming, "Who's there?" But silence followed.

Flaring his nostrils, now closer to panic than he had ever been, he breathed deeply through his nose, searching for a scent that might provide some sort of explanation.

"I am here," came a deep, monotone voice through the fog. The voice seemed to vibrate within him, and the last remnants of hope that this was his friend faded away. For the first time in his long life, he could taste his own fear.

A dark abyss began to open within the heavenly white fog in front of the man's eyes. A black, cloaked being exited, levitating gracefully over the ground. The man's terror, now all-consuming, rooted him to the spot.

There were no features to the ghostly sight. A hood was pulled low, and an empty black hole where the face should have been looked towards the man. He had never faced anything like this before. The cloaked figure extended one of their arms, draping a long part of the cloak with them. The hooded figure started chanting in a language unknown to humans, a language which the man knew belonged to witches.

Frozen with fear, the man was ripped from the security of the ground without warning by a mighty unseen force, hurling him into the air. An unbearable pressure squeezed the man's body as if he were deep underwater. He could not move, could not so much as blink, barely able to breathe. This force was like nothing he had ever known, but he did know that this was the end.

"You foul creatures are a curse on this earth," said the cloaked figure, revulsion rich in their voice. The imprisoned man attempted to reply but failed, when unexpectedly, there was a slight release in pressure that had constrained the man's voice as if the cloaked figure wanted him to reply.

"Who are you?" he breathed.

Laughing in a deep and mirthless tune, the cloaked figure replied, "It has been many years but, my powers have returned, and I have returned to finish what I started. I am after your leader. He has something I require."

"You'll never have it," said the man, using all his strength to spit these words at the ghostly figure.

The immense pressure grew once again around the man's throat, silencing him as he attempted to speak.

"The first death shall be the beginning…" said the cloaked figure before they started chanting in a language which even the vampire knew was not known to witches – instead it belonged to something darker, something Mayhemic.

The cloaked figure made a final guttural noise, like a command, and then the fog suddenly began to move into a formation of a hand. The fog hand reached out and grasped the man within its palm. The man began to sing a blood-curdling scream as the fog burned the man's skin, his hair singed away before his lips disintegrated revealing his blood-stained teeth. The man's scream thinned, becoming a distant hissing sound. The fog started churning around him, no longer white but a dark, cherry red colour. The dark red colour was spreading, leaching into the surrounding fog. The hooded figure lowered its arm and watched the Mayhemic spell do its work. Spitting on the remains of the burnt body, the hooded figure turned and disappeared into the fog. The fog disappeared as suddenly as it had arrived – the people of Oakdale going about their business as if nothing had happened. The night sky returned once again, and the cars on the bypass were once again prominent. All was as it should be, as if nothing had happened. This was for the exception of the grisly new addition of a burnt and blistered dead vampire, who was securely impaled through the abdomen upon a long, dark wooden stake set deeply into the ground high among the trees. Brandished on the wooden stake was a sigil which the world hadn't seen for years. Two dots, one on top of the other, with inverted brackets either side. The Dark Witch had begun their ancient plan.

1
The Beginning...

The teenage boy was gasping and almost out of breath. He was running as fast as his legs could carry him. The people behind… they were gaining on him. This was the final push. Aiden wanted to look behind, but he didn't want to see how close they were. The wails of the surrounding people filled the air, everywhere he looked he could see people shouting and screaming; he could not tell if they were cheering or just screaming for the sake of it. Aiden could hear the pounding footsteps approaching. He was almost there, almost to safety. The sweat that curled his dark hair attempted to blur his vision, but his eyebrows protected his eyes. A voice echoed in the back of his head, *Never give up, keep going*. Aiden knew the voice; it belonged to his father. Turning the final corner, the words of his father still in his head, Aiden saw it – the finish line.

Only another hundred metres to go and he would be victorious in the 400-metre race.

The patriotic American accents continued to scream and shout as the race entered its final leg. Aiden was in the lead, members of the opposition trailing behind him, but Aiden was not going to let them catch him. He rotated his head to see where his dad said he would be, but as he looked, Aiden realised his father wasn't there. Aiden felt his heart tighten. *Was his father actually here?* He said he would be when he'd dropped Aiden off earlier. Beginning to doubt whether or not he could win this race, Aiden scanned through the crowd in a last attempt to locate his father, but he was nowhere to be seen.

Aiden was almost there, only a few metres away. His feet were burning within his shoes, the friction between sole and track felt as if his feet were being boiled, but the red ribbon lay ahead of him.

Anticipating breaking through the ribbon, Aiden realised that wasn't going to happen. In the corner of his eye, he watched his rival storm past him, claiming victory in the race and tearing apart the ruby-coloured ribbon. Aiden felt his heart drop to the bottom of his stomach. He looked towards his teammates and coach on the side lines and the shock on their faces. He'd been so certain he could win for them.

Crossing the finish line, watching the opposition's team throw the winner up in the air, Aiden saw what could have been his. Struggling to remain standing, Aiden collapsed to the ground, cradling his head in between his legs, embarrassed by his loss and wanting to be left alone.

The minutes turned into hours as families and teams left the club, leaving Aiden alone with his teammates outside the club talking.

"It's not your fault, Aiden," said Dylan, one of the first boys who spoke to Aiden when he had arrived in California. It was the middle of April, and in a couple of months he and his dad will have been in California for two and half years. In Aiden's opinion, it was by far the best country they had been to. His dad, Jason, had a unique job in engineering. The company he worked for required them to move around the world. So far they had been to eight countries, with the United States being their ninth. It wasn't often that they stayed this long, and Aiden was glad to have finally settled somewhere.

"Yes, it is. I doubted myself," said Aiden sulkily.

"Where's your dad?" asked Chase, another teenager who helped Aiden settle into California when he'd arrived.

"That's what I would like to know," Aiden said, his head in between his legs as he sat on the kerb of the athletics club.

"Alright, well Chase and I are off, see you tonight? Arlo's?" asked Dylan.

"Yeah definitely." Aiden gave a small smile at the thought of having one of Arlo's famous milkshakes.

Leaving Aiden alone, Chase and Dylan walked off. Aiden picked at the grass by his feet. A burst of anger bloomed in his chest when he thought about the race. Maybe he shouldn't have been as disappointed as he was. Second place wasn't bad, but he knew he could have done better. If he hadn't been so distracted searching for his dad, he might have won.

An engine hummed nearby, and Aiden looked up as a car pulled into the car park. It was his dad. The red four-by-four skidded to a stop at the kerb. Black smoke pumped out of the tailpipe, and Aiden coughed from the cloud of dust that filled the air. Rising to his feet, his head popping out of the dust, Aiden's eyes locked with his father's. The anger which had suddenly appeared seemed to reach boiling point when Jason flicked his hand, gesturing his son to hurry up. Aiden gritted his teeth. He threw his bag into the backseat, slammed the passenger door closed, and Jason drove off.

"Did you win?" Jason asked immediately, seemingly unbothered by not attending his son's race.

"I was winning. I had it, and when I looked over to see if you were there. You weren't. You promised me you would be." This was just one of many promises his father had broken.

"I was working and couldn't get away. If you were winning, why did you lose?" asked Jason.

"Don't turn this around on me, you promised me you'd be there. And besides, you are always working. You never have enough time for me." Aiden hoped his father could hear the resentment in his voice.

"I need to tell you something. It's the reason why I am late."

"That would be a first," said Aiden waspishly. Crossing his arms, he leant back in his chair waiting for the excuse when a sudden thought crossed his mind. Something he thought he wouldn't hear again. Could he be talking about the call? Could his father be preparing to tell Aiden that he had received the call from the deep and lifeless voice that told them they would be moving? Feeling the world slow down, feeling his heart beat in his throat, Aiden listened to his father.

"We are moving. Back to England, back to Oakdale," said Jason. Aiden felt his chest tighten as his stomach shrivelled up. Aiden knew of Oakdale, in the briefest of conversations he had had with his father in the past, Jason had told Aiden that Oakdale was his birthplace but also the place where his mother, Amy, was killed. A place in which he had never spent any time in.

"How many more times, Dad?" Aiden said, crestfallen. So many emotions warred inside him, each trying to steal focus, yet Aiden didn't feel able to process any of them. Today just got a whole lot worse.

Aiden looked out the window, taking in what he knew was going to be his last few moments of seeing California. After moving so many times, Aiden knew there was nothing he could do or say that would change his father's mind.

"We leave tomorrow." *Tomorrow*, Aiden found himself thinking. This would be the quickest they'd ever been moved before, normally they were given a week. Aiden didn't reply. Feeling the anger finally reach breaking point, he clenched his seatbelt, hoping it would release some anger, but it failed. Aiden knew there was one question he could ask which would annoy his father.

"Dad, what happened to Mum?" Aiden suddenly felt the seatbelt tighten round his chest, and he was thrown forwards and then back against the chair. Aiden looked towards his father who had pressed down on the breaks at a crossroad, his brown hair now covering his face.

"I have told you this before. You are too young. When the time is right, I will tell you about her." Aiden could see the hints of red in his face.

"Okay." It wasn't the reaction Aiden had expected – or wanted – and he shrank back into the chair, knowing that he would not dare challenge his father when he was in a mood.

They pulled into their drive, not having spoken a word since Jason's sudden breaking. Aiden stormed out from the car, slamming the door behind him, preparing himself for his last night in California.

"I'm going to Arlo's," said Aiden, looking forward to leaving the house, which his father had already started packing.

"Okay, be home by nine," said Jason coldly, carefully and strategically packing up the kitchen into boxes. Taking his father's blunt reply as approval, Aiden left the house.

Arlo's was the ice cream parlour in which Dylan and Chase had taken Aiden to after his first week in California. Heavily reminiscing about his time in America, Aiden wasn't sure how he was going to tell his two friends that he was moving again. He was considering not telling them, but he knew it would have been unfair on them as they would be expecting him in school the next day, and he wouldn't turn up. Jumping on the bus, which Aiden had to run for before it left the station, it wasn't long before he was greeted by Chase and Dylan outside Arlo's. The sky was decorated in the most magnificent colours of pink, orange and purple as the sun set beyond the horizon. Aiden was going to miss these views.

The three teenagers sat down in the multicoloured booth and ordered their milkshakes. This was the moment Aiden decided to tell them he was moving.

"When do you move?" Dylan asked in disbelief, gently lowering his spoon. Chase remained silent as he looked at Aiden.

Aiden took a breath, hating how upset his friends looked. "Tomorrow."

"Well, let's have a good night. A night you'll remember before you head off to rainy old England," said Dylan smiling, raising his milkshake glass for the other two to cheers to. Aiden smiled, thankful to have met such a positive person in his life. The boys left Arlo's in search of entertainment in the array of street performers near the beach, enjoying the warmth the evening had to offer. Aiden still had a few hours to enjoy his friends' company.

"You…" an elderly woman pointed towards Aiden. Aiden turned to face the peculiar-looking woman who had interrupted his conversation with Dylan and Chase. She was sitting outside her sapphire-coloured tent, a parrot perched upon a metal tower, with several tables filled with the most unusual necklaces, bracelets and other objects which Aiden had never seen before.

"Yes?" Aiden glared at the woman. He looked towards the *Fortune Teller* sign beside her, which explained why she was wearing peacock-coloured clothing, and there was the strong aroma of shisha-smoke in the air.

"You have an intriguing fortune, come and take a seat." She opened the curtain into her tent, gesturing towards a chair on the inside.

"I'm okay, thank you," Aiden replied kindly.

"I guarantee you it will be worth your time. I will give it to you for free."

Aiden and the woman stared at one another for a while. Behind Aiden, Dylan and Chase pressed him to get his fortune told. Her peacock gown didn't invoke confidence in Aiden.

"It's only a bit of fun," Chase said, and he was right. *Surely, what is the worst that could happen?* Aiden found himself thinking before he gave into the woman's stare and slowly walked into tent. The last remaining strain of light disappeared as the curtain was closed, but as quickly as it disappeared, a candle lit itself when the peculiar woman whispered *Photia*.

"Nice trick," said Aiden. "Where did you get those necklaces and bracelets from outside?" he finished feeling a warm and comfortable atmosphere appear as the women sat down. The woman took a seat at a round table, and Aiden sat opposite her. The tent was warm and cozy, and there was a sweet scent in the air that made Aiden's head feel light.

"My brother's shop in the Witch's Market in London – The Marvelous Shop in Peculiar Artefacts and Possessions," she replied.

Aiden felt his mouth slowly fall open, but before it was gaping, he pretended to yawn, stretching out his arms. He'd never heard of any Witch's Market. It sounded like a novelty shop full of fake charms and trinkets.

"That sounds nice," he said, stuck for words.

Aiden's attention fell on the crystal ball in the centre of the table, and the woman began to hover her hands over it delicately.

"Now all I ask is for you to be quiet and allow me to hold your hands," the fortune teller spoke. She moved her hands from the crystal ball and towards Aiden who hesitated at first but knew that all of this was part of the *act*. He gave his hands to the fortune teller. Sitting in darkness with only the light of the candle for Aiden to concentrate on, the clear crystal ball began to fill with a light grey colour.

"I see… I see… I see a dark future, full of pain and misery," started the woman, her eyes now closed. "People you will meet and know will die, but I see happiness and fortune towards the end. There is light at the end of your tunnel, but the tunnel is very long. It will take you to places you thought would never exist, where black is not the darkest colour, where tombs are coated in gold."

Aiden accidentally snorted. *I wonder how many other people will face a tunnel where black isn't the darkest colour.*

"You were born on the morning of a red sun. The power you possess will be the death off you." The crystal ball changed to a desert sunset red colour. "We shall meet again one day, but the day we meet will be during the darkest of days." The woman opened her eyes, taking her hands away from Aiden, smiling at him.

"Well thank you for that. It was very moving." Aiden could hear Dylan and Chase giggling outside. "I must be off." Aiden rose from his chair, bowing his head to the fortune teller.

"They are real, Aiden Dyer. Never doubt yourself, everything I have told you here tonight is a warning." Aiden stopped and looked at the woman. He didn't remember telling her his surname. In fact, he was almost one hundred percent sure he hadn't. Goosebumps circulated his body as he turned, leaving the tent.

It wasn't long after Aiden's fortune reading that the three boys called it a night. The goodbyes had taken a long time and despite how much he'd enjoyed the evening, Aiden felt deflated on his journey home.

Aiden's father had finished packing the house and was now in his bedroom, packing his clothes neatly away into his suitcase. Jason had thrown Aiden his old, faded brown suitcase that had been with Aiden since he remembered. Knowing the drill, Aiden began packing his pants, socks and clothes, leaving any items which would be useless in England.

"Swimming trunks," said Aiden, placing them in the donation pile, knowing full well how cold and wet England was.

The next morning came faster than any morning before. It had shocked Aiden at how quick time went and how little time he'd had to prepare for this moment. He and his dad were already standing outside their house, Jason eagerly anticipating their taxi which should have arrived five minutes ago.

"Honestly, these drivers have one job. Be here on time. And yet somehow they are still late." Despite moving several times, Aiden knew his father was a stickler for lateness, something which he had come to learn and despise about his father over the years. Always first to every event, party and celebration. It wasn't much longer before the taxi driver arrived and Aiden was sitting in the back of the threadbare, leather taxi seat looking at his Californian home, knowing this would be the last time he would see it.

Everything seemed to go by like a blur after that: they checked in at the airport, walked through duty-free, and were sitting down at their gate waiting to board.

Having boarded the plane, their takeoff was another realisation for Aiden that his new life began now. He was used to moving around and starting at new schools and making new groups of friends, but it never got easier, and every time they went somewhere new, he couldn't help but feel like at any moment they'd be leaving again.

The plane journey seemed to go by swiftly with Aiden dozing in and out of sleep. Before he knew it, he and Jason had landed, gone through immigration and were in the taxi on the way to their new lives in Oakdale.

"So what's Oakdale like, Dad?" Aiden asked as they passed the sign into the town, watching how the scenery changed into hills and empty lands, completely different from California. The sun was setting behind dark clouds along the horizon.

Jason shrugged. "It's a lovely town."

"Yeah, that's before you make us move again," said Aiden, but Jason ignored him.

After several hours of travelling and not so much chat between father and son, the night sky descended over England. They finally arrived at 126 Greenland Gardens under the cover of darkness. The lampposts of the street highlighted their new house, which was smaller than their old house in California. Aiden surveyed his surroundings, struggling with tiredness to completely appreciate their newly built semi-detached house. Their front garden was pleasantly laid out. A small, straight pavement led towards the door, and the garden spread out on either side of it. A white picket fence separated the house from the road.

Jason opened the door with ease, and they were greeted by an immaculately clean hallway, the warming smell of new carpet lingering in the air. Aiden looked round the landing noticing there wasn't an inch of dust to be seen. Aiden inspected the lounge room and kitchen, and each room had the faint smell of fresh paint and new carpet.

"Wow, your company hasn't done too bad," said Aiden sarcastically, appreciating the clean canvas of the house. Jason stood in the kitchen searching all the startling white cupboards for food. After searching tirelessly, he found nothing.

"Well, we have no food," he said.

"Don't worry about me, I am off to bed." Aiden took his shoes off and walked up the freshly painted grey spiraled staircase. Making his way to his room, there was no doubt this house was nicer than their one in California, which was made evident by Aiden's room.

The outside seemed to be inside with the help of a large bay window which enveloped the wall, allowing as much light into his room as possible. Unable to see the landscape beyond their generously sized garden, Aiden made sure he didn't trip over his mattress, which had been carelessly dropped on the floor, before pulling his curtains closed. The wardrobes that lined the wall were opened, and Aiden peered inside to find his new quilt and cushion newly bought and wrapped in plastic.

Aiden unwrapped the quilt before shaking it in the air. Wrapping himself in his unmade quilt, and still fully clothed, Aiden dived into bed where he was greeted with space and comfort, unlike on the plane journey, and already felt himself drift off into a dreamless sleep.

"I'll be there," said Jason tersely, placing the new phone down, his eyes struggling to stay open. The heavily tiled, pristine white room beneath the house was one room Aiden wasn't going to see for another few years. It was well hidden. The only time Aiden would ever enter a room like this would be when he turned sixteen, and he would finally be told the family secret of what every Dyer had done since they turned sixteen for the past thousand years.

Leaning back in his seat, drinking a cup of coffee, something in the corner of Jason's eye caught his attention. Jason's new weapon wall was neatly displayed. Guns, wooden bullets, a crossbow easily designed to remain hidden under clothing, an expandable bow and arrows, and in the centre of it all, a long, thick piece of wood, sharpened at one end.

Jason turned his attention back to his desk, where a beige folder was neatly positioned in front of the computer. He flicked it open to freshly printed pictures of an impaled man. Jason found himself staring at the insignia. The same insignia he had seen on Aiden's wall fourteen years ago, when his wife was killed. Two dots, one on top of the other, with inverted brackets on either side. *Could it be?* Jason studied the sigil. There was no denying the similarities were uncanny. *Could it be possible?* Had the same being that had killed his wife returned?

2
Vision

Aiden woke with a start. He was sweating, and his heartbeat was pounding in his ears. He scanned the room. For a moment he couldn't remember where he was or how he got there. He grabbed his phone and checked the screen.

"Two minutes past nine," he whispered. This was the third time he had awoken with such a start, and he was beginning to wonder when it would end. Rising in his freshly made bed, courtesy of his dad making it the night before, Aiden wiped the sweat off his forehead. The electric blue walls of his room stood out in the darkness and cast an eerie glow over everything. Aiden moved to the side of his bed, looking towards his brown suitcase, clothes still bulging out the side. He wasn't willing to unpack any of his clothes, knowing that doing so would mean admitting to himself that this was their new home. Yet he knew his clothes couldn't stay in there forever.

Having decided that today was the day he would go running, he flung his suitcase open and searched for clean clothes. He grabbed one of his loose-fitting shirts and pressed it to his nose, taking a deep breath. He could still smell California. *Home*, he found himself foolishly thinking, knowing that he would never be going back. Throwing on his running clothes, Aiden opened the curtains, showering his room in the glorious warmth and light of the day. He squinted against the light and peered down the road, studying the distant hills and surrounding houses and deciding which route to take. The houses were built down a long stretch of road, all in the same design and with matching gardens, though it wasn't until now that Aiden realised just how far the road stretched into the distance.

Since arriving, Aiden had been between his room and the front room, adjusting to English TV, but he knew today was the day he was going to explore Oakdale, the town that he was born in yet knew little about it.

Marching down the stairs noticing that the smell of the fresh carpet was slowly diminishing, Aiden headed towards the kitchen, where a scribbled note had been stuck to the fridge.

Aid, I won't be home till late tonight. Food in the fridge, remember you start school tomorrow. DAD.

Aiden sighed, hating the fact he would have to start school again soon, hating all the questions and interrogations from the other students about his previous life in California and what it was like and the one question Aiden hated and despised the most: "Why did you move here?" Without giving it any more thought, Aiden tore the note off the fridge, yanked the refrigerator door open and grabbed any food in sight before making his way back to his bedroom.

The blacked-out four-by-four vehicle stood out amongst all the cars. These were the best vehicles for Jason's job. They purred smoothly along the level road, dwarfing any car, swallowing them up within its shadow before it took a right turn, entering private property. Jason was being driven to headquarters; it was his first day back since he had left Oakdale. The once young woodland had now become dense and overgrown, and it wasn't long before the trees shrouded the road ahead, consuming the black vehicle in their shadow. Passing several *Turn Back Now* and *Danger Ahead* signs, Jason knew they were getting closer.

"Are you alright back there, sir?" asked the driver who peered into the rear mirror.

"Yes, I am fine," Jason replied shortly, enjoying the perks of having a personal driver again.

Continuing their climb to the apex of the hill, where an old, abandoned factory surrounded by high-walled fencing and camouflaged guards were to greet them, Jason tightened his grip around the door handle, feeling a fresh wave of nerves pulse through his body, reminding him of his first day. This would be the first time in years he would be seeing these co-workers again, some of whom believed Jason to be dead.

The car glided to a stop, and Jason looked through the front windscreen where a towering, barbed wire fence greeted them. It was almost impossible for someone to climb, with peculiar and irregular indents – perfect for keeping people out. Noticing movement outside the vehicle, Jason's hand moved to his hip automatically, ready to grab his gun when he realised he didn't have one. The driver lowered his window, and Jason knew the driver was talking to the Guardians of the Palace. Looking through the tinted windows, Jason noticed the heavily painted men and women, no skin visible, concealed by heavy camouflage clothing that blended in with the surrounding forest.

"Jason Dyer, Master Hunter," announced the driver, daring not to lower his window any more than necessary. People moved around the car, searching and looking on the inside.

"Clear," said the woman at the window, who waved her hand in the air. And before Jason knew it, the people who had quickly appeared suddenly disappeared into the surrounding shrubbery, invisible again. Jason sighed, wiping his hands against his trousers, remembering a brief encounter he had with the Guardians of the Palace when he was younger, but now he readied himself for his first day at work.

"You can do this. You can do this," Aiden found himself saying as he performed his pre-run stretches. It had taken all of Aiden's effort to remove his clothes from his case to find his running shoes. He had commanded enough courage to go and explore Oakdale today, but as he left the front room and placed his hand on the chilled door handle, an unforgivable wave of apprehension took hold of his body. He could hear his father in his head, questioning him about his day when he arrived home from work, whenever that would be, and Aiden knew he would rather leave the house than deal with the relentless questions and comments from his father. He stood outside the house and took a few deep breaths, glancing around the street for any neighbours, but he was alone. With a final deep breath, he set off for his run.

On his way to his new office, Jason passed through a black-painted room the size of a warehouse lit with powerful floodlights on the ceiling. The space was filled with filing cabinets and desks occupied by other hunters. Several hunters had stopped to watch Jason as he passed, his name legendary in the business.

"Excuse me, sir," said a nervous voice. Turning to see who the voice belonged to, Jason noticed a young black girl stood at the entrance to a glass cubicle classroom.

"Hello," he said, curious to know what she wanted.

"I must ask you, what was it like when you killed the Midnight Madners? What weapon did you choose and why? Is that why you are back from California? Is it—" Jason raised his hand to stop the girl, whose voice grew with confidence with every question she asked. Intrigued and honoured that she already knew about his success in California, Jason moved towards the girl, hearing people whisper in the background, unaware that an audience had gathered around them.

"What's your name?" he asked.

"Shanika," she answered.

"Well, Shanika, I hunted down every member slowly and carefully. Information, common sense and advanced knowledge of their abilities and strengths helped me. I killed three of them with a gun and the last with a wooden stake as I wanted to watch the life, if you can call it a life, leave the man's eyes." People in the background muttered to one another. "And yes, that is one reason why I am back."

Shanika glanced at Jason in awe.

"Now I must leave as I am meeting my equals," said Jason, briefly smiling at the young trainee, knowing one day that might be Aiden.

Having left the crowd of people and entering the office department, Jason made his way to a room he had been directed to in his welcome email. Jason turned left down a dark marble corridor with doors on either side, and at the end, he saw the door he had been directed to.

J. DYER had been imprinted in gold on one of the doors. Without hesitating, he walked into his office.

The dimly lit room had been filled with the minimalistic furnishings. A desk and chair were in the middle of the room, a single bookcase stood next to the door which led into Jason's project room for his current missions, and maps of the local area and UK were plastered over walls, each showing precise locations of roads and abandoned buildings. The books which he had also requested filled the shelves of the bookcase. Everything was perfect, but he noticed something on his desk, a yellow Post-it note stood out amongst the dark colours of the furniture.

The familiar handwriting made him smile.

> *Hey you. I am glad to have you back, finally you won't make as much mess with me being around. Be at board room for 12.*
> *Much Love, D.*

Jason quickly read before he checked the time – 11.17 am. Placing the note gently down on his desk, Jason grabbed the green, bulging book from the case, *Ancient Killings and What They Mean* by William Bold. Sitting down, he dived into the new book, hoping for something that may help with the task at hand.

Music was blasting through Aiden's headphones, giving him the motivation to run faster. The sun was out and shining brightly, occasionally hiding behind a bubble of clouds, the complete opposite to what Aiden had been told about England. Wiping the sweat from his forehead, he moved towards the shade, enjoying the temporary coolness. Aiden had enjoyed his run so far, having passed the local school, Oakdale Secondary School, which he knew he would be attending tomorrow. He'd seen a few teenagers around the newly developed shopping centre, and

Aiden wasn't sure what kind of friends he would make here. Would they be different from Dylan and Chase?

Aiden caught his breath and let his heartbeat settle before starting off again and heading towards the forest. The path into the forest was well worn and cut through tall, twisting trees that made the sun shine through in dapples. He would easily be able to lose himself inside, enjoying the peace and tranquillity of the world… That was until he felt the ground beneath his feet change. The once soft, comforting and uneven flooring of the forest had disappeared, only to be replaced by a stone pathway. Coming to a halt and glancing down at the stone, wondering why there was a pathway in the middle of the forest, Aiden followed the track, now walking, making sure he didn't lose it under the thick layer of grass and moss.

Following the route, it wasn't long until Aiden found where it led – an abandoned, burnt-down church. Taking his earphones out, his mouth dropped open, Aiden stared at the crumbling building. The forest trees swallowed the church in their eerie shadows. There was something eerily fascinating about the church that made Aiden want to know more. The structure of the walls remained intact, but Aiden saw the heavy layers of ivy that consumed the face of the church. Despite the charred appearance, the long grass by the entrance seemed untouched by the damage.

Aiden didn't realise he had walked forward until he reached the outskirts of the crumbled stone walls. Ancient tombstones fought the overgrown grass to remain visible, each battling one another to stand taller. The majority of tombstones were noticeably wonky and bore faded writing, leaving a question lurking in Aiden's mind as to who was buried here. The church cross, which would have once stood proudly on top of the roof, was now cemented deep into the ground where the unearthed soil filled the air with a musty smell. Walking gingerly around the premise of the stone wall, an opening appeared in the ancient wall. The strange curiosity came over Aiden again, and he was drawn closer to the church. Lurching forwards and into the premises of the church grounds, Aiden made his way towards the entrance of the church. The classical gothic wooden doors, which barely hung on their hinges, greeted Aiden. He managed to slip through a chink, his back scraping the doors.

The church was daunting, and Aiden shivered in the dim light. Droplets of water echoed throughout the church, magnified by the emptiness. A pungent smell of stagnant water forced Aiden to cover his nose. Walking carefully over the soaked floorboards, Aiden looked into the skeletal ceiling where gaping holes let light into the church.

Walking down the aisles, his attention was drawn to the windows. Surprisingly, some eye-catching stained-glass windows remained intact, whereas others were broken, their shards of glass littered across the floor. Shrubs grew in the dark crevices in between the charred floorboards, and Aiden realised that this church must have been abandoned for some time.

The creaking floorboards reverberated around the church as Aiden moved up to the podium. Something in the corner of Aiden's eye caught his attention. In between the two stained-glass windows, a scratch mark had been embedded deep in the stone wall, and it taunted Aiden to come closer. He walked over to the claw-like marks slowly. Wondering what on earth could have done this to the stone, Aiden reached out to touch it…

"Lesa, where are you?"

Opening his eyes, Aiden fell backwards in bewilderment. The church was on fire, people were scrambling as a teenage boy no older than Aiden stood down the aisles with his back to him. A cackling laugh echoed throughout. Aiden covered his ears, feeling like the laugh belonged to a dark presence when goosebumps pricked his skin.

"I'm over here," a female voice taunted.

The boy, whom Aiden's eyes were now glued to, turned to face him. Aiden was backed against the wall, breathing heavily as he caught a glimpse of his horrific face. His eyes were blood red with black slits for pupils, and pulsing red veins consumed his face. The boy's clothing was stained with blood, and a shiver raced down Aiden's spine. The boy smiled from ear to ear, bearing his elongated white fangs, and searched the surroundings of the church amongst the fire.

"There you are," he yelled, looking directly at Aiden. He lunged forwards at lightning speed, his arms outstretched to attack. The boy missed Aiden by centimetres, leaving a large claw mark in the stone pillar of the church. Aiden looked around frantically, noticing the boy did not aim for him but a woman floating through the air, speaking another language. The boy roared over the blazing fire, his black spiky hair standing out against the orange flames. Aiden tried to move away but he couldn't.

"*Liiykufureous*," shouted the older woman. Beams of lightning were fired from her hands towards the boy, which propelled him through the air towards a roaring inferno. Thinking he was about to witness the murder of the devil-like boy, Aiden was flabbergasted when he somehow avoided the fire by bouncing off the church pillars, using what Aiden could only think of as enhanced strength. Using the power from jumping from pillar to pillar, he aimed and propelled himself through the air. He tackled the woman to the ground and threw her in Aiden's direction.

In that instant, she hit the scratch on the wall, and Aiden was back in the burnt, desolate church. Alone. He looked around the church, sweating profusely and breathing heavily, looking for the woman and boy, but no one was there. The church was the same state as when Aiden entered it.

There was no roaring inferno, there was no fight, no floating woman and there was most certainly no monstrosity of a boy. Terrified, Aiden leapt from the church podium, gracefully sliding between the gap of the gothic church doors and ran home, he didn't stop. But in the distance a roaring sound echoed from the church. Refusing to look behind at the cursed church, he ran, ran back home to the safety of his bedroom.

Jason arrived at the board room, walking straight in without knocking. Four familiar faces sat at the rectangular table. Closing the door behind him, the room became silent as they all looked towards him. One face he saw was of a woman he had missed dearly.

"Hello, Mr Dyer." Jason looked towards the white-robed woman, whose vibrant purple hair contrasted against her serious expression. "We have been expecting you."

"Hello," Jason said, in a tone equally as dramatic as the woman's.

"My name is Alicia, and you already know Cambal." She gestured towards the black man who sat next to her; he too was wearing white robes.

"Welcome, Jason, it is nice to see you again," said Cambal, nodding his respects to Jason. He was of a similar age to Jason and wore thick glasses which hugged his face.

Jason returned the nod, remembering how many times Cambal had looked after him in the infirmary, and Jason, in return, had protected him on missions.

"We are the Master Healers who work in the infirmary; we have been looking forward to meeting you. You obviously know your co-workers," Alicia said.

"I know who you are, this isn't my first time," said Jason, feeling like Alicia was forgetting her place and, most of all, who Jason was.

"Oh," said Alicia, and returned to her seat.

"Look at you with your grey hairs… you're getting old," said a friendly female voice, who noticed the blossoming lightness in Jason's hair.

"Don't forget you're older than me, Diana." Jason grinned, looking towards his best friend. "Where is the boss?" he asked.

"Unfortunately, she cannot join us as she is away with Neil on a mission," said Hayden, his chair larger and sturdier than all the rest due to his large body and muscles bulging from underneath his tight shirt.

"Okay, let's begin." Jason paused. "I have one question and one question only, who would want one of Shun Yun Li's most trusted men dead?"

"Tomorrow there will be a new boy in your class called Aiden Dyer."

"Dyer," snapped the spiky-haired boy. "I know that name." It was late at night. Diana had returned home after spending several hours with Jason and was now sitting at her dining room table with her daughter and, what her daughter now called, her friend.

"Yes, he is the son of Jason Dyer, one of the greatest in our generation."

"Diana," said the boy.

"Tyler," interrupted Diana, barely giving Tyler a chance to finish his sentence. "I have hacked the school system so that Aiden will be in your class. I know Jason, he is my best friend, and he will be thinking about Aiden at school so I want you guys to make him feel welcome and become friends with him."

"But Mum…"

"Just be friendly with him. Please," said Diana.

"Diana, I don't think you understand," said Tyler, looking at her cautiously. Knowing what Tyler was going to say, Callie began fiddling with her pyjamas.

"What don't I understand?" Diana almost snapped, her irritation growing.

"He smells different. Since they arrived in town, Callie and I have smelt something that only belongs to someone who was born on the morning of a red sun."

"That's impossible," said Diana, knowing what Tyler was implying. "Look out for him. Jason's wife was killed here, so make sure you protect him." A headache began to throb in Diana's temple, and she desperately hoped what Tyler was saying was wrong.

3
A New Day

"Aiden, are you up yet?" shouted Jason. Aiden awoke to a start as Jason came marching into his room and opened the curtains. Aiden moaned, covering his face with his bed sheets as the sunlight flooded his dark room. Jason ripped the bedsheet from Aiden's grasp and body.

"Dad," moaned Aiden, wanting to stay in bed a little longer but at the same time surprised he was still at home.

"You have school. Get ready," Jason yelled before leaving Aiden alone in his room. The day had come, the day which Aiden had resented since they'd arrived in Oakdale – the first day at school. Rising from his bed, Aiden remembered his dream. The black spiky-haired boy with crimson eyes, toxic red veins which covered his face and the ear-to-ear smile of razor-sharp fangs had haunted Aiden whilst he'd slept. Feeling tired before his day even started, Aiden once again heard Jason shout from downstairs hurrying him to get ready.

"Do I have to go today? I am so tired," said Aiden, appearing in the archway of the kitchen, washed and ready for school. Jason looked at his son, first confused as to why he was wearing a striped black and red tie with the school blazer before remembering he had to wear a school uniform.

"Yes, you do. You look smart," Jason added, acknowledging his son's effort to tame his curly bed hair and his top button done up with his tie correctly made.

"Well, if I wasn't, you would have made me redo it," Aiden said coldly. "Besides what are you still doing here?"

"Can't a father wish his son good luck on his first day at school?" Jason shrugged, smiling, an odd look which Aiden never really saw on his father's face.

"So you can watch me go to school yet you can't make it to any of my running events? That's nice, Dad," said Aiden, still upset his father never made it to his race, though it felt like a lifetime ago.

"Have you got everything you need for school?" Jason said, ignoring his son's comment.

"Unfortunately, yes."

"Do you want breakfast?" asked Jason.

"No, otherwise I'll be late, and you hate me being late despite you being late to everything." Aiden felt some pent-up anger exit his body with every comment.

"That's enough of that," Jason warned, and joined his son in the hallway whilst Aiden did his shoes up.

"I remember tying your shoes up on your first day in school in Australia, you were so nervous," Jason reminisced as he watched his son, leaning on the banister.

"Yes, but then do you remember forgetting about me and leaving me at school till ten o'clock at night because you had work?" Aiden remembered the incident very well, thinking Jason had forgotten about him or worse, abandoned him, at school.

"I was—"

"Working," said Aiden quickly, throwing his school bag on his back. "Yeah, I know. That's your excuse for everything. I'll see you later." He pushed through the front door and let it slam behind him, leaving Jason standing in the hallway.

The warm spring day bombarded Aiden with the rays of sunlight as he walked down his road. He was trying to build his confidence before he got to school, but the mixture of heat and nerves wasn't helping. He unbuttoned his top button and loosened his tie, trying to cool down, but the warmth of the sun seemed to intensify. He needed a distraction, but each step closer to school made it harder not to think about what awaited him.

Thinking about what could go wrong with his day, Aiden followed the route he took yesterday on his run, passing overgrown fields in desperate need of a trim and approaching a busy road, signs directing the cars in multiple directions.

Castle Nort, Aiden read in his head, wondering what that was, noticing cars driving in the general directions which also led to Oakdale Train Station. A cooling breeze brushed his hot face as he walked down the busy road, following the sign which directed him towards Oakdale Secondary School. It wasn't long until he noticed he was almost there.

In the distance, he could see students jump out of their parents' cars and disappear into the herd of students which were swarming into the gates of the school. Realising he was at the back of the throng, comforting as it was, he now knew school was going to start imminently, and he was not ready.

The students entered the school with Aiden slowly approaching the red cast-iron gate. *Oakdale Secondary School* was written over the entrance in black, spiky writing that didn't look inviting. Aiden's heart dropped to the bottom of his stomach when he reached the cast-iron gates. Before him, a sweeping drive shrouded by oak trees and built over a small waterway led the way to the reception. Aiden followed the other students to the main entrance. His legs felt like lead, and he was certain everyone knew he was the new kid. He stopped outside the front doors and drew a steadying breath. Then he walked in.

The clock struck nine, and Aiden was sitting patiently in reception. Several school students, varying in size and age, walked past staring at Aiden, knowing he was the "new boy". Separated by thick glass doors, it made Aiden feel like he was on show at the zoo. He looked back towards the entrance tempted to walk out, but the lady at the desk was staring at Aiden, drinking her cup of tea, watching intensely behind her cat-like glasses. The woman had checked Aiden in, ignoring him once she had done her job, but she was now intrigued as to who he was. Rubbing his clammy hands together, wondering how long he would be seated here for, it wasn't long until a very noticeable woman started to run back and forth, struggling to carry the three very large folders, which probably wasn't helped by the six-inch-high heels she wore. Aiden watched her run past at least seven times with the three folders, her bleached hair trailing behind her. She reappeared, pulling the handle down and struggling to open the heavy door.

"Hello, Aiden," she said hoarsely. "I'm Mrs Thompson, and I will be helping you around the school for the next week." She smiled.

"Hi," Aiden replied, caught off guard by Mrs Thompson, who sadly had noticeable signs of sweat through her blue blouse.

"Now, let's take you to your tutor," she said.

The hallways were long and lifeless. The faded blue carpets and white walls were dissatisfying and depressing. Only a few large pictures hanging from the walls and office doors lined the hallway. Looking closely, Aiden noticed the photos were taken every year, each picture commemorating the Year 11s leaving school.

"So, Aiden. When did you arrive in Oakdale?" asked Mrs Thompson, searching for a topic of conversation.

"Only a few days ago," Aiden replied, turning to face Mrs Thompson who had finally regained her breath.

"Wow, you haven't been here long then. Well just so you know, Oakdale has a tremendous amount of history. We are in the top ten for most historical towns in all of England. So if you ever have any spare time, I would recommend going to the Oakdale Library and Museum, it's quite fascinating." Aiden felt like Mrs Thompson was trying to sell the local area to him.

Reaching the end of the claustrophobic hallway, where the carpet beneath changed from pale blue to a cheap plastic flooring, a strong chemical smell overwhelmed Aiden's sinuses. Taken aback by the strong smell, which seemed not to bother Mrs Thompson, he ascended the quiet stairs towards the top floor.

"Alright then, let's begin," said Mrs Thompson, her pace quickening.

"Your tutor's name is Mr Burton. He is head of languages here at the school and a very good teacher. He will be your German teacher, and he will most likely tell you that he has never let a student fail before." She pulled out a red and black diary.

"This is your diary, Aiden. If you look at the first few pages, you can see your timetable. Then the rest allows you to keep on track with your homework." Mrs Thompson smiled, blinding Aiden with her whitened teeth.

"Thank you," said Aiden. They approached two double doors at the top of the staircase where Aiden began to feel his nerves return, almost having forgotten about them since meeting Mrs Thompson.

"Did you bring your PE kit in with you today?" she asked quietly.

"Yes, I did." He was looking forward to PE more than anything, the only lesson where he didn't have to think, where he let his body do whatever it wanted.

"Okay, Aiden, this is where you will come up every morning for tutor at 8.45 am." They walked through the pair of blue doors, that opened far too easily, slamming against the wall and sending an echoing vibration down the short hallway.

"When we go into class, I'll introduce you to Mr Burton, and he will introduce you to the class." They approached a poorly painted, vibrant blue door with U5 engraved in the top right corner. Aiden was convinced the only colour in this school was blue.

"Are you ready?" Mrs Thompson asked, but before Aiden could reply she opened the door, bursting into the lively classroom.

"Hello, Mr Burton." Mrs Thompson walked in with confidence, extending her arm.

"Oh, hello, Mrs Thompson," said Mr Burton who had been caught off guard, shaking her hand, his oversized suit engulfing both their hands.

Aiden slowly poked his head into the classroom, his body following shortly. The classroom was plunged into silence with Mrs Thompson and Mr Burton now murmuring to one another. Aiden began to smile, but behind his smile was great trepidation. Standing alone in front of the class, Aiden felt like a sitting duck, all the students looked towards him with hungry eyes. He studied the classroom, gulping, noticing two teenagers at the back, one boy and one girl, who were engrossed in their own conversation, concealing their faces until the boy removed his hand from his face.

Impossible, Aiden immediately thought to himself.

It was the boy from the vision. Aiden had a sudden flash back of the devil-like boy from the church, but where were his bloody eyes? His evil ear-to-ear smile with razor-sharp fangs?

Aiden stared at the boy, with the boy returning a dubious look himself.

"So, this is Aiden Dyer then?" said Mr Burton, shattering the glacial silence of the room with his voice, looking at Aiden through his glasses, which were too small for his head, and down his pointed nose.

"A bit messy, aren't you? Especially for your first day." Mr Burton winced, having looked Aiden up and down, bunching his mole-like face together. The teacher looked at Aiden with disdain, taking immediate notice of his top button being undone and the lousy knotting of his tie.

"Sorry," Aiden found himself saying, quickly fixing his uniform.

"Well sorry does not help first impressions," he snapped back. Aiden looked at Mr Burton's awful clothing in return. His suit was far too big for him, and his shoes looked like he had stolen them from a Year 7 student.

"Well. Will you look at the time," said Mrs Thompson looking at her watch. "I've got to get going, Aiden, and if you have any questions you want answering, just come and find me."

Aiden couldn't form any words in return. He wanted Mrs Thompson to stay; she was friendly and calm – the complete opposite to what Aiden was feeling from Mr Burton. Leaving the room and closing the door behind her, it wasn't long until the silence returned. Until…

"What time do you call this then?" roared Mr Burton. Aiden turned to see a red-faced man staring at him. "And look how untidy you are!"

"Pardon? Have you seen yourself?" Aiden replied scathingly.

"Excuse me," Mr Burton said through gritted teeth. Most of the students in the classroom had heard what Aiden said, and some started murmuring and talking to one another. Aiden, himself surprised at what he just said, noticed the two teenagers at the back of the classroom exchange wary looks.

"How dare you… how dare you say that to me!" Mr Burton's voice seemed to have grown louder, filling the classroom and most likely the hallway outside. Aiden was in shock, all the traces of politeness Mr Burton had shown Mrs Thompson had now disappeared, only to be replaced with rage.

"No student ever speaks to me like that. Especially on their first day," he spat. "You've just earned yourself a lunch time detention. Find a seat and I will collect you later." Mr Burton raised his hand to his head, walking towards his cluttered desk in the corner of the room. Aiden stood awkwardly in front of the class, feeling slightly embarrassed and annoyed that he had already earned a detention on his first day.

Feeling the pressing eyes of the other students, Aiden moved slowly, scanning the rows looking for a seat, but there were none. The only seat available was next to the girl who was sitting next to the spiky-haired boy. But the girl caught Aiden's attention;

he didn't know why he didn't notice her earlier. She was beautiful. Her wavy brown hair sat just past her shoulders, and she watched Aiden curiously. Aiden was mesmerised by her, but as quickly as the butterflies appeared, they disappeared as he felt his chest tighten once again. With the class slowly picking up in conversation again, Aiden knew this was the only seat there was. Next to a beautiful angel, with the devil-faced boy on her shoulder.

"Hey." Her voice was calm and mellow as Aiden took his seat. Aiden looked at the girl and was instantly lost for words. He felt his mouth move but no words exited.

"Hi," he managed, rubbing his clammy hands over his school trousers. He noticed the girl's fingers fidget with her skirt.

"I'm Callie."

"And I'm Tyler," said the spiky-haired boy.

"I'm Aiden. Aiden Dyer." He was surprised at how nice they were being; Aiden remembered a time in Russia when none of the other kids spoke to him for days, when they all thought Aiden was an alien.

However, Aiden was unsure of what to think of Tyler. Could this boy possibly be the kid from Aiden's vision?

"So, you're the new kid then?" Tyler stared at Aiden over Callie's shoulder.

"I guess I am," said Aiden through gritted teeth, hating that expression but not wanting to deter the only two in the class who were speaking to him.

"Well, let us give you the personal welcome to Oakdale Secondary School," said Callie joyfully.

"Thank you."

"Dyer," Tyler said suddenly.

"What?" Aiden asked.

"Your surname, it sounds odd." Tyler continued leaning forward, before he was elbowed in the stomach by Callie, which Aiden found peculiar. They were both staring at him intensely, as if his life depended on the answer.

"Oh yeah… um… my dad has mentioned something to me in the past about our family history." Aiden scratched the back of his head.

"By the way, don't take it to heart how Mr Burton treated you, he is like that to us two as well even though I am one of his best students," said Callie. Aiden suspected a little boast towards the end.

"See, all the teachers think he's nice and wonderful, but he is actually kind of a jerk. He has given me at least twenty detentions in the last month for just being me," said Tyler.

The classroom was full of chatter, so nobody could possibly hear the trio at the back, especially Mr Burton. Aiden chortled, it was nice that Tyler and Callie were making an effort with him so far. He felt his nerves slowly fade away with any lasting fear that Tyler was the boy from the vision.

"I'm glad I am not the only one," Aiden said.

"So, what's your first lesson then?" Callie asked inquisitively.

"I don't even know." Aiden realised that some students in the class were now placing their bags on their desk. He reached for his diary, which Callie easily took from his grip. She opened his diary immediately to the correct page and both she and Tyler studied his timetable.

"Science, that's your first lesson," said Callie.

"Looks like we have PE together," Tyler mentioned, grinning at Aiden.

"Awesome," Aiden replied, overwhelmed by the two. Handing Aiden his diary back, their hands grazed each other, and Callie pulled her hand away immediately, turning to face Tyler. For a moment, Aiden swore he could have heard the groaning of someone's stomach.

Callie turned to Aiden with sore, red eyes.

"Are you alright?" he asked. "Your eyes have gone bloodshot."

"Oh, yeah, don't worry. It's just…" Callie paused.

"It's hay fever season," Tyler said quickly. " Callie suffers badly from the pollen, better she sneezed on me than you. Wouldn't be the best first impression, would it?"

Aiden furrowed his brows. It was weird how she acted and how Tyler covered for her, especially when he could have sworn she hadn't sneezed.

"Okay then," said Aiden cautiously, feeling the atmosphere turn strange between the three off them. But determined to not let this possible companionship end on his first day, Aiden changed the subject. "What's science like then?"

"It's alright. We are starting to begin the Year 10 topics now. The teachers have decided to give us a look at what Year 10 science will be like."

"At the moment, we have just started to look over chemistry," Callie added onto the end of Tyler's response. Aiden noticed how they were almost in sync with one another. They continued to speak for the remainder of tutor before the bell echoed through the school.

"Alright, you lot. Get up and get going to your lessons," Burton shouted.

"Let's get going to science then," said Callie with a cheeky grin.

"I'll be seeing you at lunch, Mr Dyer, or you'll be in serious trouble," Mr Burton said. "And Tyler Steede, you best be joining us as well for your rudeness yesterday." Aiden sighed in relief to have some company, realising that Tyler was in detention as well.

"As you say, sir," Tyler replied on behalf of himself and Aiden.

"What did you do wrong?" Aiden asked.

"I *accidentally* said he looked like he stole his shoes from a Year 7 quite loudly in class yesterday, which he heard and didn't like."

"That's what I thought." Aiden smiled. *This may not turn out to be so bad after all*, Aiden found himself thinking as he marched off to science with Callie and Tyler.

4
CARA

It was an early Friday afternoon, and Aiden, so far, had survived his first week at school. He owed this to Callie and Tyler, who so far had not left him alone, escorting him to all his lessons and spending all their lunches with him. He would dare to say the three of them were becoming quite good friends.

Mrs Thompson, who at the beginning of the week was at Aiden's beck and call, would meet him in the reception every morning and interrogate him to see how he was settling in. However, when she learnt about Callie and Tyler, she soon began to back off, and on Aiden's fourth day, she left him alone, due to the constant companionship from Callie and Tyler.

It felt as though a weight had been lifted from his shoulders and he was finally free to be himself and completely settle into his new school. However, this relief was short lived when he realised he had to be in the presence of Mr Burton every morning for tutor. His detention with Mr Burton on Monday was something he did not want to repeat. The teacher had given him and Tyler the chore of cleaning the overflowing cupboard at the back of the classroom. The dust layered thick over all the books had decorated Aiden's and Tyler's uniforms, turning their jet-black blazers white. When the bell heralded the end of lunch, Aiden and Tyler left the classroom before Mr Burton could say anything to them, but distant shouts from the classroom, that could be heard by the pair of them down the hallway, suggested to them Mr Burton wasn't happy. It wasn't long before the relief Aiden felt was diminished when he learnt he had German after lunch – almost instantly regretting running out of Mr Burton's detention early, with Tyler chuckling under his breath as he walked off to his French lesson.

A mutual dislike between student and teacher had blossomed between Aiden and Mr Burton during German and it wasn't long until German became his least favourite lesson. He was constantly picked on by the mole-faced teacher, who would ask him questions in German, fully aware that Aiden didn't understand a word he had said. However, it turned out PE was always after German. German lessons always felt like a lifetime, but as soon as the bell rang, Aiden would leave Callie and run for the boys' changing rooms, meeting Tyler and ready to partake in their PE lesson for the day. A budding rivalry unknowingly emerged between Aiden and Tyler. Tyler, who was naturally good at sports, felt the pressure when Aiden was able to keep up with him compared to the others in the class.

It was on the Friday that Aiden finally felt settled at Oakdale Secondary School, taking notice of things he hadn't seen before. One thing he noticed was a picture of an auburn-haired girl with Callie and Tyler in the back of Callie's phone.

"Who's that?" Aiden asked. Bewildered as to who he meant, Callie looked at what Aiden was pointing at. Flipping her phone, she saw the Polaroid picture of herself, Tyler, and another girl.

"That's Lydia," Callie said. Aiden remained silent, waiting for Callie to explain herself further. "She's currently away in France for a year on an exchange programme with her twin brother and her family. She will be back in September, but she already knows about you."

The two teenagers walked down the distasteful hallways with the faded blue carpets and chemical smell in the air on their way to meet Tyler for lunch. Callie began to fill Aiden in on the popularity ladder at Oakdale Secondary School in the meantime. It seemed she and Tyler were in the middle; people knew who they were, but Tyler and Callie were happy enough to keep their distance and stay as a threesome before Lydia left for France. Which Aiden found weird with how he watched the boys swoon over Callie as she walked down the hallway. Aiden, however, was used to starting at the bottom and working his way up slowly.

"You're doing better than people who have been here since the first day," said Callie, reaffirming Aiden, who couldn't help but think it was due to his friendship with Tyler and Callie and nothing to do with him that he had been able to do so well. "But then there is that thing," said Callie coldly. Aiden was taken aback to begin with. What did Callie mean? He had no idea what Callie was talking about nor the reason for the sudden change in tone, but when he followed where Callie was looking, Aiden spotted a blonde-haired girl with an eye-catching beehive hairstyle.

"That's Amber Monroe. The school tart and a horrible girl," said Callie, walking off to meet Tyler who was sitting in a four-person, off-brown, plastic school table. Knowing that this was not the moment to question Callie about Amber, Aiden refrained himself knowing that his next lesson was with Tyler who would happily tell Aiden about the drama.

"Would you guys want to come to mine after school for some dinner?" said Tyler, his voice barely audible over the wild cursing and shouting of the other students in the canteen.

"Only if Cara makes one of her specialities," said Callie, crossing her arms and leaning back in the chair, which seemed close to breaking from the years of wear and tear.

"Of course," promised Tyler, as if it were only natural for this woman named Cara to make one of her special dishes.

"How about you, Aiden?" Tyler looked at Aiden who still hadn't spoken. He hadn't expected to be invited around so soon after arriving. Never had he made such good friends this quickly.

"Yes," said Aiden. "Please," he finished, feeling like his dad would have whacked him in the back if he hadn't said please.

"Great. I'll let her know."

It wasn't long until the bell echoed throughout the school, signifying the end of break. Going their separate ways off to their lessons, Aiden watched Callie disappear into the crowd of students as he and Tyler walked towards the boys' changing rooms for PE. This was the perfect time to ask Tyler about Callie and Amber.

"Why does Callie hate Amber?"

Tyler grinned at Aiden, his face almost implying that he had been waiting for this question.

"When Callie moved into our school, she immediately started receiving attention from the boys which Amber didn't like, so she spread a rumour about Callie which wasn't very nice. In true Callie fashion, after some teasing from boys in the years above, Callie went and confronted Amber in the canteen where she proceeded to beat her up and give her a black eye." Aiden's mouth dropped open as Tyler continued. "I was only new at the time, and we had been hanging around, so I jumped on Callie, ripping her off Amber before she broke a bone or killed her." Tyler chuckled at the memory.

"Wait… you were a new kid as well?" Aiden questioned, remembering how Tyler had called him the new kid on his first day, whilst feeling an odd but particular bond suddenly appear with Tyler.

"Yeah, I joined a week before Callie. We hit it off immediately because we were both the new kids, but then we became friends with Lydia, and ever since then, it became us three until you arrived," said Tyler.

"Obviously our class is the *new kid* class," joked Aiden. "How come you moved to Oakdale?"

"I lost my parents in a car crash, I used to live up north but my nan, Cara, decided to move us here because she wanted to get me away from bad memories."

"I'm so sorry," said Aiden instantly feeling rude for asking.

"Don't worry about it. It was a while ago. Besides, we are here now and I'm going to beat you in PE today." Tyler nudged Aiden before they walked into boys' changing rooms.

"Not a chance," shouted Aiden in return.

It wasn't long after PE finished and Aiden was walking side by side with Tyler and Callie. Aiden and Tyler, having met Callie at the school gates, were now listening to how she successfully hit Amber in the face with a ball during PE, leading

Amber's face to turn red. Walking in the opposite direction, in which Aiden would take to his house, the three followed a sign to Oakdale Hills which led them towards the outskirts of town and a private road. Trees lined the roads as hedgerows grew high, sealing the houses away in a layer of secrecy.

"These aren't houses," said Aiden. "These are mansions." Aiden looked at the grander and more opulent houses. Climbing the hill, which seemed harder than usual for Aiden after he had just pushed himself in PE, they shortly approached a pair of black cast-iron gates.

"Here we are," said Tyler, who entered a PIN into the gate. The cast-iron gates hummed to life, slowly moving inwards and disappearing into the white walls that curved around the house. A lavish garden greeted them – tulips, sunflowers and other assortments of flowers danced in the wind. The rainbow-coloured area smelt of the coming summer. Taking in a deep breath, Aiden's attention was drawn to the single-storey house, ivy consuming the face, leaving a handsome large black door visible.

"Cara likes to garden," mentioned Callie. Tyler opened the front door, and Callie and Aiden respectfully took their shoes off. Aiden flinched as his foot touched the cold black and white marble flooring.

"What are all of these?" Aiden asked, taking note of several ornaments that were hung on the yellow walls or neatly placed upon stalls that lined the hallway which led to stairs.

"My nan likes to collect items. When she was younger, she travelled the world extensively." Tyler led the way. The chilled hallway retained Aiden's attention until Callie pulled him away from a blue and white vase that had a dragon curled around it.

"They are amazing," said Aiden, never having seen anything like this before. He descended the stairs at the end of the hallway, and a grand marble fireplace caught Aiden's attention in the large kitchen-diner living room, where a black katana hung handsomely over the mantelpiece. This kept Aiden's attention until his breath was suddenly taken away; the living space boasted an entire wall of floor-to-ceiling windows that looked out onto Oakdale. The houses in the distance looked like tiny dots.

"Aiden, I want you to meet my nan," said Tyler. A woman, who looked in her early sixties, sat comfortably on a lavish sofa covered in soft blankets, a glass of wine in one hand whilst she watched TV. She turned to face the trio. She did not look old enough to be Tyler's grandmother. Her skin had few wrinkles and was in almost perfect condition, and her hair had been curled into her neck. Her black clothing was complimented by a sapphire diamond that was concealed in a moonstone brooch in the style of a bee.

"Nan, this is Aiden," said Tyler. The woman rose from the sofa easily, her eyes darting towards Aiden. Her face was calm but her eyes were intense as if they were looking for Aiden's soul. She smiled brightly and Aiden's doubts eased.

"What a pleasure it is to meet you. I've heard so much about you, struggling to comprehend you actually exist baffles me. I'm Cara." Cara pulled Aiden in for a hug, taking a deep breath as though she were smelling him. Aiden, surprised at the woman's strength, pulled away smiling, being polite to the elderly women.

"It's lovely to meet you," said Aiden, exaggerating the words that came out of his mouth.

"I have the bits you wanted, Nan, I'll just put them in the office for you," said Tyler, walking towards a wooden door in between two bookcases.

"Oh, you are such a good grandson, now I can continue my research," said Cara.

"What are you researching?" Aiden queried.

"Oh, just witches of the fifteenth century."

"Witches?" Aiden questioned.

Callie handed Aiden a glass of water and replied, "Ignore her, she's crazy."

"Crazy as the most sane person in an asylum," muttered Cara.

"What are you cooking, Cara?" asked Callie.

"Chicken fajitas bathed in human blood."

Aiden coughed his water back into his glass in shock.

"Cara, you can't say that," said Callie warily.

"Human blood?" Aiden asked the elderly lady, who was staring at the young teenagers, taking a large sip of red wine.

"Yes, human blood," she replied innocently.

"It's my nan's fajita mixture. When I was younger, I thought it looked like human blood, so now she calls it chicken fajitas bathed in human blood," said Tyler reappearing back in the room. Aiden sighed with relief. Cara was definitely a peculiar woman.

"Sounds amazing, I look forward to it," Aiden added.

"So polite you are, I'm glad you haven't been killed yet."

"*Nan*," Tyler hissed. Aiden looked between Cara and Tyler. The way Cara spoke and the things she said made Aiden think this is what all grandparents must be like – confused and short. The three teenagers sat happily at the table as Cara served up dinner. Tyler was right, it definitely looked like human blood. A thick layer of sauce was drenched over the chicken and chunks of tomatoes and peppers looked like pieces of flesh. Despite this, Aiden indulged in the food. Cara told stories of when she travelled the world. She spoke several times about things which Aiden did not understand, saying how plants and flowers had magical powers which only a certain few people in the world could utilise, calling them herbalists – a term which Aiden had never heard of before, but Tyler pulled her back to reality.

"Okay that's enough for one night, Nan," he said as Cara continued to make unusual comments.

Cara looked displeased and muttered something under her breath. "It's getting late," she said to Aiden. "I bet your father will want to know where you are." She collected the plates and made her way back to the kitchen, having instructed Callie to remain seated and not help her clean up.

"Don't worry about him, he is always at work. Can barely make it to anything important for me." Aiden sighed.

Jason sat quietly in the office, Diana next to him, along with three other men and another woman. They were sitting at a long polished black oak table that had been recently moved into the room for this meeting. Sitting patiently, Jason studied the contents of Daria's office; the subdued lights layered the room in levels of darkness. A blind covered the window, and adjacent to it was a bulky black and chrome desk where a large mahogany red chair sat behind it. A powerful, sweet scent lingered in the air as the remaining incense sticks burned, forcing

Jason to remember his trips to the Buddha temples in Thailand. The large black vault door swung open with ease, illuminating the dark office with the lights of the hallway, but a tall, broad woman stood in the doorway, her hands behind her back.

"Hello, everyone," the woman spoke in a calm and toneless voice. Her heavy boots echoed in the office, and a plain black outfit did nothing to accentuate her figure. Her black shoulder-length hair was in perfect condition, not a single hair out of place, as she took her seat in her mahogany-coloured chair. She sat stiffly and eyed her employees with dark eyes. "Pleasure to see you in the flesh again, Jason Dyer." The woman extended her masculine hand, but there was no hint of kindness in her stern expression.

"The pleasure is all mine. Daria the Great leader of the VHA," Jason replied, shaking her hand quickly.

"We have a lot of work ahead in order to figure out what happened the other week, but firstly," Daria paused, turning to face Alicia and Cambal who were sat at the end of the table, their white clothing standing out in the dimness. "What happened to my men?" A sudden change in Daria's tone and facial expression made the unease in the air grow. Jason looked towards a nervous Cambal who seemed to begin fidgeting with his robes.

"Well," said Cambal nervously, not knowing how to break the news to Daria. "Unfortunately, we have lost two of the six which were bought in a week ago."

"Two," Daria interrupted, she rose from her mahogany chair, limiting the little light in the office. "How?" she added curtly before she advanced menacingly towards Cambal. Jason and Diana caught each other's eye.

"Their injuries were far too advanced, and the only option would have been the transformation," said Cambal, his voice shaking.

"Unfortunately, they are dead now. *Dracas De Ramores*," said Jason, bringing the attention away from Cambal before Daria reached him. Jason didn't like seeing Cambal uncomfortable, especially when he knew from past experiences Cambal would have tried everything in order to save the men.

"May the dead stay dead," said Diana, remembering the first time she had heard the association's motto.

"You are right," said Daria, her cold eyes fixed unblinkingly on Jason. She leant back standing taller. "Anything about the man who was murdered?"

"It was one of Shun Yun Li's men," said Jason, who was now challenging Daria's stare with his own.

"How do you know?" asked Daria shortly.

"Shun's insignia was tattooed onto the man's back," answered Alicia. "And after looking through the archives, I confirmed with Hayden that he worked for Shun." Daria shot her a look of concern; Alicia seemed to retract in her chair once she had answered.

"What was this man doing here though?" queried Diana.

"To spy on us, I would assume, but for now I think we should wait," said Jason.

"Well, Jason, I will leave this to you," said Daria.

"Of course," said Jason.

"That will be all today, please leave," Daria dismissed them. The hunters rose from their chairs, Jason and Diana exchanging looks to one another. Leaving the heavily incensed dark room and stepping back into the hallways, Alicia and Cambal walked off in the opposite direction to Jason, Diana and Hayden, whilst Neil remained in Daria's office. Hayden walked in front, leaving Diana and Jason.

"What did you think?" asked Diana, knowing it was safe for them to talk without any prying eyes.

"What I expected," said Jason.

"But why didn't you tell her about the sigil?" Diana asked.

"Because the last time I saw that sigil was the night my wife was killed," said Jason.

"Have you heard about the party that Jasper is having?" said Callie. Having eaten all the food that Cara had provided and more, Aiden was enjoying his walk home from Tyler's, both Callie and Tyler accompanying him.

"No. I haven't heard anything," said Tyler. Aiden remained silent; he didn't expect to be invited to a party after only being at school for a week, but he was surprised that Callie and Tyler were talking about it in front of him.

"Well, it's happening next weekend, and I am pretty sure Jasper won't mind us three turning up," said Callie.

"Three?" Aiden asked.

"Yeah, you're coming, of course. You're one of us now," said Tyler, smiling. Aiden grinned exultantly, he had never felt so comfortable and so included before.

Within minutes, they were at the top of Aiden's road walking towards his house. The evening sky was in an array of blue, pink and oranges.

"Well, this is me," said Aiden, stopping in front of the immaculate front lawn of his house.

"Cute house," said Callie, looking at the golden thatched roofing.

"I guess I will see you guys on Monday."

Callie embraced Aiden in a tight hug which caught him off guard. He returned the hug, feeling her cold body within his grasp.

"You're cold. Are you okay?" he asked, withdrawing from the hug.

Callie looked suddenly alarmed. "I-I-I'm just chilly that's all."

"Night." Tyler winked as he and Callie walked away.

Aiden entered the silent house – his dad still wasn't in from work.

The remaining strains of sunlight danced off the walls as Aiden entered his bedroom. Pulling the curtains closed, he jumped into his bed, thinking about the hug with Callie… and the smell of her hair…

"Peaches," he whispered, heaving a great sigh. Aiden felt relaxed thinking about everything that had happened that evening as he fell asleep. However, it wasn't long before his subconscious took control of his dreams. Once again, he saw the vision of the boy and the woman fighting, this time it was far more graphic, depicting Tyler's face. Despite everything, a sneaky suspicion entered his mind, feeling like there was more to his new friends than they were letting on.

The dark cloaked figure levitated high above the ground, blending in with the night sky, inches from the golden straw that formed the newly built roof. If it were possible to see the face of the Dark Witch, they would be grinning with triumph.

"Oh, how you have grown," said the figure in a monotone voice, knowing that the time to come was approaching, whilst remembering it had been a night like this fourteen years ago when they first held the boy realising who he was. "My powers have returned, and I will come for you last!"

5
THE LAST NORMAL WEEK

It had been another draining week at school for Aiden, with another detention given by Mr Burton; however, this time he was accompanied by Tyler whom had laughed when Aiden did an almost perfect mimic of the teacher. A detention from Mr Burton seemed to be a weekly trend which Aiden was unable to break, and Tyler seemed to be joining him for more and more. Having not told his dad about any of them, knowing full well that they would argue with Jason perceiving Aiden to be a terrible student and his new friends to be a bad influence, Aiden kept the information to himself.

The only thing that was helping Aiden get through the week was the talk of Jasper's party at the weekend. But with no time to relax at school, there was certainly no chance to relax at home. Jason and Aiden's remaining items had arrived from America, meaning Aiden had to once more sit through the painful unpacking process with his dad. "This is not packed properly… Slackers… Jobs worth", were the constant comments his father had when something wasn't done to his standards. The once empty house had now been filled with all their belongings, with a cluster of boxes left untamed in the corner of their living room. With Jason working late, he had tasked Aiden to finish the last few boxes, but Aiden did everything in his power not to.

It was Tuesday night when Aiden finally had dinner with his father for the first time since they had arrived in Oakdale. Jason had cooked Thai food, a treat for Aiden for doing so well at school and settling in far quicker than Jason had hoped. They sat in silence for some time, Aiden enjoying his Pad Thai.

"How was your day then, Dad?" Aiden asked, before taking a big mouthful of noodles. Jason waited several seconds before he replied, his head was still spinning from his busy day at work.

"It was very good, thank you. We are working on a new project which would hopefully help prevent Oakdale from flooding by building stronger bridges and better flood defences."

"That sounds interesting," said Aiden, trying to not sound bored.

"How about you? How are your two friends, is it Timmy and Cindy? No, that's not it, Tyler and…?" Jason paused struggling to remember the girl's name.

"It's Callie," Aiden snapped.

"Got a crush on her?"

"What? No!" said Aiden immediately, feeling his face suddenly flush.

"I would believe you, if you weren't blushing," Jason grinned looking at his son.

"Yes, okay, I do have a crush on her. She's beautiful, Dad," said Aiden, knowing it was impossible to lie in front of his father. Something drastic would have to happen in order for Aiden to lie well to his dad.

"Well, when you get the chance, make sure you tell her," said Jason. Aiden remained silent, knowing this to be the first and only time that he had ever spoken about a girl like this in front of his father.

"Dad," said Aiden, not wanting to change the subject but thinking this would be the best time to ask his father about Jasper's party. Aiden felt more confident when his father replied in a calm tone. "On Friday there is a party at this boy Jasper's house. Me, Tyler and Callie are wanting to go…"

"No," his dad spoke sharply, cutting Aiden off.

"Why?" Aiden glared at his father.

"Because there was a murder recently in this town, and I want you to be safe."

"But Dad, that was the other week, and it could be good for me and Callie," said Aiden, feeling like this would help his case.

"Besides, I was going to be with Tyler and Callie all night, and Tyler said I could stay at his after."

Pausing to check his father's expression, Aiden continued, "Tyler's house is only two minutes away from the party." Aiden wanted to go to the party badly. Tyler's house was not two minutes away but more like twenty minutes away, but Aiden was desperate to go; he did not want to miss out on something that could bond his relationship with Tyler and Callie more. "Also, you aren't even here this weekend, you already told me you were planning to have a long weekend at the office. So rather than being on my own, I would be with Tyler and Callie."

Jason remained silent as he listened to his son's plea but smirked at his son's optimism. "You promise to be careful?" said Jason with a different tone of voice. Aiden's face illuminated at the change of tone.

"Yes."

"Okay, you can go then, but if anything happens I want you to run as fast as possible."

"Yeah, of course," said Aiden, totally ignoring Jason's last sentence, having already picked up his phone to text both Callie and Tyler about the news.

"Oh, the corridors of this school are an adventure," said Tyler sarcastically with the eruption of students into the hallways, witnessing Year 11s shoving the tiny Year 7s into the walls. It was the Friday, the day of Jasper's party, and it was fair to say that the entire school now knew of the event.

"I spoke to my dad, and he said I was allowed to stay at yours tonight," said Aiden.

"That's good, did he say anything else?" asked Tyler.

"Not really, only if I was in danger to run which I found weird," said Aiden, remembering the odd comment.

"Oh well, what's the worst that's going to happen," said Callie, joining in on the conversation.

"Everybody to the left side of the hall please," shouted the short, gorilla-like teacher, Mrs Zeros, who waved her hairy arms in the air, but students ignored her and began mimicking her voice. The hallways were far too busy for any teacher to try to control, leading to Mrs Zeros disappearing back into her room, slamming the door behind her. With the crowd of students eventually dispersing, revealing the sticky flooring beneath, the trio approached the stairs that led towards to the canteen.

"Aiden, Tyler!" a sudden shriek broke over the remaining students. Callie rolled her eyes, knowing who the voice belonged to. Amber appeared from a small crowd of students, walking arm in arm with a boy. "Hey, you two. Callie," said Amber contemptuously, glaring at her. "This here is my friend

Jasper. Obviously, you've heard he's having a party tonight and you two are more than welcome," Amber said slyly.

"Actually," said Jasper, looking towards a spoilt Amber. "It was just a friendly reminder that my party starts at six, just want to make sure you guys knew. Would be nice to see you all there." Jasper looked towards Callie and then Tyler.

"Thanks, Jasp," Callie mumbled back. Amber shot a dirty look towards Callie, not enjoying the fact she had just called him Jasp, while also giving Jasper a discreet look of disappointment.

"We shall see you later then," said Callie.

"Nice to see you guys. Aiden, Tyler, I'll see you both in PE," said Jasper. The two boys nodded as Amber barged past them, dragging Jasper with her, who seemed unable to escape her grip.

"Poor boy," said Aiden turning to walk, when suddenly someone walked into Aiden from the stairs, forcing Aiden to backtrack from the sudden force.

"Aiden," Callie yelped.

"Hey," said Aiden, looking towards the taller boy who had forcefully walked into him.

"Hey, you are that Aiden Dyer kid, aren't you?" the boy with white silver hair spoke, catching Aiden off guard.

"Yeah I am, and I'm sorry but who are you?" Aiden was taken aback. He had never met this boy before.

"I'm Tobias." He was older compared to Aiden, suggesting he was in either Year 10 or 11. Aiden had noticed him around the school, especially how all the girls would swoon over him as he passed by, but this was the first time they had ever spoken or even looked at one another directly. Tyler and Callie watched from a distance, both seemingly wanting to evade joining in the conversation.

"Are they your friends?" Tobias grinned, looking past Aiden at Callie. His natural silver hair complemented his grey eyes and tanned skin.

"Yeah, they are," said Aiden, only now noticing how far Tyler and Callie were from him.

"How are you finding Oakdale so far? You haven't been here long, have you?" Aiden was put off by the questions, he was surprised Tobias knew so much about him but at the same time a little cautious.

"Just under a month," said Aiden gingerly, as an unpleasant silence followed.

"Well," said Tobias calmly. "It was nice to meet you. I get a feeling we will see each other again." He walked off, passing Tyler and Callie, both of whom were still acting weird and keeping their distance.

"That was weird," said Aiden, approaching Callie and Tyler.

"Yeah that was, you know how I told you about the popularity ladder," Callie said, glancing towards Aiden, who nodded in return. "Well, you just met the prince of Oakdale Senior School, Tobias Irwin." She looked worried but Aiden wasn't sure why.

"Let's go to break before we miss it," said Tyler, before Aiden could ask about Callie's worrisome look.

"By the way, Aiden, I'll be at yours for six. I thought we could walk together to the party?" said Callie. Aiden's face lit up. *Time alone with Callie*, he thought as butterflies erupted in his stomach.

"Yeah, of course," he said, grinning all the way to lunch.

"What are you looking for?" Diana asked, her arms crossed. She had walked in Jason's office, which was now full of boxes, books and maps which were plastered to his walls. She looked at her long-time friend, who was digging deep into a box dated fourteen years ago.

"You know what. That night, the night I received that threat from Giovanni, I ran home only to find a burnt body in Aiden's baby room, with this sigil." Jason slammed down the pictures onto his desk, which Diana promptly picked up, immediately noticing they were the same. "And my wife gone. Amy was a mysterious person indeed, with a lot of secrets, but the moment Aiden was born, we were finally a family, and then I lost her. I believe the being who killed this person is the same being who killed Giovanni and my wife."

"That's why you didn't tell Daria about the sigil then," said Diana. "But please just listen to me." Diana knew from past experience that Jason was sensitive with this subject. "If this being did kill Amy, why did they disappear for fourteen years and return to kill one of Shun Yun Li's men?"

"That's what I was thinking," said Jason who pulled a pile of paperwork out of the box, slamming it against his desk before he delved deeper into what he thought was a forever expanding box.

"Besides, who is Daria? I've heard rumours about her when we were younger, but I had never seen or heard of her until a few years later," Jason added.

"Her family was killed, and she was brought in," said Diana. "She trained and gained a reputation quickly, a reputation which could almost rival yours, but then she disappeared on a mission and resurfaced years later. When the old boss left, she was the only candidate despite the International Seven wanting you to become the next leader."

"Finally," said Jason, his eyes lighting up.

"Interesting, I did find it peculiar when she appeared out of nowhere," said Jason, quickly exchanging a look with Diana. He pulled out a brown folder titled *Giovanni* with a red stamp on the cover.

"Extended research needed?" Jason said aloud, remembering last time he saw this folder it was heavier and without a red stamp.

"Yes, a few years ago when we had an influx of employees, the archive master wanted help in sorting out the decades of cases and information. I made sure that one stayed so I stamped it for you," said Diana.

"Thank you."

A lengthy silence stretched between them. "How's Aiden getting on?" Diana asked, leaning on Jason's cluttered desk, always finding it funny that despite him being so professional and tidy in his line of work, his office was to be this messy.

"Good. He's going to a party tonight with his two friends, Tyler and Chloe..." Jason paused, scrunching his face up knowing that to be the wrong name for the girl after the brief conversation he had had with Aiden the other night. "No, it's Callie," said Jason, opening the folder, when he heard Diana let out a small whimper.

"Callie?" Diana whispered under her breath. One of her hands quickly reached for her neck. Jason looked towards Diana realising what he had just said.

"Di... I'm so sorry... I... I..."

"It's okay," said Diana, a tear forming in her eye. Jason quickly closed the folder, moving towards Diana and placing a hand on her shoulder.

"It will be two years soon," said Diana, feeling her breath leave her body. Jason was lost for words. How could he be so stupid and self-absorbed to remember not to mention Callie, the name of Diana's dead daughter? Especially after feeling so guilty when he couldn't make it to her funeral to support his best friend.

"I'm sorry, Di," Jason said, remembering how Diana moved from Essex to Oakdale within the week of her daughter's death and took a short leave of absence from the company.

"It's honestly fine, Jason. I'm just happy I have you back. Besides, we have other things to focus on now," she said, wiping the tear from her cheek. "Let's try to find a connection and reason as to why this being has returned. Despite my daughter being dead, I still have a duty to protect others."

Jason nodded, not sure what to do but to listen to his friend, knowing full well that this case would be the best way to distract her.

6
The Party

It was half past six, and Aiden was waiting for a late Callie. At one point he was actually questioning whether or not she was going to come, but all these thoughts faded when he heard a loud knock on the door. Swinging open his front door, he saw Callie standing there applying lipstick and playing with her already perfect hair.

"Hey, you ready?" she asked putting her lipstick away in her purse.

"Yeah," said Aiden awestruck.

"You okay?" she questioned.

"You look beautiful," Aiden said bravely. Callie gulped. Aiden couldn't tell if she was blushing due to her foundation, but he knew she appreciated the compliment. The butterflies in Aiden's stomach seemed to intensify as he continued to look at Callie.

"Let's get going, shall we?"

"Of course," said Aiden closing and locking the door behind.

Walking down the road, following Callie as if he were a dog on a leash, Aiden admired how perfect she looked, the way she walked, her beautiful smile. He flexed his hands as they turned clammy. Her black sparkly heels were the same style as her obsidian sparkly jumpsuit; her brunette hair was buffed up with hairspray and curled with elegance.

"Where is Tyler?" asked Aiden, only just realising he never asked why Tyler wasn't walking with them earlier.

"He said he would meet us there, he's talking to Lydia," said Callie.

"Why Lydia?"

"They are good friends and before she left for France, they were spending a lot of time together. When she found out, she…" but before Callie finished her sentence, she bit her tongue sharply as if she was about to say something she shouldn't have.

"But then?" Aiden prompted, trying to make her carry on the sentence. "What did she find out?"

Callie struggled to form the words – she was struggling to form a sentence at this rate.

"Callie?" Aiden persisted.

He looked at her, and she continued to search her brain for a reply. She bit her lip anxiously. "Well… well everyone knows

Tyler's rich, but they don't know he is bisexual," said Callie, finally answering Aiden who was taken aback.

"That's cool," said Aiden. He wasn't bothered, but by the way Callie was speaking earlier it sounded like it was something far sinister. Callie looked at Aiden with appreciation. She knew some people would be put off by learning something like that about their friend's sexuality, and her stomach started to erupt in butterflies for Aiden. If she were able to blush, she would.

Eventually, they approached Jasper's house. The small cul-de-sac was filled with stylish Tudor-fashioned houses. Prominent black beams were visible on the outskirts of the houses, as the small lattice windows occupied the façade, with crooked chimneys rising above the roofs.

Callie came to a sudden stop. "Can you hear that?" she said apprehensively. Aiden stopped, turning to look at her. She moved her hair away from her ear, trying to concentrate on the surrounding sounds.

"Hear wh—"

"Shh," Callie snapped, concentrating. "Listen," she whispered. The two teenagers stood in silence, Aiden shut his eyes, concentrating, trying to understand what Callie could be hearing; he could only hear the faint sound of music in the background. But then a rustling noise erupted from the bushes on the other side of the road.

"Callie," Aiden murmured quietly, opening his eyes to see Callie had crossed the road and was by the bushes when something jumped out at them. Callie yelped, but it was only a small rabbit.

"Oh really," cried Callie as the rabbit started hopping away into another set of bushes. "Alright, let's get to this party then," she said, walking back to Aiden.

That was weird, Callie thought to herself. She swore she heard something else, something heavier instead of a rabbit. She watched as Aiden started walking again towards the party. Aiden placed his hands in his pockets and was speaking to her, but her mind was elsewhere. Taking in deep breaths, smelling the all-powerful and mouth-watering scent that belonged to the boy she walked next to, she forcibly controlled herself. Thinking of the compliment Aiden gave her when he saw her at his front door made her feel something which she thought she would never feel again... warmth. She smiled, when suddenly she heard a voice speak to her which made her still heart jump into her throat.

"Good little girl," whispered a male voice, the voice knowing that only Callie would be able to hear them and not Aiden. "If that cute little bunny rabbit never jumped out of that bush, then you may have found me." The voice chuckled hauntingly. Callie looked over her shoulder, knowing she was being watched, but she couldn't see the man the voice belonged to. The voice was only inside her head. "Oh, and by the way your friend smells… tasty." The malevolent tone made Callie shudder before it dissipated into the surrounding sounds of the forest.

Callie grabbed Aiden's hand, holding it tight, which took him off guard, but he seemed to enjoy the moment. Her stomach growled with discomfort, knowing it wasn't the hunger but something else. She felt as if her stomach was warning her about the party. All she knew was that she had to keep her eyes on Aiden at all times; she would not be able to forgive herself if something horrible happened to him.

Arriving at the party, still hand in hand, Aiden knocked on the door, and she muttered under her breath, "Callie Shaw, you need to protect Aiden Dyer!"

Tyler answered the door and beamed at the sight of his friends. He led Aiden and Callie through the crowded hallway and to the kitchen. Another door to the side led to the dance floor where loud music was pumping through multiple speakers.

There were more people here than Aiden had anticipated and he was glad to have Callie and Tyler on either side of him.

Time seemed to fly by. They filled their night with chatter and dancing. Confidence, happiness and the thought of being able to talk to anyone flooded Aiden's body.

The dynamic music was up-beat and exhilarating, having kept Aiden and the others on the dance floor for the entire night. Strobe lighting was bouncing off the corners of the room as Aiden danced happily with Callie and Tyler. Since arriving, Callie and Aiden hadn't left each other's side. So far, this night felt like the best night of Aiden's existence. To top Callie's night off, Amber had shown up to the party in a not-so-flattering black bodysuit that made her look dull and bloated. Callie laughed in her face when they arrived, almost causing a fight, but Aiden pulled her away before the first punch could be launched. Amber had attempted to make her way towards Aiden on the dance floor, but Jasper had pulled her away, telling her to stay away from them. It wasn't long before Aiden, Tyler and Callie had all retreated outside, into the fresh air escaping the stuffy, sweaty and overcrowded dance floor.

"How are you finding this?" Tyler yelled over the music.

"I am loving every second of it," said Aiden. "I need to go to the toilet. I'll be back in a minute," he shouted back. Callie and Tyler nodded as he walked off.

Aiden marched up the stairs, making his way to the toilet, wanting to rejoin Callie and Tyler downstairs as quickly as possible.

Slamming the toilet door closed, he splashed water on his face and then patted himself dry. All the dancing and loud music had made him dizzy. He wasn't used to strobe lights and crowded dance floors. He took a moment to collect his thoughts and then slipped out of the bathroom to join his friends again. "You smell nice," said a thin, drawling voice from the darkness as Aiden exited the toilet. Aiden looked to whom the voice belonged to, and a man walked forward from the shadows of the landing.

"What do you mean?" Aiden gulped, taking note of the older man, knowing he didn't belong at the party with his ancient leather jacket and baggy blue jeans. He found it strange someone like this was at Jasper's house when Jasper had made it clear his family was out of town. Aiden looked around, and they were the only two on the first floor.

"You smell amazing," said the man, grabbing Aiden's arm fiercely.

"Let go of me," yelped Aiden. The man tightened his grip, and it felt as if the man was about to break his wrist.

"Never, you are all mine," the man said malevolently. He pulled Aiden forwards and threw him against the wall. A darkness descended within the house, with the strobe light following the beat of the music and, now, Aiden's heartbeat. A growl came from the shadows, a growl which Aiden had heard before and recognised… back in the church. This was all happening too quickly. *What was happening?* Was his mind playing tricks on him? As the strobe lighting illuminated the landing, Aiden's worsts fears were confirmed.

For what was once the man's cold and pale face, was now a creature of the devil. His blood red eyes stood out in the darkness, with black slits for pupils, a fountain of red veins consumed his face, blood pulsing from under his eyes. His teeth had turned into razor sharp fangs; his smile elongated from ear to ear, showing every fang in pristine condition.

Aiden gasped and struggled against the man's grip, but he was powerless against the man's strength. His stomach shrunk and his mind panicked. Instinct told him to run, but before he could, the man's hand went to Aiden's neck and pinned him against the wall. Feeling the floor disappear from below, he was elevated into the air by the man's spectacular strength. Quivering with fear, unable to breath due to the man's immense grip around his neck, he tried his best to speak but nothing came. Suddenly, the man was ripped away and Aiden fell to the floor. The man disappeared from in front of him like magic.

Coughing heavily, relieved to feel oxygen once again bless his body, Aiden looked over to see the man had been thrown to the floor at the end of the landing.

"Tyler," Aiden coughed.

"Aiden, run!" shouted Tyler. Aiden noticed a distinct redness in Tyler's eyes as well. He didn't need to be told twice, and he massaged his neck as he ran down the stairs, leaving Tyler and the monstrous man. He barged out the door and onto the littered lawn and, remembering what his dad had said about danger, he ran and did not look back, running towards the forest which lay at the side of Jasper's house.

The forest was forever expanding. Branches slapped Aiden in the face, and the damp ground made it tricky to not fall over. Aiden continued running fast; he didn't know how fast he was running, but he was certain of one thing, that he had never run this fast before in his life. The adrenaline pulsing through his body was forcing him to carry on and not stop. He looked back a couple of times, but he didn't see anyone following him. Aiden couldn't stop wondering who the man was. Red eyes, red veins that covered his face, and the fangs that erupted from his gums. It reminded Aiden of Tyler in the vision. But one question popped into Aiden's head, why was he after him? And how was Tyler able to save him? He didn't know what to think, but his body kept telling him to run and to not stop.

Realising that he must have been a considerable distance away from the party by now, Aiden came to a slow stop. His stomach churned with the possibility of being sick, and he focussed on slowing his breathing. Aiden closed his eyes, he was scared, terrified – had he just avoided death tonight? The questions kept popping into his head, but he did as his father had said, run away from danger. He kept his eyes closed as the night life of the forest continued to sing around him when Aiden suddenly heard a twig snap. His eyes snapped opened, and the man appeared out of nowhere, grabbing Aiden by the shirt.

"Hello, boy." He raised Aiden off the ground with immense strength. "It's just me and you. Your friend won't save you this time. I am going to enjoy draining you." He was salivating, looking into Aiden's eyes with pure hunger as the growls from the man's stomach grew louder and louder. Aiden's feet dangled in the air as he tried to escape the grasp of the man but failed.

"You are about to make me the most powerful being in existence." The man's face returned to its devilish form. The thick veins erupted under his eyes as his red, soulless eyes with black slits returned.

"What are you?" Aiden coughed out. The man pulled Aiden close to him, breathing his disgusting breath onto Aiden, who could only describe it to be a mixture of dried blood and out-of-date meat.

"I'm a vampire." The man laughed as if it were obvious, his pristine white fangs appeared from his expanding upper jaw. Aiden gulped. He never knew this fear was possible. The man threw Aiden through the air. He hit a tree with force, falling to the hard ground with a loud thud. Aiden roared with the excruciating pain that followed. He looked down to see his leg broken and the bone protruding through the skin. Blood came rushing out, trickling onto the grass. Aiden cried, knowing tonight was the night he was going to die. He looked everywhere but at the man's face, trying to see if there was anywhere for him to escape to but then a lurch of hope ignited as Callie and Tyler had appeared out of nowhere. Both of them looked at Aiden warily.

"Back for more are we, boy?" the man said, standing over Aiden, ready to pounce. He looked at Aiden with hungry desire, and Tyler and Callie leapt forward, but it was too late. Aiden screamed with horror. The man had his mouth round Aiden's neck. Every single razor-sharp fang pierced his skin, entering his neck – Aiden could feel his inner warmth leaving his body. What seemed like forever was only a mere few seconds. Tyler tackled the man off Aiden. Aiden felt the instant relief as if life had returned to his body. Callie appeared next to him, cradling his head in her arms.

"You're going to be okay," she stuttered, grasping her soft hands around Aiden's bloody and bleeding neck, looking towards his broken leg. Aiden looked at Callie, taking notice as red veins appeared and disappeared from underneath her eyes, her pupils switching back and forth from slits to her stunning eyes.

"You're a vampire," he said weakly.

After having hit the man with all his power, Tyler and the vampire rose to their feet. Tyler's face had changed as well, and in a glimpse, Aiden saw his friend's haunting face and knew for certain that Tyler was a vampire and the boy from his vision. The man had started to act like a wild animal who was craving Aiden, screaming his name trying his best to reach him, but Tyler defended Aiden.

"Aiden, look at me," Callie muttered under her breath, trying to distract herself and Aiden, but Aiden couldn't pay attention to her. He was far too weak; all he could do was watch Tyler and the crazed vampire fight. Tyler was throwing quick punches, attacking the man's abdomen, but this seemed to have no effect. The man grabbed Tyler by the cuff of his shirt throwing him aside and moving towards Aiden and Callie. Callie held her hands against Aiden's neck, trying to stop the bleeding, but as the man approached menacingly, she was readying herself to fight. Tyler appeared from nowhere, tackling the man backwards into a tree. Retreating and jumping into the air, the crazed vampire shuffled forwards with Tyler landing behind. Advancing, Tyler locked the vampire's head in a headlock before kicking the man in the back with his knee, the vampire fell forwards, groaning, before Tyler forced his hand into the back of the man. The man roared in agony, and Aiden could hear the distinct sound of bones breaking.

"He's my friend," said Tyler, ripping the man's heart from his back. Tyler held the man's heart in his hand, and the body fell forwards with a thud, turning grey instantly.

"We have to get Aiden out of here," said Callie. Walking over to a numb Aiden, who had become paralysed with fear, Tyler leant down, his eyes red and cheeks flushed.

"I'm sorry," said Tyler, whilst Callie watched, knowing what he was going to do.

Before Aiden could speak, Tyler's fangs appeared, and he bit Aiden's neck. Aiden gagged for air. The sensation was opposite to what he felt earlier, he felt Tyler inserting a cold liquid into his body, feeling the cold liquid move throughout his body and down towards his broken leg.

Tyler withdrew his mouth, but before he could say anything, Aiden felt another bout of excruciating pain, which was far too much for him to handle. He blacked out peacefully, welcoming the realm of sleep where he could no longer feel any pain.

"Callie, let me take him home to Cara. You take care of the body." Callie nodded. As much as she didn't want to leave Aiden, she knew, from previous experiences, Tyler always knew what to do in situations like this. Tyler picked Aiden up quickly, leaving Callie to deal with the dead vampire body, and zoomed off at an amazing speed.

Aiden, the Perfect Blood, was far more important and more powerful than Tyler thought he was. All he knew was that he didn't fancy any more fights this evening.

7
Finding Out

Aiden slept heavily. His dreams were full of horror. He was cornered by a creature, a creature with a face of a monster. The red eyes with black slits glaring at Aiden, and the most all-devouring mouth, a grin from ear to ear showing every razor-sharp white fang possible. Aiden tried to look away, but he couldn't; nothing could stop him from seeing the face of a vampire. Trying his best to block the sight out of his head, he woke up, gasping for air.

Minutes passed and Aiden was looking down at the white sheets knowing that they were not his. For a mere second, he was hoping his dad would walk in any minute, reassuring Aiden that last night was all a dream, but as he glanced around the room, he remembered last night was not a dream. He was not in his own room but Tyler's. He looked around warily. Everything that had happened was not a dream but reality. He threw the covers off, looking at his leg, remembering he had broken it. Expecting to see a bandage, he saw nothing. His leg looked completely normal as if nothing had happened. Furrowing his brow, he searched for an answer as to what had happened and how his leg miraculously healed itself. Wondering what to do, he instinctively thought of his dad.

"Where's my phone?" he questioned himself as he scrambled around Tyler's room looking for his jeans, for which his phone would be in.

"Your phone is downstairs," said a voice.

Aiden jumped to his feet, having been on his knees looking under Tyler's double bed for his phone. Hobbling towards the wall, feeling his heartbeat in the region of his Adam's apple, Aiden looked towards the doorway where Cara stood, holding clothes and a tray of food.

"I think you need to come downstairs," she said, walking calmly into Tyler's room, placing the tray of food on the bed. Aiden remained silent, his tongue was twisted, too scared to talk.

"You can trust me. I am human," she said. Aiden looked at her apprehensively. He stood against the wall, hoping she wouldn't come and pry him away.

"I want to speak to my dad," said Aiden, these being the only words able to exit his mouth.

"You'll have time to do that, but first you need to learn the truth." Cara paused, looking at Aiden standing awkwardly in his boxers. "Are you going to stand there all day in your boxers, or will you put some clothes on? Eat your breakfast that I kindly prepared for you and come downstairs for a chat."

Aiden remained still, not knowing what to do. He glanced over to the food, noticing she had made him pancakes in the shape of fangs. His belly rumbled with hunger. He wanted the food, yet all he could think of was his dad.

"Eat it because if we wanted you dead, you would have been dead the instant you walked into my house." Aiden's eyes widened as he looked back towards Cara who had left the room silently. He was alone again, and the thought of knowing someone could have killed him at any point left a nasty taste in his mouth. But he ran for the pancakes, scoffing them down quickly, the hunger in his stomach pleased with the offering. Wiping his mouth clean, he looked over to the clothes Cara had given him. Fear, caution… he could taste it… but most of all curiosity flared within him.

What do I do? Aiden wondered. Why wouldn't they let him talk to his father? As Aiden gave it a greater deal of thought, what would he say to his father? *Hi, Dad, my friends are vampires, and I was almost killed last night.* The more Aiden thought about it, the crazier it sounded. Looking towards the open door, Aiden knew the only way to get answers and to leave Tyler's house was to go downstairs. Throwing on the clothes provided, Aiden left the safety of Tyler's room and headed downstairs.

He walked cautiously into the open living room. He was greeted with surveying looks from Tyler, Callie and Cara, who sat calmly on the sofa. It reminded him of his first day at school – the glaring looks trying to pierce his soul.

"Hi," Aiden murmured, looking between the three of them.

"Hey," said Tyler and Callie in chorus. This was the first time Aiden had seen them since the night before, and despite all that he had seen, there was no thought or feeling to run away or fear them.

"Sit," said Cara, pointing towards the armchair opposite Callie and Tyler. Aiden did so reluctantly and placed himself on the edge on the seat. Cara sat up straighter, acting like a judge in a court room.

"Where do we begin?" said Callie gingerly. She was rubbing her hands up and down her legs. She seemed like she was trying her best not to cry but at the same time struggling to think what to say.

"Where would Aiden like to begin?" said Cara. She looked towards Aiden, awkwardly smiling as if this were a counselling session.

"What are you?" said Aiden immediately. Despite knowing what the answer was, he felt like he needed to hear them say it one more time.

"We are vampires," said Tyler.

Aiden felt his stomach drop. Even though he saw what they were and what they were capable of the night before, it still made his spine tingle hearing them say the word. "How did you guys become vampires?"

Tyler and Callie exchanged looks. Cara looked towards Tyler, and Aiden felt the unease in the air.

"You go first," said Callie quietly, looking towards Tyler.

"I was born on May 15, 1916," Tyler began. "I grew up in 1920s America, during the Boom era. When the Great Depression hit, my father committed suicide because we lost all our money. My mother went insane and disappeared. During that time, I ended a relationship with this girl, Lesa, as I cheated on her with a guy."

"Lesa?" Aiden interrupted, remembering hearing that name before. "And you're old," said Aiden dealing with the extraordinary amount of information Tyler was saying.

Tyler laughed, rubbing his hands together. "You've heard that name before?"

"Yes."

"Where?" queried Tyler.

"During the first couple of days of being in Oakdale, I went for a run and came across a church. When I went inside I touched this scratch mark and saw you there fighting this woman, who was flying through the air." Aiden recalled the events, now realising how much had changed. Cara and Tyler looked at one another, understanding what Aiden was talking about.

"Yes, she was a witch, and before you ask, witches do exist," Cara said pointedly.

"Our friend Lydia is a witch," Callie added as if it were nothing.

The world which Aiden knew was expanding dramatically. Vampires and now witches? He didn't know if this was amazing or scary.

"But let's get back to Tyler's story," said Cara, trying to return the conversation.

"But I want to know," said Aiden.

"Aiden, you are not going to be able to learn about the entire supernatural world in one day. Let's just stick to the basics," Cara snapped. Aiden retracted his head into his shoulders, feeling like he had just been told off by a teacher.

"So," said Tyler. "It turns out I broke Lesa's heart and she didn't really take it well. After breaking up with Lesa, she asked me to meet her in Central Park where we used to hang out. When I approached our spot, I found a hole and a coffin. I called her name and turned round to meet two red eyes in a bush, staring at me. A man pounced out and attacked me. Lesa watched from a distance; she had bewitched the vampire to kill me, but instead he transformed me. A day later I awoke in a coffin as a vampire. I met Cara in 1934." Tyler went silent for a while after. Callie seemed to console him by touching his hand, but Tyler waved her off before returning his gaze to Aiden, seemingly anticipating his next question.

"So, Cara isn't your nan then?"

"No, she isn't. She found me confused and dazed; it turns out a witch wiped my memory between when I was transformed into a vampire till when I met Cara. Since then, Cara and I have travelled together. We came to Oakdale in the late 1980s. We lived here peacefully until Lesa returned when she found out I was still alive. One night she attacked me, and we ended up in the church where I killed her. After I killed her, we left Oakdale and moved up north." Tyler shrugged, finishing his story.

"How many vampires are there in the world?" asked Aiden, the questions now coming easier.

"Not as many as you would think," answered Callie. Aiden looked towards Callie, who was smiling sweetly at him. Despite what he had learnt, he felt oddly guilty that he hadn't asked Callie about her transformation into a vampire.

"How did you become a vampire?"

"I was transformed by Tyler," she answered.

"Transformed?" questioned Aiden.

"Transformed from human to a vampire," answered Cara. Aiden bore a puzzled face. He understood what they meant but how did it happen? Cara observed this look before she continued. "Vampire venom must be inserted into a human and then you must die with it in you. Once you die, you will awake, and the tricky part is that you must drink the blood of the vampire who transformed you. If you don't, you die within two days… that's if you aren't killed by the sun or other factors."

"Am I going to become a vampire then?" Aiden felt his heart sink. "I remember you biting me last night. Why did you do that?"

"Calm down," said Callie, briefly smiling towards Aiden, hearing his heart rate increase.

"Tyler did it to heal you. He inserted vampire venom into your body, which quickens the rate of healing in a human, the only downside is that you feel the pain you felt when you sustained that injury. It will leave your system within twenty-four hours, which is one reason why we want to keep you here."

Aiden felt a wave of relief, exhaling heavily. The brief thought of him becoming a vampire was truly horrifying, especially when he knew nothing about it all. Aiden took another deep breath in, whilst at the same time wondering what they meant by "one reason". Turning his attention to Callie, realising she hadn't finished her story, he asked, "How did you become a vampire?"

"I was born July 24, 1996, and I was transformed by Tyler. When I was fourteen, I was diagnosed with bone cancer and by the time I was sixteen," Callie paused, her voice broke and her eyes flickered. Aiden noticed a tear in her eye, and in that moment, all he wanted to do was hug her. "The cancer had made its way to other parts of my body. My mother refused to lose me, so she did everything in her power not to. The day before I died, my mother went out. When she returned, she bought Tyler. Tyler offered me the chance to live, and I took it. I had to become a vampire," Callie finished.

"I have so many questions," said Aiden. "How did your mum find Tyler? How did she know Tyler was a vampire? She knows you're a vampire? Why are you guys still here?" Cara raised her hand before Aiden could ask any more questions, Aiden himself feeling like he had been asking a marathon of questions.

"My mother has a particular job, that is the second reason why we want you to stay here. That will answer your first two questions. My mum does know I am a vampire. I moved to Oakdale with her for her job, and Tyler moved back here to teach me to be a vampire. Please trust me when I say you will get the answers." Callie looked deeply into Aiden's eyes.

"Okay," he replied, despite his eagerness to know everything. Another question popped into Aiden's head, and he said, "How are you guys able to walk in sunlight?"

Tyler exchanged a quick grimace with Callie, as if he had been anticipating this question from the start. Within a blink, Tyler had disappeared then reappeared in front of Aiden holding a jar of discoloured yellowy water, with peculiar pieces floating on the inside. Aiden leapt backwards, deeper into the comfortable chair.

"Yeah, we are very fast. Vampires have increased strength and speed," said Tyler casually as if it were nothing special.

"This is our protection from the sunlight," said Callie, trying to make Aiden focus on the murky water. Aiden looked at the water, readjusting the way he sat. *It looks like drain water*, he thought. "What is it?" he squinted into the jar, almost afraid to touch it.

"It is a sunflower ointment which is created by a different type of witch. It protects us from sunlight for a year so we have to make sure we keep topping up, otherwise one day we could start to disintegrate and burst into a miraculous fire," said Tyler, once again in a casual tone, as if this was all normal.

"When you say a different type of witch, what do you mean?"

"We are only going to focus on vampires. We will let Lydia educate you in the community of the witches," said Cara, looking at Aiden who nodded in return. Tyler returned to his seat, placing the yellow water on the table.

The sunlight of the day pierced through the floor-to-ceiling grand windows and illuminated the room. Aiden massaged his hands against his legs. He was finally understanding everything, but there was still one thing, one question, that would help him understand why he was attacked last night.

"What am I then?" he said in a calm tone, looking towards his two friends and Cara. "The man… the vampire," Aiden corrected. "When it attacked me last night, he said I smelt delicious, and when I was bleeding he changed and became… like a wild animal." Aiden found it hard to explain how the man had been acting when it was all a blurred vision.

The atmosphere in the room seemed to change. Callie pursed her lips. Cara looked towards her wine cabinet in the corner of the room Tyler begun scratching his head. It was Callie who spoke. "You are what is known as the Perfect Blood."

"What's the Perfect Blood?" Aiden replied immediately. "How do you know I am the Perfect Blood?" The panic that had once subsided now returned.

"The Perfect Blood is a mortal being with the most powerful blood in existence," said Tyler. "The individual's blood is so pure it can create a vampire that is so strong that it can change the fabric of the supernatural world. The vampire would become the Ultimatum."

Aiden gulped as he struggled to digest the information, feeling his stomach turn and a sudden sickening feeling grow. "How is it created?" Aiden bravely asked, whilst also wishing he hadn't.

"From what we can guess, the vampire must feed off your blood, draining you entirely… killing you," said Callie.

Aiden let out a little whimper. "Am I the first Perfect Blood then?" he asked.

"No, you aren't," answered Cara.

Tyler once again zoomed off, leaving his seat on the sofa for a few milliseconds before returning, holding a frail bound book. He handed the book to Aiden, who slowly opened it, taking note of the weak binding. On the front page was a table.

"They are the previous Perfect Bloods."

Name	Location	Born	Died	Age	Death
Jacob Smelt	UK	1200	1220	20	Vamp
Gretta Roberts	Germany	1418	1430	12	Vamp
Rowan Drukheim	Poland	1560	1612	52	Suicide
Mizuki Mou Feng	Japan	1706	1731	25	Witch

"So, how come the Ultimatum has never been created then, if two previous Perfect Bloods were killed by vampires?" questioned Aiden. He pointed his finger towards the two names that stated they had been killed by vampires.

"We don't know," Cara muttered calmly.

There seemed to be a peace in finally knowing who and what he was, but that seemed to dwindle knowing the blood that circulated his veins could create the most powerful vampire in existence.

"But still, how do you know I am the Perfect Blood?" said Aiden, in some small way hoping that they could be wrong.

"Bloods have different types of scent. If you are a human, you smell sweet, a supernatural creature has a neutral smell, whereas the Perfect Blood has a mouth tingling sour smell. We were unsure whether or not you were the Perfect Blood to begin with as your blood goes through phases, one moment it has the sour scent and the next it smells sweet; it's like your blood is changing... evolving almost," said Tyler. "As vampires have never smelt a sour scent before, it's intoxicating. A young vampire would easily lose control of their hunger in order to hunt you down; maybe that's why the vampire attacked you and may explain the deaths of the previous two Perfect Bloods, but we are quite unsure as to how the Ultimatum is created."

"What do you mean, when you say my blood is evolving?" Aiden asked, feeling like he was now interrogating them.

"It means that right now, at certain moments, you blood switches into the Perfect Blood and the next is switches back. It's only a matter of time before your blood makes the permanent change. When that happens, you'll be the most hunted being in the supernatural world," Cara muttered. Her tone had darkened. "And with that said, I need a drink." She rose from her chair, heading towards her silver embossed bar cabinet, pouring herself a healthy measure of red wine.

"Cara," said Tyler, yet his tone lacked any surprise.

"It's five o'clock somewhere, boy," Cara said sharply.

"Have you got any more questions?" Callie asked, her voice soft and mellow, distracting Aiden from the others.

"Yes. Only one."

Callie felt her insides flip knowing the time was coming to tell him the truth about his father.

"Why have you wanted to keep me here?"

Tyler and Callie exchanged cautious looks at one another. "Do you want to tell him?" said Tyler, pointing his head towards Callie. Callie sighed, knowing it would probably be best coming from her as their two parents both worked for the same company.

"Aiden," Callie began. Aiden sensed the severity in her voice; she had never said his name in a manner like that before. "The world is a dangerous place for humans and vampires. Despite us being the apex predator, vampires are also hunted. There is a reason why we stay hidden and out of sight. We are hunted by a secret organisation that will kill any vampire, no matter if they are good or bad, without mercy. All this organisation worries about is the eradication of vampires. My mother works for this organisation and is different to the other employees. When she knew the only cure to save me was the very thing she had hunted and fought, she knew she was only seeing the world through one pair of eyes. She is probably the only one in the organisation who, in my eyes, is reformed. My mum saved Tyler, but Tyler had to transform me. I just want you to know that this organisation is very dangerous; many of its employees travel the world, to different countries in fact, hunting and killing vampires and then moving onto their next mission." Callie paused.

Beginning to think about the past, Aiden was suddenly understanding. *Could it be possible?* His dad in the past had mentioned, "When you reach sixteen, I'll have a good job for you" or when Aiden also remembered the constant vigilance he suffered on days out as a kid. Could this be linked?

As he remained silent, deep in his thoughts, Callie continued. "My mother, Aiden, is a vampire hunter. Your dad is a vampire hunter."

8
The Bloody Rock

"No," said Aiden indignantly. "He can't be. He isn't. I don't believe you." Aiden felt his voice grow louder.

"The secret organisation is called the Vampire Hunter Association but VHA for short…" Callie started. Aiden listened to her, feeling a deep anger within start to erupt, not knowing where it came from and whether he would be able to control it.

"Stop," he whispered, but neither Callie nor Tyler heard.

"Your father is a notorious and dangerous hunter. Your family, the Dyers, has a rich history with the VHA. You will become a part of this organisation when you reach sixteen."

VHA! Vampire Hunter! Dyer! These were all the words that were circulating Aiden's mind before the room started to spin.

"Your father is known as a Master Hunter. One of the most elite and talented hunters in the world."

"Shut up!" Aiden silenced Callie, spitting with anger. "That's not my dad. He's…" but as quickly as the anger appeared, it began to dissipate. Aiden couldn't find the words to finish his sentence. He stood up, flushed, with his mouth wide open, but everything was now finally making sense.

"We haven't lied to you," said Callie, rising from her seat. She walked forwards, standing in front of Aiden, their faces centimetres apart. Aiden looked into her gorgeous hybrid eyes; never before had he seen a mixture of brown and green before, almost resembling a forest. Feeling her body millimetres away was in some way comforting, despite knowing that she could kill him within seconds.

"Besides, we can take you somewhere to show you we are telling the truth," said Tyler.

Aiden pondered with his thoughts as Callie slowly took Aiden's hands; feeling her soft skin in his hands gave him the power to speak. "Take me there then," said Aiden.

"Firstly, go have a shower, you smell," said Cara abruptly, breaking the tension of the room. Tyler, Callie and Aiden's heads turned to face the older women, who was most likely on here third drink by now. She seemed to sway as she turned to face them, one of her eyes looking wonky.

"A shower will do you good, honey," she finished before walking off.

"Meet us in the garage when you have finished," said Tyler before zooming off to Cara who suddenly tripped.

It was mid-afternoon on a Saturday, and the VHA continued its day-to-day operations. Jason Dyer and Diana Shaw sat in the back of the sleek black four-by-four, being driven to a site by their chauffer.

"I've never heard of this warehouse before," said Diana.

"Neither have I," agreed Jason, equally as suspicious.

They arrived shortly at the abandoned warehouse complex where vegetation now ruled. Jason and Diana were led to one warehouse in particular where the metal doors had been forced open. The site had already been searched by other hunters before the arrival of the two Master Hunters.

The site before the Master Hunters was a site of astonishment. At least twenty Asian men, dressed in once-spectacularly well-fitted black suits, lay dead on the floor. However, they were not people; they were vampires. Their bodies had been cleanly sliced apart as if it had been as easy as tearing a piece of paper. Diana sighed, looking at the grey and disfigured bodies.

"Good riddance," spat Jason walking forwards, looking down at all the bodies. They all lay in a scarlet puddle of their own blood. Jason remembered the first time he had seen a dead vampire, remembering how if their hearts were removed, they would turn into a grey corpse. Far more merciful than igniting into a roaring fire if a vampire had been killed with a wooden stake.

"These men look familiar," stated Jason, before a hunter from the other side of the warehouse waved for Diana and Jason to join them. The two Master Hunters walked over, Diana stepping carefully and meticulously over the bodies, whereas Jason walked over the bodies as if they were nothing.

"*Oi Chi*," said Jason in perfect Vietnamese. Standing at the doorway of the office, a body lay on the desk, blood oozing and dripping off the side of the neatly organised desk.

"Is that?" Diana paused. Jason walked deeper into the room, examining the site. "Wye Mun Gong?" Diana asked rhetorically, knowing it was after seeing his face in many pictures taken by VHA hunters.

"It was Wye Mun Gong." Jason looked at the dead man.

"How did this man get into England without us knowing? And why has someone killed him?" Jason said aloud, knowing Diana would be thinking the same thing.

"We have all of the UK airports linked to our security and facial recognition systems, so that means they came in another way," said Diana.

"Well for someone to kill Shun Yun Li's right-hand man, they are obviously trying to get his attention but why?" Jason began pacing the length of the office, the dead body not bothering the grown man at all. "For now," he continued, turning to face the hunter who stood at the doorway, "take pictures and send all the evidence to us and only us. Once this has been done, then burn it down." The hunter nodded and ran off.

The two Master Hunters exited the warehouse and made their way back to the blacked-out four-by-four. "Someone or something is after Shun Yun Li. A very skilled being," said Jason. He and Diana entered the air-coned car, the leather interior chilled. "There is no coincidence that these killings are linked but" Jason continued, remembering when he had received the phone call about a man who had been impaled by a mighty stake, leading to his return to Oakdale, "this attack was more physical and the other was magic." Jason stroked his chin. Something wasn't adding up. To begin with, Jason was sure the being who had impaled the man was the one responsible for his wife's death, but now he doubted himself.

"There is no such thing as a coincidence in our line of work. Maybe they are trying to throw us off?" said Diana. She looked at Jason who was deep in thought. "Shall we tell Daria about Shun Yun Li's men?"

"No, not yet. I haven't got enough evidence. I'll tell you when it's time."

Jason remained silent until they left the site, and it wasn't long before he looked in the rearview mirror of the car to see the abandoned warehouse go up in flames. He felt his phone vibrate as he received the pictures. But one matter lingered on his mind. Why was someone killing Shun Yun Li's men? What was this being trying to achieve?

Despite his utter revulsion for vampires, Jason couldn't help but have a sense of admiration for Shun. The man was intelligent and cunning. He had completely eradicated the VHA from Japan in the early 1900s and now ran one of the world's largest weapons empire. Could it be possible that this being was trying to pull Shun away from safety to the UK where he would be open to be attacked? But then would Shun be that stupid to fall for it?

As the car drove off, Jason thought about Aiden. He wondered how his weekend had been. If he had had a good time at the party with his friends. Jason took a sigh of relief knowing that his son was safe at his friend's house, far away from anything dangerous. Especially vampires.

Cara was right: it turned out a shower was the best thing Aiden needed. The warm and powerful jets of Tyler's all-consuming shower head gave Aiden what he needed most – time to digest what he had learnt. Having dressed in clean clothes that Tyler had provided, Aiden made his way back down to the dining room.

"You ready?"

"Yes," he replied. He turned to face Callie who stood behind him smiling, her hands behind her back.

"I hope this doesn't change anything between us," she said.

"Never," Aiden felt himself say by instinct as he knew he wanted Callie to be more than a friend. Aiden wanted nothing more than to reach out and grab her, but some hesitancy still lingered, knowing full well what she was capable of.

"Good." she smiled. "Come with me, Tyler is waiting."

He followed Callie up the stairs towards the front door. She took a sharp right turn into an open door which Aiden hadn't noticed before. The two teenagers made their way into the immaculate garage. Four car shapes stood out underneath a protective cloth like ghosts. "Tyler, where are you?" yelled Callie. Aiden was too preoccupied with looking around the garage when a deep voice echoed, making Aiden jump.

He spun around and his heart missed a beat. *Does Tyler have a brother?* was the first thought that popped to Aiden's mind as he locked eyes with an older version of Tyler.

"Who are you?"

"It's me," the voice spoke. "Tyler." It was Tyler, but he looked different. He had grown another few inches now being well above six feet tall. His body and face were more toned, and he now had prominent stubble.

"What happened to you?" Aiden said gingerly, looking Tyler up and down.

"Vampires have a special hormone called Vamporosium. It allows us to increase or decrease our age by five years from the age we were transformed at. So, as we were both transformed at sixteen, Callie and I can age ourselves up to twenty-one or down to eleven."

"That's amazing." Aiden grinned, studying Tyler.

"We can use Vamporosium whenever we want. It's a defence mechanism our bodies came up with that allow us to go unnoticed. It's a hard skill, one which I am trying to learn still," said Callie, educating Aiden further.

"I've used it so I can drive, otherwise it would be weird seeing a fourteen-year-old driving," Tyler joked. Aiden laughed as he admired the power of Vamporosium. It made him wonder what he would look like himself as he grew up.

"So what car are we taking?" said Callie, grinning.

"I'm thinking the Aston?" Tyler replied with a cheeky grin.

Driving to the outskirts of Oakdale, past the forests and winding hills, Aiden sat in the front, the smooth, luxury leather mixed with the all-body relaxing seat made it an experience not just a drive. Bright, summery leaves danced in the wind as the Aston Martin drove smoothly over the roads, and it made Aiden realise that the scenery Oakdale had to offer was almost incomparable to anything he had seen before. "It's beautiful," commented Aiden.

Within the hour, they reached Oakdale Forest Hiking Route. Parking the car in the almost abandoned car park, Tyler returned to his regular age, twitching his head and body throughout what seemed like a painful process.

"It will take us just under an hour to get there," said Tyler, twitching his jaw back and forth.

"So other than speed, what else can you do?" They were halfway into the journey to the Bloody Rock. Aiden was almost certain it was a cover-up and that Callie and Tyler were about to take him somewhere super secretive. His active imagination was playing up, *Was it a person? Or a person inside a rock? A person inside a rock who had the powers to compel people to tell the truth?*

"Let me show you," said Callie, and without warning she jumped high into the air, as if gravity had magically turned itself off. Aiden watched, mesmerized. Callie seemed to linger in the air for a while, her hair floating, but then she came slamming down, karate chopping a fallen tree, breaking it into a million wood chips as if it were a twig.

"Amazing," said Aiden awe-stricken. A thin layer of golden dust filled the air as thousands of little splinters littered the forest flooring. Callie walked out unharmed, clapping the dust off her hands.

"I have the power to Silvertongue," said Tyler.

"Silvertongue?" questioned Aiden.

"It's a rare and special ability that only certain vampires have. It allows us to access the mind of humans. We can control their thoughts and make them do whatever we want, and we can change the events of a certain time in their mind."

"Lucky you," said Callie sulkily. Aiden watched her, guessing that Callie did not acquire the power to Silvertongue when she was transformed by Tyler.

"You never used mind control on me, did you?" said Aiden in a reedy tone.

"No, I haven't. Or have I?" Tyler joked.

Approaching an opening in the forest after what seemed to Aiden like a day's trek, the ground turned from a soft moss into hard stone. Aiden looked around, panting and sweating.

"Where's the Bloody Rock?" he said, regaining his breath.

"Here," said Callie. She and Tyler looked towards a rock. Aiden turned to face the mouldy, cracked rock with disappointment.

"It's literally a rock?" Aiden said scornfully. Aiden looked at it; his expectations had been too high, for the rock was literally a rock. He studied it further, gracing his hand over the soft and surprisingly warm moss. There was a crack in the centre that seemed to be covered by a splutter of deep dark stains.

"Blood," Aiden whispered.

"Yes," said Tyler.

Aiden stared at the two vampires bewildered as to what this rock was. Callie answered, subduing Aiden's curiosity. "This is the Bloody Rock. A few hundred years ago, a powerful witch fell from above and cracked her head on this rock. She was killed instantly, but somehow her powers were transported deep inside. Our friend Lydia brought us up here when she realised we were vampires."

Aiden's eyes widened, learning what he was in the presence of. "So it's like a lie detector then? What do we do then?" he asked.

"It's exactly that. We place our hand on the rock at the same time, and within a few seconds, you will feel this tingling sensation once we speak, you will know the truth," said Tyler.

Aiden nodded. They moved around until they were standing in front, all looking at one another.

"We have to touch it at the same time, otherwise it won't work," Tyler stated, holding his hand out with Callie and Aiden following. "On the count of three… One… two… three."

They placed their hands, simultaneously, on the warm moss, Aiden having slammed his hand harder than the other two, not knowing if that was correct. Within moments Aiden felt a wonderful sensation move through his arm, making its way to the centre of the body; he felt warm, cosy and most of all relaxed. He leant his head backwards, feeling like he was floating on a cloud.

"Now, for you to learn the truth so you can trust us, we will say a few things which you already know," said Tyler.

Aiden returned to the moment and nodded.

"I'm a vampire," said Callie. The rock sent a tingling sensation through Aiden and Tyler, making them both smile. Aiden couldn't help but giggle.

"Lemme try," Aiden grinned. "I am the Perfect Blood." The same warm sensation made its way round the group.

"I am going to kill Aiden Dyer." Aiden winced at Tyler's comment. He looked towards Tyler who was smiling devilishly. For a mere few seconds, the same comforting sensation remained. Aiden felt his stomach drop. Then suddenly a monster of fear surged through Aiden's body. Any desire for love, peace and hope was eaten by a cold, toxic feeling. Aiden felt his stomach turn. Somehow his mind would not let his hand remove itself from the rock as if it had been glued on. Callie, witnessing Aiden's discomfort, intervened.

"We like you," she murmured under her breath. Squinting from the discomfort, Aiden welcomed the immediate relief. The empowerment had fought off the negative thoughts and feelings, showing Aiden that they meant him no harm. He smiled towards Callie and Tyler, content with what he had learnt.

"You are our friend, Aiden. Over the past month with you being here, I couldn't think of my life without you. You have already had a big effect on our lives," said Callie.

"Everything we have told you is the truth," said Tyler solemnly.

All their hands were still touching the Bloody Rock, and Aiden knew he could trust them both. The constant sensation of warmth and love kept pouring out of the rock and into their bodies. In that moment, Aiden felt like he knew who he finally was. He was the Perfect Blood. The life he lived before was not for him; the supernatural world was where he belonged, and he could not be any happier that he was going to be able to explore it with his two best friends.

Leaving the Bloody Rock and walking back towards the car, they returned to normal as if the weekend of horror had never happened. Aiden emitted a different aura than before: he was confident, he felt more alive.

"Well, thank you guys for everything. It's been a hell of a weekend!" said Aiden, as Tyler pulled up to Aiden's house.

"No worries. I'm glad we have been able to stay friends and that you won't report us to your dad and have us killed," said

Callie teasingly. Aiden couldn't think of anything worse; these two now played a prominent part in Aiden's life and protection.

"One thing though, Aiden," Tyler said before Aiden went to get out the car. Aiden turned to face him. "Whatever you do, don't allow people to come into your house unless you know them or your dad is there."

"Why?" Aiden questioned.

"Vampires can't get into a house unless they are invited in. For me and Callie to be able to walk into your house, you have to say something along the lines of 'Come into my house.' if you don't, then we can't get in. It's something you must remember. Also", said Tyler warningly, gaining Aiden's attention with his sudden changing tone, "no matter what, do not tell your father you are the Perfect Blood. No matter what. Cara is currently working on a bracelet that will help hide your scent," he finished sternly.

"Of course," said Aiden. Saying their goodbyes, Aiden walked into his house, and Callie and Tyler drove off.

"Well, he knows now," Tyler spoke, driving off from Aiden's having watched him walk into his house.

"It's for the best," Callie replied with a concerned tone.

"What's up?" Tyler asked, knowing Callie all too well.

"Mum texted me. Telling us to be careful. More of Shun Yun Li's men have been killed."

"That's not good." These being the only words he could think off whilst focussing on driving. "Why is someone or something killing his men?" he questioned.

"No idea, but it's not good, and why does it feel like it's not a coincidence?"

"What do you mean?"

"Well, these attacks began, then Aiden returned, and we smelt him for the first time the day after." Tyler knew what Callie was implying.

"There is no such thing as coincidence in the supernatural world," said Tyler, quoting Callie's mum, only to feel a little apprehensive.

"We don't tell Aiden. He has been overloaded with a lot of information. We will tell him at the right time," said Tyler. Callie listened but didn't reply. Instead, she sat watching the world go by, wondering what would happen to the Perfect Blood.

9
THE BASEMENT

The town of Oakdale remained silent. The sun rose slowly, and Aiden stirred, having slept pleasantly. He welcomed the feeling of waking up in his own bed. His dad was due home today. It had been his first weekend away since arriving in England, and Aiden had spent Sunday on his own. Despite learning that his dad was a vampire hunter and killed for a living, it offered some relaxation to Aiden, who knew he was the Perfect Blood, the most hunted supernatural being in the vampire world.

But everything now made sense. His dad always being late to events and the cold, uncaring mood he would be in. It made Aiden feel guilty about how he had spoken to him in the past, but the more Aiden thought about it, the less he felt guilty. His father hunted and killed vampires for a living, the very thing that Aiden was best friends with.

Then he began to wonder more, did any of this have anything to do with his mother? His dad had always said Aiden would understand one day, would that day be the day Aiden was told about the VHA? Aiden had only ever seen a handful of pictures of his mum, but by entering the supernatural world, he couldn't help but think he might be on the verge of learning the truth. He rose from bed, ready to begin his day.

"One more question," said Aiden. He was walking side-by-side with Callie on their way to school. She grinned, having answered and reiterated some from the other day.

"Okay, what is it?" Callie smiled.

"What are your weaknesses?" said Aiden feeling like this was a good question. "I just didn't want to assume that a wooden stake would be your weakness," he added.

"Okay," she mumbled before she answered. "Well, we can be killed by wooden stakes, and that is one of two main weapons used by the VHA. Over the years, the VHA has been able to make them into little wooden bullets, as well as customise them to other weapons, making it easier to kill vampires. Another weakness of ours is a poisonous flower called Wild Rose. The VHA has manipulated this flower to turn into a liquid where it can be used in grenades, stun grenades and other weapons," said Callie, whipping out her mascara quickly and applying a thin layer while she looked in the mirror.

"Hang on," said Aiden. "I thought vampires couldn't be seen in mirrors. That's what Google said." Callie laughed and Aiden blushed. He had been Googling vampires over the last day to learn more, but now he was embarrassed that he had told her.

"That's a fairy tale," Callie laughed. "My body still reflects light, when you look at a dead person, they can still be seen in a mirror. I'm not invisible; an invisible person can't be seen in a mirror because there is nothing to reflect light on; an invisible person changes their surroundings and uses light to hide themselves. It's physics really. Light reflects off my body and allows me to be seen." Callie answered the questions easily, having conducted several hours of research into understanding it herself. Reaching school and joining Tyler at the cast-iron gates, they followed the herd of students into the school grounds.

"Okay, there is something we need to tell you," said Callie. The school day had ended, and with minimal interaction with Mr Burton, Aiden had deemed it a successful day at school… apart from the constant questioning of Callie and Tyler.

"Okay," he said, feeling a little nervous with the tone of her voice.

"In your house is a secret basement. I have one in my house. It's where my mum does all her work and keeps her weapons."

"What?" said Aiden, suddenly paying close attention to what Callie was saying.

"We chose not to tell you the other day because you had enough on your plate, but now you seem ready," said Tyler quickly, knowing they would be separating on their way home soon.

"It will give you insight into your dad's life at the VHA," said Callie.

"Wasn't he due back yesterday?" asked Tyler.

"Yeah, but he phoned to tell me that apparently they had to go upriver. Something about a riverbank needing work," said Aiden, reiterating what his dad had said to him with a little less enthusiasm knowing it was now all a lie.

Before he knew it, Aiden waved goodbye to Callie and Tyler as they watched him walk down his road. Arriving home, Aiden manhandled the front door handle, forcing it open. Throwing his school bag on the stairs and locking the front door behind, Aiden made his way to his father's office. Passing through the living room, tossing his school blazer on the sofa, loosening his tie, Aiden stopped at the office door. Was he ready for this? Aiden trusted Callie and Tyler, but seeing what might be down there, the evidence, the weapons, he knew he would never be able to unsee it. Having unknowingly placed his hand on the door handle, Aiden walked into the heavily furnished room.

Books filled the walls, with large A3 copies of bridge designs and flood defences stubbornly stuck to the walls. Aiden frowned at his father's ability to hide the truth from him, even going as far as to display engineering and architecture books on his shelves to deter his son from any suspicions of his job. The desk was impeccably clean and well organised, just how his father liked it. Aiden looked at the neatly placed pile of paperwork to the side of his dad's computer, quickly scanning the top document, *Oakdale Targeted Areas*. Aiden's eyes widened. Treading carefully and sitting down in his father's brown leather office chair, Aiden gently peeled the first page back... *We hereby commission Jason Dyer to search and update the Mayor's Office quarterly on revised plans for the protection of Oakdale Monuments with the Flood Defence Bill.* Rolling his eyes, almost laughing at his father's commitment to the lie, Aiden placed the top page down, making sure it was in line with the others, to avoid his father's eagle-eyed vision. He reclined backwards, sighing loudly when he heard a loud squeaking noise from below.

Aiden looked down at the red Persian rug seemingly intact.

"What's that?" Aiden murmured, noticing a long, thin line in the rug. The large area underneath the desk seemed big enough to fit a fully grown adult. Moving the chair away and onto his knees, his eyes were inches away from the rug. A now visible square-shaped line appeared within the rug. Carefully caressing the soft material, Aiden swiftly inserted his finger into a gap. He peeled back the large square piece of material, and a large metal door appeared underneath.

Aiden's heart skipped a beat. He had found it, the entrance to his dad's secret basement. Aiden couldn't help but feel proud of himself, while at the same time feel a little nervous.

Aiden grappled the cold, thin handle, pushing himself forwards to discover what was underneath. Pulling it upwards, the door folded into itself, fitting perfectly under the desk. A ladder was below leading downwards. Aiden manoeuvred his body underneath the desk and slowly onto the ladder.

Jumping off the ladder and into a cold and musty concrete hallway, a large, vaulted steel door stood out. He moved towards the door, feeling more and more anxious with every step, his footsteps bouncing off the walls. Aiden placed his hands on the metal door and pushed it with all his strength. The vaulted door glided open effortlessly.

Aiden was met with a jaw-dropping sight. The pristine, white-tiled room seemed like another world. Feeling his stomach drop against the chilled tiles, Aiden walked down the stairs and into the secret basement. The walls were decorated with weapons, maps and medieval devices.

A wooden stake hanging in the centre called his name. Picking the splintering wood up, a sense of foreboding came over him – this was the weapon used to kill vampires. Gulping, Aiden placed the stake back.

Moving around the room, taken aback, Aiden studied the maps. One map of Oakdale had three large circles drawn on, one not too far from Aiden's house and the others surrounding towns which couldn't have been that far from Oakdale. Continuing the exploration of the room, a fountain of books covered the face of the table in the centre of the room. *Powerful Witches of the 20th Century* and *Ancient Killings and What Do They Mean?* were the two open books. For some weird reason, Aiden didn't want to leave the basement. He could have happily stayed down there for the next few hours, but when he heard a loud knock from the front door, he knew he had to leave. To his surprise, a computer monitor on the wall switched on, showing a man standing at the door, holding a toolkit dressed in overalls. Another loud thump came from the door as Aiden watched the man knock from the camera. Feeling slightly infuriated, Aiden left the secret basement, sealing the vault door shut and closing the entrance to the basement in his dad's office.

One final slam echoed throughout the house as Aiden opened the front door to the impatient man.

"Hello, I've been trying to get into your house to check your gas for the past couple of days. It needs to be done immediately. Can I come in?" said the man matter-of-factly.

"Yeah, of course, come in," said Aiden irritable, noticing he was a gas man. Walking away from the door and into the kitchen, Aiden wanted to return to the basement.

"The boiler is just under here…" Aiden spoke before he realised what he had just done. His brain stopped thinking and reverted to what Tyler had said to him the other day. Aiden gulped; had he just let a vampire into his house? A human would not need to be invited in but a vampire would.

Aiden moved away from the boiler cupboard to notice the front door was wide open and the man was not standing there anymore, his toolkit left teasingly outside as the front door came to a gentle close. *Stay calm*, Aiden thought to himself feeling his mouth suddenly dry. Aiden placed his back against the wall.

"Hello?" said Aiden hoarsely through the dryness of his voice, feeling his heartbeat in his throat. He didn't know what to do. He was hoping the man was going to reply and say sorry for accidentally leaving the front door open, but as time went on with no reply, it seemed the chances of him being a human and an actual gas man were dwindling.

Slowly moving from the kitchen and towards the front room, planning on making his way back to the basement, Aiden kept his back against the wall. Entering the small hall, looking into the front room before he entered, he listened carefully. The house was quiet, and to anyone else, it would be empty. Aiden was thinking about the abilities of vampires – speed, strength and exceptionally good hearing. He was trying his best to move as quietly as possible, trying not to alert the vampire of his whereabouts, but Aiden had a sickening thought that the vampire knew exactly where he was. Moving slowly to the corner of the front room, Aiden looked around, and still there was no sign of the man. He pulled the curtain back to see if anyone was outside, but there wasn't. The taunting toolbox still placed on the ground sent a daunting shiver through Aiden's body.

Aiden looked directly at the office door on the other side of the room. He was weighing his options up as to what to do. Should he walk slowly, trying his best to be as silent as possible or make a run for it? Not knowing whether or not his scent was active at the moment, Aiden decided to run. Breathing in deeply and with a good push off from the wall, Aiden ran for it…

He was almost at the door. Just a few more feet to safety when a blinding pain erupted in his ankle. Aiden tumbled to the floor screaming, slamming into the front room furniture. He looked down his leg; a deep scratch mark appeared on his ankle as blood boiled out the wound.

Aiden cried as the vampire went crashing into the wall. The vampire, still wearing the gas man outfit, roared as his face had transformed. The all-consuming red abyss with the black slits for pupils stared at Aiden. Quivering with fear, Aiden looked deep into the eyes of the vampire, transported back to the night he was attacked. Aiden crawled backwards as the vamp now loomed over him, each razor-sharp fang ready to drain Aiden of his blood.

"You ready to die?" the man sneered, staring down at Aiden. Aiden groaned as he began to accept his fate. There was no way he could fend off the vampire.

He glanced to the side where a squared-shouldered man with dark features stood at the entrance to the front room.

"Dad?" Aiden said breathlessly. His father stood in the doorway in disbelief.

The vampire started chuckling to himself. "You don't smell as delicious, but I will kill you after, eh?" he teased malevolently. The vampire turned back round to face Aiden. Aiden tried desperately to move back, but his ankle stung with a vengeance.

Before the vampire could pounce, an illuminating flash filled the room, blinding and deafening both Aiden and the vampire for several seconds. Aiden's screams filled the house as he squeezed his eyes shut, feeling them burn beneath his eyelids as he held his hands against his ears.

Opening his eyes by a millimetre, a white veil of Wild Rose mist filled the air. Aiden coughed as he inhaled the toxic mist. A burning sensation followed as if a razor blade was being dragged down the back of his throat. Everything seemed to move in slow motion as the flash faded. Aiden's ears were filled with a ringing noise; however, compared to the vampire, Aiden had it easy. From what he could see through the white mist, the vampire was on the floor screaming. Jason stood behind wearing a gas mask that covered his eyes and mouth.

His dad grabbed the neck of the vamp and pulled him to his feet. "Nobody goes after my son," he spat with venom. He threw the vamp to the floor, who had succumbed to the paralyzing effect of the Wild Rose. His dad loomed over the body, pulling an eight-inch stake from his back pocket before plunging the stake deep into the vampire's back.

Almost instantly, the body erupted into flames. Aiden felt himself fall to the ground, slamming his head against the wooden floor. The last images he saw were his dad running towards him shouting his name. Aiden felt his dad pick him up, but it was too late. A dark, taunting voice called Aiden, and within seconds he was plunged into a dark abyss, feeling only pain and suffering once again.

10
THE VHA

Jason sat quietly in the white room below the house, his nerves putting him on edge. Aiden laid on the table with a cannula in his arm. *OXY-Friadam* was being injected into his body to remove the essence of Wild Rose, while at the same time, aid in healing Aiden's ankle which Jason had bandaged up.

How could I have been so stupid? Jason thought to himself as he ruffled his hair. In the heat of the moment, he had forgotten how dangerous Wild Rose was to humans. All he wanted to do was kill the vampire before it pounced on Aiden. He now couldn't believe the day had arrived. The day his son would learn what he did for a job. He was wondering where he would begin, wondering how he would tell his son everything, the lies that he had made. He needed to tell his son that he was a vampire hunter and that vampires were real, but would Aiden be able to handle it?

With the hours passing giving, Jason more and more time to construct an explanation in his head, he had already phoned the VHA, alerting them to the situation. A car was sitting out the front waiting to take Jason and Aiden to the VHA. The cleaners, who specialised in cleaning scenes and removing bodies, had attended to the scene in the living room. Before Jason realised the time, it was early in the morning. With a new day beginning, Jason had already sent the school an email, telling them how Aiden had been ill in the night so he would not be attending. The thought of a new day lingered in Jason's mind. It was a new day indeed; another Dyer was about to join the VHA. Aiden was going to be inducted early. That's what protocol demanded, but as more pressing thoughts continued, Aiden began to stir. Jason rose from his seat ready to talk to his son.

"Hey, Aid, it's me," Jason whispered gently.

Aiden slowly opened his eyes, wondering where he was. He looked around the pristine white room, recognising the decorative wall of weapons. Realising he was downstairs in his father's basement, Aiden's eyes opened wide with shock before he bolted back to life, adrenaline surging through his body as if he had been electrocuted.

"Where am I?" he said frantically, knowing he had to act terrified to deter any suspicions.

"Where do I begin?" Jason questioned himself. Aiden looked at his father, who was being very attentive.

"Where am I?" Aiden asked once again, putting on his best acting skills.

"You are in the basement, Aiden. There is a lot I need to tell you," Jason said in a calm and comforting voice.

"Basement? But what was that upstairs? And we don't have a basement," said Aiden warily.

"That was a vampire, and this is my secret basement," Jason answered, almost acting as if he were guilty of something.

"A va-vam-vampire?" Aiden stuttered. The sharp feeling of bewilderment and fear spiked in his stomach again, remembering how it felt the first time he heard Callie and Tyler say the V word.

"Yes, a vampire."

"You're joking. Vampires aren't real," said Aiden breathing heavily, wondering if he was being believable. Jason looked at this son with a fierce and grim look, knowing that Aiden should know his father didn't joke.

"You aren't joking," said Aiden clocking on. Jason nodded before removing the cannula from his son's arm and watching him closely. Aiden twitched from the sharp pain, feeling like his legs had turned to jelly, but once again his ankle had been miraculously healed.

"You don't seem scared or as surprised as I thought you would be," Jason murmured. Aiden slowly rose, feeling his blood rush to his legs.

"A vampire... it's something out of the movies, how can they be real?" Aiden replied. Jason nodded understandingly, remembering when he learnt vampires were real, it had taken him some time to adjust.

"I understand how you are feeling." Jason heaved a great sigh, pausing. "But they are real. A group of vampires killed my mum and dad. The company I work for took me in and educated me. At first I didn't believe them, but eventually I accepted the truth."

"Your mum and dad?" Aiden said in disbelief. This was the first time Aiden had ever heard his father mention his parents. Aiden knew nothing of them, apart from being told they died when his father was young. "What happened to them?"

Jason looked at his son. "They were killed by a group of vampires whom they were hunting. When I was old enough, I hunted the vampires down and killed them all. But enough of that. Right now, I'm surprised you aren't as shocked as I thought you would be."

"I'm freaking out!" Aiden shouted, reaffirming his stance. "Of course, I'm shocked, scared and surprised. You have just told me vampires are real, I was just attacked by one, and I saw you kill it and now I'm learning you've killed more than once." Jason looked at his son, taken aback by the sudden burst of emotion.

"Okay," said Jason.

"So what are you then?" Aiden asked once he had calmed down.

"I am a Master Vampire Hunter, Head of Missions. I have been a hunter since I was thirteen, and you will be one too. I work for a company called the Vampire Hunter Association, otherwise known as the VHA. Our goal is to rid the world of vampires," said Jason, reciting what he had told several people many times before.

"So you're not an engineer? Why have you never told me this before?"

"No, I'm not. That's a cover and I've never told you because you are under the age of sixteen. The VHA has a rule where all sons and daughters of vampire hunters become hunters at the age of sixteen."

"What's the VHA?" Aiden asked. A strong sense of déjà vu hit him like a train; he knew this was his opportunity to find out more about the VHA, filling the gaps which Callie and Tyler were unable to fill.

"You are about to find out."

"What do you mean?" said Aided in a shortness of breath.

"Due to the attack and the protocols we have, you are being enrolled into the VHA from today."

"I'm what?" Aiden's felt his chest tighten. He already knew he was going to be told about the VHA when he turned sixteen, and he was okay with that because he was hoping something would have happened by the time he was sixteen for him not to join; now he was finding out he had been enrolled.

"Now let's go. Daria has requested a meeting," said Jason.

Being dragged from the basement and through the living room that had been cleaned from top to bottom, Aiden desperately wanted to text Callie and Tyler. But he remembered Diana, Callie's mother, would be the only way for Callie and Tyler to find out what had happened. Aiden and Jason left the house quickly as they were greeted by a large black vehicle that Jason escorted Aiden into the back of.

"Have you heard from your mum?" questioned Tyler as he and Callie sat at the back of the class.

"No," said Callie curtly, when her phone suddenly buzzed on the inside of her blazer. Like lightning, Callie pulled her phone from the inside pocket. She had sent her mother hundreds of texts, questioning her on why there was a VHA vehicle parked outside Aiden's house.

"Aiden was attacked by a vampire last night. He is being taken to the VHA," Callie read aloud. She began caressing her hair violently. What should she do? She was worried about Aiden, but at the same time she was worried about herself and

Tyler. What happened if Aiden told the VHA about them? She was panicking. She knew Aiden wouldn't. Even if he did, her mother would tell her and Tyler to run.

"He will be in school tomorrow, everything will be fine. Your mum will keep us up to date," said Tyler, noticing her great discomfort. Callie looked at her dear friend, who seemed calm. If he was not panicking, then there was no need for her to panic. She calmed herself down before Mr Burton stormed over, demanding an answer as to where Aiden was. Callie, not in the mood for one of his tantrums, could feel her hunger rising, demanding her to rip the head off Mr Burton and drain his body dry of blood, but she resisted. Tyler explained the reason for Aiden's absence. Dissatisfied with Tyler's answer, Mr Burton walked away, leaving the two to worry.

Shrouded by the dense forest, Aiden studied the insides of the large vehicle; the leather seats often disturbed the silence of the car with Aiden's constant fidgeting, trying to get comfortable. Jason kept looking over to his son. The black interior of the car suited the tinted windows and made it hard for Aiden to see anything. On the rare occasion a burst of sunlight would pierce through the dense forest and into the car, Aiden was able to see a variety of buttons and compartments built into the seats before the light dissipated.

"Why is everything black and made out of leather?" said Aiden, noticing the constant combination.

"Easy to hide and clean blood," said Jason matter-of-factly. Aiden retracted into his seat, feeling uncomfortable in what he now called the Wagon of Death.

"So, who's Daria? And you're a Master Hunter?" Aiden asked, trying to make conversation with his father.

"Daria is the leader of the VHA, and I am a Master Hunter," replied Jason sternly. Aiden had noticed a change in tone from his father. All his answers were now precise and blunt, and the once-attentive father was now long gone. Was he in the presence of Master Hunter Jason Dyer instead of his father?

"We are almost there," said Jason. Aiden looked forwards out the windscreen. The shadowed road ahead looked like it was heading nowhere, only into darkness, but that's when Aiden saw it. It wasn't shadows but a towering black fence that seemed to go beyond the trees, wrapped in heavy barbed wire. Feeling the car slow, Aiden watched the driver force the car into a crawling stop. He almost seemed like he didn't want to take his foot off the accelerator. The driver lowered his window by a centimetre, while the car continued its snail pace crawl. Aiden went to speak, but as he looked towards his dad, he saw movement on the outside of the vehicle that made him jump back into his seat, keeping his mouth shut. Three beings appeared from the bushes and trees, heavily camouflaged, carrying what Aiden could only think of as the most heavily armed weapons in the world.

"Jason and Aiden Dyer," spoke the driver, Aiden sensing the trepidation in his voice. The man who stood at the window seemed to grunt as he looked into the car. Aiden wanted to retract into his seat further but couldn't – although Jason remained seated, calm as if nothing was wrong with the world.

"Move," said the man, backing off from the car and back into the wilderness of the forest. The others followed, having quickly scanned and searched the car. The driver needn't be told again and pressed his foot on the accelerator, and the car moved forward into the opening gates.

"Dad, who were they?" asked Aiden, slowly feeling his confidence return.

"The Guardians of the Palace, they protect the VHA. I had a brief encounter with them when I was younger. If it was between me or them, you would beg to fight me," said Jason hauntingly.

Leaving the shaded forest and onto a tarmacked wasteland, Aiden noticed the large black fencing that encased the baron grounds.

"Dad, where is the VHA?" said Aiden, noticing the lack of building but just an old, decrepit factory that seemed like it was close to collapsing.

"In there," said Jason. Aiden felt like his father was being awkward in not telling him, but as the car continued to drive towards the old factory, something odd began to happen. The floor beneath the car was lowering downwards. Rather than driving into the factory, the car was now about to drive underneath the factory towards the downward spiral road.

"It's underground?" Aiden questioned, but Jason remained silent as if it were obvious. Not knowing what to expect next and deciding not to ask his father any more questions as he seemed to officially be in work mode, Aiden remained silent, watching the lights pass the car as they continued deeper.

They arrived in a crowded underground car park. The car pulled into its own bay, and Aiden exited the vehicle, mesmerised by other hunters and mechanics continuing their day-to-day duties. Hunters were restocking cars with guns, stakes, grenades and first aid, whereas the mechanics were preoccupied with fixing the destroyed or barely reparable vehicles. One vehicle caught Aiden's eyes. Claw marks scraped against the doors, and the roof had been ripped clean off.

"That was a good mission," Jason stated. Aiden looked towards his father who was smirking.

Walking past doors that had been left ajar with hunters walking in and out, Aiden began to feel more and more uncomfortable, standing out against the legion of black uniformed men and women. All the hunters greeted Jason whilst at the same time ignoring Aiden. It wasn't long until Jason pulled themselves away and waited in front of an elevator.

Doors opening, Jason gently pushed his son inwards. The loud sounds of metal drills and chatter were cut off as the elevator doors closed. The elevator moved quickly up three floors, and Aiden began to wonder why there were so many floors.

"Floor seven," said the elevator voice. The doors opened smoothly, and a long, black hallway appeared in front. *Silence.* That's all Aiden could notice. Jason led the way down the hallway, his footsteps echoing off the walls. The red carpet led towards two magnificent black doors at the end of the hallway. The industrial style lighting reminded Aiden of the church, and how light had tried its best to fill every dark corner. Jason and Aiden arrived at the towering double doors, which had seemed far smaller from the elevator. Two red door handles captured Aiden's attention; they were designed to look like a vampire's head, with the two fangs used for door handles.

"Are you ready?" Jason questioned. Aiden felt his voice stick. He was rubbing his clammy hands up and down his trousers, and before Aiden could reply, Jason pushed the two doors inwards.

Aiden found his breath sucked from his mouth. Thinking the VHA couldn't be any larger after passing several floors, Aiden had never seen a cavernous room like this. The once-silent hallway was now filled with the voices, screams and shouts of hunters inside the great room. The large room seemed to be split into four. In one corner was a canteen where many hunters were eating and laughing; another part was divided into see-through glass cubicles where Aiden noticed teenagers sitting down, furiously writing on pieces of paper. Another part seemed to be devoted to black mats where hunters were fighting one another, throwing each other to the side and punching dummies relentlessly and the final quarter was devoted to hunters running and participating in what Aiden could only guess was fitness tests.

"This is the VHA," said Jason. "Let's go, Daria is waiting." Aiden looked towards his father who was looking into the distance. Aiden followed his line of sight to see a balcony looking out onto the VHA, where a towering broad pale woman with shoulder-length black hair was staring at the father and son.

"Hello, Aiden Dyer," the masculine woman spoke. Aiden walked into her office, it was her, the woman who had been staring at them. "My name is Daria Charpman, leader of the VHA." She looked towards Aiden, taking a deep breath in, as if she was trying to smell Aiden through the heavily incensed office. Aiden sat down in front of her as Jason remained at the back in the shadows.

"Hi," said Aiden apprehensively. The chair he had sat down in was far smaller compared to Daria's luxury mahogany chair.

"Well, well, you have had an interesting twenty-four hours, now haven't you," Daria said softly, pacing behind her desk, looking at Aiden with the utmost interest.

"I guess you could say that," Aiden said warily.

"Welcome to the VHA. I am glad we now have another Dyer in our ranks, you are going to be a very busy boy this week." Daria paused, having almost condescendingly said *boy* to remind Aiden that he was nothing more. "I would like you to meet my other Master Hunters, you already know one." Daria gestured her hand towards the back of the room. Aiden swung his head round. Four figures, including his dad, were now standing at the back, all different shapes, sizes and builds. They all stood strong as if they were superheroes.

"You have your father," Daria started, "who is Head of Missions with Diana." Aiden took one look at the only woman Master Hunter. *Callie*, he thought, noticing the similarities in their facial features, especially their nose and mouth. "Then you have Neil, Head of Combat, and Hayden, Head of Finance and PR." Aiden looked at the difference between Neil and Hayden. Hayden dwarfed Neil with his muscles and height, and Aiden was surprised that their roles were not the other way round.

"Nice to meet you all," said Aiden to the three Master Hunters. They all stared back at him, especially Diana. She seemed to be trying her best to see Aiden's soul through his eyes.

"Anyways, down to business," said Daria pulling the attention of the room to her. "I am the leader of the VHA, and every leader has failed to rid the world of vampires. I plan to make history by ridding the world of this deadly infection called vampirism. I also want you to know that we have one rule. One very important rule." Daria's gaze was so intense Aiden had to force himself not to look away. "Rule one. It is forbidden for any member of the VHA to love, be friends with, or care for any vampire. If a hunter is found to do any of these, they will be sentenced to death and face a public execution in front of the V-H-A," Daria finished, emphasising every letter of the VHA.

Aiden felt his heart drop to the bottom of his stomach. He immediately thought of Callie and Tyler, but then his mind changed to Diana. Diana knew the rules and had happily taken the risk; he wanted to turn round and look at her, but he didn't want to make anything obvious. He was too preoccupied with looking at Daria, who's aura was radiating around the room, a feeling Aiden had never felt before, and in some weird way, it felt like she was trying to drain Aiden of his power.

"I understand," said Aiden gulping.

"Wonderful," said Daria, gently sitting herself down in her mahogany chair. "You will attend school, and then from 3.30pm to 7.45pm, Monday to Friday, you will be at the VHA and on Saturdays from 8.00am to 7.00pm training." Daria flicked her hand in the air. Aiden heard someone from behind approach. Neil walked over from out the shadows. His perfect combed-over brunette hair and clean skin seemed to make him appear too pretty to work for the VHA, but then a scar that appeared on the side of his cheek suggested otherwise.

"I look forward to seeing you in my classes," he said, handing Aiden a black duffle bag. Aiden looked inside. "That is your VHA uniform and books. We expect you to read everything within the next week," said Neil. The books varied in size and width; Aiden was only beginning to realise how much he had to learn. "This is your schedule, and I look forward to seeing you tomorrow." Neil handed Aiden a piece of laminated card. The laminated card detailed everything from times and locations to the lessons from combat training to vampire anatomy.

"Thank you," said Aiden, not knowing why he had said it.

"I think that covers everything for now," said Daria. "Unfortunately, we have to return to our work. You were lucky we were able to squeeze you in but don't worry. Your dad's schedule has been cleared, so he will be returning home with you now. I am expecting big things from the son of the most renowned Master Hunters we have had in recent years and the most important family in the VHA. Good luck," said Daria.

Aiden grinned, feeling the pressure mount on him, he could feel the four Master Hunters watching him closely as he engaged with Daria.

Muttering their goodbyes, Daria watched Aiden's every move. He left the office escorted by his father, who was carrying the heavy duffle bag. Jason and Aiden left the VHA quickly, it almost felt to Aiden that they had been kicked out.

Exhausted from the wild rush of the day, he welcomed his bed when they arrived home. Aiden sat up and opened one of the five books that Neil had given him to read. *VHA: For Beginners* sat in his lap. Side light on, sitting in bed comfortably, he had told Tyler and Callie everything over text and was looking forward to seeing them at school. Sighing deeply, Aiden turned his head downwards and began to read.

> *The VHA is believed to have been founded during the early 9th century, by Caber Dyer, when Vampire creation is believed to have begun (certain geological and historical factors support this assertion). Not much is known regarding the creation of vampires, or who the first vampires were or their creators, therefore this book will be here to guide you through the modern-day Vampire Hunter Association and how to best understand vampires as well as the basic information regarding the structure of the VHA, previous leaders*

and legendary Master Hunters, including Arkadian Armstrong and Jason Dyer, both of whom are still alive to this day (2009).

Aiden read the introduction. *Dyer? Caber Dyer?* A Dyer was the founder of the VHA. Feeling the weight of the world pile on his shoulders, Aiden began to wonder if he belonged in the world of the VHA.

11
Aptitude Test

At 3pm sharp, a blacked-out four-by-four parked up outside Oakdale Secondary School, waiting for Aiden Dyer. The driver sat still, black sunglasses covering his face, watching parents pick their children up, while at the same time, noticing parents exchanging worrisome looks with one another about why a mysterious vehicle was parked outside the school. But the parents seemed to have their trepidations put to rest when Aiden walked out and towards the car, opening the back door and jumping into the vehicle.

"Good day, boy?" the driver grunted before he drove off, thinking it was degrading to be picking up a teenager. Aiden sighed, not being particularly jovial about heading to the VHA. He was happy to be rid of Mr Burton but at the same time sad he wasn't able to hang out with Callie or Tyler. It had been a busy day for them, Callie had been chatting non-stop, telling

Aiden everything she knew about the VHA and what to expect before she turned on Tyler, pressuring him for an answer as to when Aiden's concealment bracelet would be ready for him.

"You need to change," grunted the driver. Aiden looked to his side to see his VHA clothing, plain black T-shirt, black trainers and cargo trousers. Heaving an even greater sigh than before, Aiden unwillingly began stripping in the back of the vehicle. He was tired. Tyler and Callie hadn't stopped asking questions about the VHA, especially Tyler who seemed to find it far more intriguing. He now understood how they felt when he badgered them with questions about being a vampire.

The car took a sharp but predictable turn, passing the *DO NOT ENTER* sign that Aiden saw yesterday. Finally changed and noticing the towering fence in the distance, Aiden strapped himself back into his seat, not looking forward to seeing the Guardians of the Palace. Once again, the four-by-four slowed into a crawl; this time Aiden watched carefully, wanting to see where the Guardians appeared from. The driver's window was lowered, and if by magic, four figures appeared from darkness, this time one drenched in a crimson liquid.

"Aiden Dy-Dyer," the driver stuttered. Aiden whipped his head round, looking straight into the eyes of a Guardian. Aiden shivered. Never had he seen a look that brandished the face of the Guardian. His eyes were wide open, wrinkled all around, covered in a black substance that Aiden did not want to guess. They seemed soulless. Dead.

"Move," the deep voice of the Guardian reverberated within the car. Aiden looked away, not being able to bare another moment of looking into the lifeless eyes of the Guardian. The gates opened in front, and Aiden had arrived at the VHA for his first day.

Neil Gauze stood short and proud amongst all the hunters in the underground car park. His hair combed in the same style, almost same positioning as Aiden saw yesterday.

"Dyer. Move, we have a lot to do," he said. Aiden jumped from the vehicle and sprinted to the elevator just before the doors closed. Aiden still didn't know what to think of Neil. Was his nice? Rude? Or another version of Mr Burton?

"You're late," mumbled Neil. Aiden stood next to the Master Hunter not knowing what to say. He knew he couldn't challenge him like Mr Burton; what would the man do if he did? Aiden was pretty sure the VHA had different rules, especially to the ones at school.

"Floor four," the robotic voice spoke. The elevator doors slid open gently. Instead of the grand hallway that had appeared in front of Aiden yesterday, now it was a hallway with peeling wallpaper. Neil strode forward, not wasting any time.

"What are we doing today?" Aiden asked, having to speed walk to keep up with Neil's long strides.

"A test."

"What test?" asked Aiden worryingly.

"The Aptitude Test. You answer the questions truthfully. The results will tell us what part of the VHA you will go into, but as you're a Dyer you'll become a hunter."

"What's the point in me doing it if I'm going to become a hunter then?" Aiden challenged, not realising what he had just said. Neil stopped in his tracks and looked down at Aiden.

"These tests tell us what each individual shall go into, mechanics, healers, hunters or desks."

"Desks?" asked Aiden.

"Stop interrupting me. People who work behind desks, ensuring the VHA runs efficiently. You're a Dyer, your family history is as rich as the VHA itself," said Neil glaring at Aiden. Aiden remained silent as Neil strode off once again. Bursting through a pair of double doors, another long hallway was in front of them, but this time doors lined the way. *Inductions, Processing, Employees.* These were the words that had been engraved in gold on the doors.

"Testing. Here we are," said Neil. Neil opened the door with Aiden following, taking note that the T was wonky compared to the other letters.

It wasn't a test room, more like an interrogation room that Aiden had seen on TV. A metallic table and two chairs either side, with a dangling light above that reflected off the table, filling the dark and humid room in little light.

"Sit," said Neil, who scraped the metal chair backwards, the legs screeching against the steel flooring. Aiden sat on the chilled chair.

"I am going to ask you several questions. All you have to do is answer the question as quickly as possible with the first thought or answer that comes into your mind. Do you understand?" said Neil taking his seat.

"Yes" said Aiden, squinting from the brightness of the metallic table.

"Right, let's begin." Neil paused before the questions being fired became relentless. "Dove or Crow?"

"Crow," answered Aiden.

"Are you fascinated by why we live or why we die?"

"Live."

"Cat or mouse?"

"Cat."

"Fight or Flight?"

"Fight."

The questions continued with Aiden trying his best to answer them as quickly as possible. He felt flushed from sitting under the light for what seemed like hours but was most likely minutes.

Neil closed the folder and crossed his arms. "One more question, then we are done," he said with Aiden nodding, who was retaining the sigh of relief. "Defining moment of your life."

Aiden took a moment to think. If he was to tell the truth, it would have been the night he was attacked by the vampire at the party, learning what his friends were and his father. "Never knowing my mother," said Aiden, ending his silence, knowing full well he couldn't have said the others.

"Thank you, I will be with you in a moment." Neil kicked Aiden out the test room and back into the gloomy hallway which seemed to suck the life out of its employees.

"Your results are in, Dyer," said Neil, walking out the room that he and Aiden were in not five minutes go.

"That was quick," said Aiden. He leant against a damp wall.

"There is no time to waste in the VHA. Out of the categories that have been assigned, you are set to become a Hunter. Congratulations, Dyer, you'll be following in your dad's footsteps. Now follow me, I'm taking you to your class," said Neil bluntly without showing any signs of delight.

This was a test Aiden was certain he would pass, though he wasn't sure yet how he felt about being a hunter. Did he want to be one of them?

Rather than walking back to the elevator, Neil and Aiden headed towards the staircase. *Three levels up*, Aiden thought. The long and steep concrete staircase was easy to climb for Aiden. It took him back to his sprint training in California, where life was normal and Aiden was a no one. Neil didn't seem to have much to say; he walked in front of Aiden, almost ignoring him.

Entering at the back of the VHA, which Aiden thought was almost like a back door, he noticed the handsome doors in the distance. He was reminded of yesterday when he stood there, overlooking the VHA in all its grandeur before he was spotted by Daria. Thinking of Daria, he turned his head to her balcony. It was empty and her blinds pulled down.

"Where's Daria?" Aiden asked.

"She is leader of the VHA, she doesn't need to tell people where she goes," Neil bit. Aiden couldn't help but think Neil was going to be another version of Mr Burton.

Guided towards the glass classroom cubicles which he saw yesterday, a handful of trainee hunters turned to look at Aiden, some gossiping about him and others looking at him for a fight, almost wanting to challenge the legendary bloodline of the Dyers.

"We are here," said Neil. He extended one of his arms which Aiden accidentally walked into. Neil looked down at him before entering the glass classroom. "This is your class," said Neil. Aiden walked in and looked at the three boys and one girl.

"Billy, Thomas, Edward, T—" Neil stopped the terse introductions before he paused. "Where is he?" questioned Neil. Aiden looked around the class and at the faces of his trainee class.

"Gone to toilet, sir," said one boy. Neil sighed with his response.

"If he wasn't my favourite, I would have kicked him out by now," said Neil. "By the way, the girl over there is Gabriella," Neil said.

Aiden looked at the girl. She was blonde and clearly shy as she didn't meet Aiden's eyes when she was introduced.

"I'll be back," said Neil before he stormed off. "And Dyer, find a seat, sit down and don't move." Aiden nodded as Neil left the class.

Turning to the other trainees, Aiden knew this was going to be different compared to his first day at school. Aiden found a seat in the middle row, something that was far away from all the others to not invade their space, but still close enough to them to be part of the group. Aiden took his seat feeling the eyes of the class on him.

"Your father is Jason Dyer, isn't it?" said a voice. Aiden was taken aback when a boy, older than he was, had walked round and was now standing in front of his desk. It was Thomas.

"Jason Dyer, the legendary Master Hunter," said another boy who decided to join Thomas. This time it was Edward, and before Aiden knew it, the other boy, Billy, joined in.

"The closet person to become a Master Hunter was Arkadian Armstrong who was thirty-five at the time," said Billy.

"Has he ever told you the story?" asked Thomas.

"What story?" said Aiden, noticing how everyone was now staring at him with a certain anticipation in their eyes.

"About Astra, the Mexican Queen," said Edward.

"It's one of the most famous stories of the last... well, last hundred years, I would guess," said Thomas eagerly. He scratched his chin, wondering whether or not he had gotten that right.

"It's one of many missions that made your father's career," said Gabriella, who seemingly chirped up. She, however, remained seated but seemed eager to join in on the conversation. Aiden whipped his neck round as they all continued to pester him about a woman called Astra, but who was she? Aiden had never heard her name before, and it wasn't until now that he had realised he had never asked his father about his hunting career.

"Back off, he doesn't know," said a familiar voice entering the glass cubicle classroom. The group that had surrounded Aiden backed off. Tobias, the Prince of Oakdale Secondary School, came striding in, his shoulders squared with an almighty confidence.

"What makes you so sure?" questioned Billy who folded his arms. Aiden couldn't stop staring at Tobias. He couldn't believe he was another trainee, and yet it made sense now how he'd known so much about Aiden.

"Well, firstly, he would have answered you by now, and secondly, I think he is too polite to tell you lot to bog off," said Tobias. Aiden looked at the Prince of Oakdale Secondary School who was smirking at him.

"Tobias?" Aiden questioned.

"Yeah, Dyer, I am a trainee hunter. Told you I would see you around," Tobias grinned confidently. Aiden noticed Gabriella blush before looking away. "Would you like to know the story?" asked Tobias.

"Yes, please," said Aiden guiltily, knowing that he should have asked his father and be hearing this story from him and not a student.

"When your dad entered his final year as a trainee in the VHA, he was sent on a mission to Mexico to aid the then-Master Hunter in a mission to hunt, capture and kill, Astra the Mexican Queen. She was a notorious Mexican criminal, responsible for thousands if not tens of thousands of deaths. She smuggled children in and out of the USA and aided in almost decimating the VHA in North America. The VHA had received intel that she was to be moving to Mexico City, this being the first true information they had received on her in months.

"Your father and others, including Diana and Cambal, were trainees at the time approaching their final exam to be certified Vampire Hunters, and this was their test.

"It was a trap for them just as much as it was for the hunters. There was an epic fight in the desert between the VHA and Astra's vampires. Gaining the advantage, an injured Astra jumped into a car and went to Mexico City, your father followed her, through the Festival of the Dead and into her apartment building. Your dad and her fought for hours before he emerged from the building, bloodied and holding her head in his arm and a woman by his side.

"Your father was responsible for killing one of the most dangerous vampires during the twentieth century. He was responsible for the resurrection of the VHA in North America. Your father is a legend in the VHA." Tobias finished the story as a certain aura filled the room. Aiden didn't realise how amazing his father was or who he even was.

Everyone remained silent, that was until, "Tobias, there you are!" Neil came in shouting, shattering the silence.

"Dracas De Ramores," said Tobias coolly, bowing his head to Neil, who seemingly ignored the student.

"Dracas De Ramores?" asked Aiden confused, looking towards Tobias.

"It's a VHA saying, it means may the dead stay dead. It's kind of a greeting between hunters and how hunters identify one another in the field; it's hard to explain," said Tobias who was making no sense whatsoever to Aiden, but before he could question him further, Neil began shouting.

"We are the last defence against vampires!" He paused now, taking a calmer but more threatening tone. "Vampires hunted werewolves to extinction. Therefore, we are the last line of defence against their disgusting kind. Now get out there and train!"

Aiden watched the students in the room panic and scramble around like headless chickens before they ran out the class.

"Dyer," snapped Neil. "You are most likely wondering what you will be learning while you are in the VHA. I am here to put that all to rest." He paused. "In the VHA you will learn personal survival, history, vampire anatomy, physical combat, weapon training and fitness. These will make you the hunter you are destined to be. Welcome to the VHA."

"Nice," said Aiden, trying to inject some enthusiasm into his voice.

"You are now done for the day. Daddy is waiting for you," said Neil condescendingly before he left the room. Aiden slowly looked around the pristine classroom, alone and with his thoughts. He'd been overloaded with information today, but what really lingered in his mind was the story about his father. He always felt like he and his father were different, and that difference was only magnified when he found out what he did for a job. Knowing the man from this story was the same man who raised him, Aiden had never felt so distant from his father before.

Meeting his father at the grand doors to the VHA, it wasn't long before they were sitting comfortably in the back of the four-by-four and Aiden was reiterating the story to his father. Jason remained silent listening to his son, the once-distant memory now returning like it was yesterday.

"The only thing that's missing from this story is that, without the help of Diana and another special woman, I would never have killed Astra," said Jason. "Diana forced me to go after Astra; she forced me to follow her and kill her; she gave me the weapon that killed Astra. Diana backed away when we returned home, giving me all the credit for the mission as she wasn't ready for any major advancement in the VHA. The woman we rescued we bought home."

"Who was the other women?" Aiden questioned, feeling like Jason left that sentence to be questioned.

"Your mother," he said, turning to Aiden.

"My mum?" Aiden's throat tightened suddenly.

"Yes, your mum was captured by Astra. I rescued her and bought her back with me. The moment I saw her, I felt my heart skip a beat. I knew she was the love of my life, but she had a chameleon personality; she wasn't ready to settle down. Surprisingly though, after a year we married. Our first year of marriage was nothing but a whirlwind. She refused to join the VHA but instead worked at Oakdale Hospital. Then shortly after, we were blessed with you."

Aiden felt warm, like a piece of his life that he had been searching for had suddenly found its way to him.

"Dad, what happened to her?" Aiden asked, not breaking eye contact with his dad. Aiden felt like he was about to receive the answer of a lifetime, but Jason remained silent as he continued to stare at him.

"I will tell you soon, I promise," said Jason, turning his head round to look out the window. Aiden wanted to probe, but he didn't want to anger his father, so he settled back and thought about everything he had already learnt today.

12
TRAINING

"Grab a gun!" roared the Asian man before his head was cleanly sliced off. The group of Asian men, wearing tight black suits, ran at inhuman speed, gathering what guns they had. The floating black figure dodged the firing bullets as if they were a ballerina, taking the men out one by one with the swipe of their sword. The men cursed in Japanese. The gun fire continued to rain, but with bodies falling quicker than the men could react, it wasn't long until one lone man was standing.

"What do you want?" the lone man said in a high-class English accent.

"Your master and your chi. Your life force will help me," the cloaked figure tilted their head. "Shun Yun Li is a smart man, and I need to grab his attention." The cloaked figure shrieked, raising an arm. The quivering man felt the floor beneath his feet begin to crumble.

"You're a witch."

"The Dark Witch," they corrected matter-of-factly. "The second sacrifice…"

The Dark Witch began to chant an ancient spell, their voice growing louder and echoing around them. There was a sudden drop in temperature, and a white mist swept over the ground. The vampire looked around frantically, but there was no escape. Before he could move, the Dark Witch opened their palm, and the vampire was propelled into the air, his limbs splayed like a starfish. A large stake appeared beneath him and he cried out.

"I will find what your boss has hidden," the Dark Witch murmured. She closed her fist and the vampire fell – impaled once again, like the Dark Witch's first victim.

It was the next day, and Aiden, Tyler and Callie were sitting on the field, a stifling hot day making it unbearable to sit inside in the canteen. Aiden had just finished reiterating the story about Astra to Callie and Tyler.

"Wow," said Tyler. "I knew of the story from Callie, but I didn't know it had something to do with your mum."

"Neither did I. My mum never told me she knew your mum, but it sounds romantic," said Callie, who had enjoyed the moment when Aiden had said, "My dad said his heart skipped a beat when he saw her."

"I feel like I've never known my dad until now. I see him differently," said Aiden, taking the moment to reflect.

"Bloody Vlad," said Tyler suddenly.

"What? What's Bloody Vlad?" asked Aiden.

"Trainee hunter, twelve o'clock."

Aiden and Callie turned their heads in sync, not being subtle at all.

"Tobias," murmured Aiden. That was the first thing Aiden had told Tyler and Callie this morning on their walk to school. Tobias was a trainee hunter. Callie had a panic, especially as she was still classed as a newborn, but Tyler had comforted her in the knowledge and confidence that she would not slip up.

"I can't believe we have a trainee vampire hunter in the school," said Callie, clasping her hands together, feeling the nerves reappear from earlier again. They watched from a safe distance as Tobias mingled with all the girls, particularly enjoying the attention he was getting from Amber.

"How did your mum not know?" asked Tyler.

"She doesn't deal with trainees," said Callie.

"Anyways, what does Bloody Vlad mean?" Aiden asked.

"Bloody Vlad is the equivalent of Jesus Christ for vampires. There was an old wives tale that if a vampire said Jesus Christ, they would burst into flames, but as I have just said it twice, it proves it isn't real," answered Tyler. "Now what have you got at the VHA later?" Tyler added as Callie seemed to dip her head, almost not wanting to be recognised by anyone.

By the time Aiden had told them his timetable for the evening, their break had ended. It seemed almost impossible that the lesson was over and Aiden was once again jumping into the back of the black four-by-four and was on his way to the VHA.

Combat training was the first lesson of the evening. Aiden was changed and standing in line with the other trainees, Tobias smirking confidently next to him. "Don't worry. Remember it's only your first day, lucky for you you have a name to fall back on," he said provokingly. Aiden looked towards the older teenager.

"Don't worry. I won't punch your only personality trait," said Aiden, taking aim at his good looks. This comment seemed to aggravate Tobias because when it came to pairing up, Tobias didn't seem to hold back. He threw Aiden back and forth, dropping to the floor and kicking Aiden off his feet. Aiden began to take it personally.

"Dyer," snapped an irritated voice, having watched Aiden fail to do an offensive move once again. Neil marched over. "You are doing it wrong. If you want to kick Tobias off his feet, you need to move faster and aim for the ankle."

"Of course," said Aiden panting. This had been his first ever combat lesson, and he had been thrown in the deep end. There was no beginner's course, just Neil's lesson where you are expected to know. The hour finished with no luck of Aiden being able to drop to the floor, spin and kick Tobias of his feet. Aiden examined his sore fists, cautious of any blood seeping from his red-raw knuckles. Without a chance to rest, fitness training was the second lesson of the evening, and Aiden had the pleasure of being put through one of Neil's atrocious HIIT sessions.

"Dyer," Neil shouted once again, halfway through the lesson. "Your fitness is superb but your hand-to-hand combat is dreadful," he said, complementing and criticizing Aiden. Neil stood on the edge of the mats, watching how the other trainees lagged behind, including Tobias.

Mercifully, the training ended, and Aiden staggered over to his bag to collect his water and towel.

"Next is history," said Tobias, squirting water into his mouth and *accidentally* pouring too much in that it dribbled down his vest. "Woah," he casually said as the shirt began to stick to his six pack. Gabriella flushed bright pink and had to turn away. "They love it." Tobias winked at Aiden, Aiden knowing full well that he was doing it on purpose to show off.

Arriving at their last lesson of the evening, Aiden was grateful he didn't have Vampire Anatomy due to a sudden surge in tiredness. They took their seats and Aiden felt his legs fall asleep. A voice entered the room before the person.

"In these history lessons, you will be learning about the VHA." An elderly man walked in supported by a walking stick. His goatee was almost white and his balding, wrinkled head reflected the light from above. "My name is Toby Pearson, and I shall be your history lecturer." He readjusted his half-moon spectacles which had fallen down his crooked nose. "Today we will be learning about previous VHA leaders and the election process," said Toby. "Billy and Thomas, hand the books out." Toby tapped his desk with his walking stick. The two boys sighed, tired from the previous lesson, but did as Toby asked.

Aiden quietly sat at the back of the class with Tobias and Gabriella, all studying the books Toby had provided. "There are two ways for the leader to be chosen," Toby began. "One way is through the four Master Hunters choosing the candidate with the I-VHA confirming the appointment, or the I-VHA choosing two candidates and proposing them to the four masters, allowing the masters to choose. However, the leader must have held a senior position in the VHA. A senior position classes as Master Hunter and I-VHA." Aiden scribbled all the notes down furiously, struggling due to his sore hands, but he hadn't reached the election process in his reading yet, so all these notes were necessary.

"Who are the I-VHA?" Gabriella asked. Aiden had heard from his father that Gabriella had also been attacked by a vampire and been enrolled early.

"The International-VHA consists of seven members, one member for each of the seven continents and those seven members report to the Master Hunters. Together, if they have a unanimous decision, they are just as powerful as the leader of the VHA – only once in the VHA history has the I-VHA united in order to remove a leader. We will have a lesson regarding the removal of Sviet the Skull later on," said Toby.

"Aiden Dyer," a voice said, interrupting the class. All heads in the room, including Aiden's, looked towards the door where a hunter stood.

"What do you want?" said Toby, not impressed that his class had been interrupted.

"Your father wants you. He says you are ready," the hunter responded, as if Aiden had asked the question. All heads in the class now turned to Aiden, who seemed as confused as they were.

"Take him but tell Jason I don't like it when my lessons are interrupted," said Toby, pointing his nose into the air. Aiden rose from his chair, awaking his sleeping legs, and packed his belongings away. Tobias stared at Aiden with the utmost interest.

Aiden left the class eager to know what his father wanted. He felt sorry for Toby and was annoyed that he had been taken out of history and not one of Neil's combat or fitness lessons.

Escorted by the hunter, who was walking in front, Aiden once again noticed the closed blinds in Daria's office. He wondered whether she was in or if she preferred to be in constant darkness. They passed other hunters, some training and others arguing about what tactics are best to be used against vampires who are classed as Ancient.

The hunter slammed a pair of office block doors inwards, and they followed the long winding corridors, turning left, then right, then another right, before the lights started to flicker and the plastic flooring started to smell new again, before making it to the final turn.

"Left here, and your father will be waiting for you," said the hunter, and he left Aiden alone in the grim hallway. Aiden turned left, greeting his father who stood at the end of the hall, once again outside another vaulted door.

"Hello," said Jason, disapproving of his son's millisecond tardiness.

"Hi, Dad. Toby wanted you to know he doesn't appreciate you interrupting his lessons," said Aiden, ignoring his father's negative tone having so often heard it.

"He will get over it. Besides, what I am about to show you is probably one of the most important rooms in the VHA. Memorial Hall," said Jason.

Jason swiped his card to the side, and the card reader buzzed. The vaulted door clicked and clanked, sending echoes back down the hallway, before it opened slowly. A long, well-lit, chilled hallway greeted them. Aiden walked in, noticing the large eight-foot statues that lined the long and forever-expanding hallway. His mouth slowly opened, slightly taken aback by what was in front of him.

His dad said, "These are the statues of VHA Leaders."

Aiden glanced across the statues. There were so many, leading further down the hallway. Most of them were men, all serious looking and well dressed. They walked down the hallway, and the statues told the tale of time. They were all different, the plaques at their feet faded and cracked. Some statues had been well maintained and repaired, others not so much.

"Between the birth of the VHA till the early 1400s the VHA didn't make statues of the leaders. This tradition didn't start until after the 1400s when we found this statue." Arriving at the end, Aiden wondering how deep they were into the mountain by now. Aiden couldn't help but notice how the last statue resembled something he could have only described as a large blob.

"This is the statue of Caber Dyer. The First, The Fierce, the founder of the VHA." Jason looked at the statue with adoration. Aiden looked towards the blob noticing how the years had erased the carvings of the face and body.

"This man is our great ancestor, Aiden. If this man could speak, the things we would learn would change the world," said Jason. Aiden looked at the statue, staring at the erased face. A powerful energy seemed to be radiating from the statue. Aiden did not know if his father could feel it, but Aiden could hear a murmur in his ears… It felt as if the statue was calling him.

"What's underneath the statue?" Aiden asked. The source of the noise seemed to be coming from the large stone base of the statue.

"Each leader of the VHA is buried with three items which belonged to them. Nobody knows what they are. Caber Dyer is probably the most successful vampire hunter of all time. Over the years, the VHA has had many headquarters in several countries, but the VHA was founded here in Oakdale," said Jason. The noise slowly died away and eventually disappeared from Aiden's ears. Aiden faced his father smiling, grateful that he was being shown his family's ancestry.

Despite hoping for an early finish, Aiden was devastated when he found out his father was called away for an emergency. Rather than relaxing in a classroom, Jason had asked Neil to give Aiden a private fitness and combat lesson. Aiden now found himself in a corner of the VHA on the training mats as Neil shouted at him.

"Come on, Dyer, keep running, keep punching," Neil bellowed. Aiden sighed with exhaustion, but he knew the quicker he got on with the circuit, the quicker he would be done. He walked back over to the dummy and began punching the doll until his fists turned red raw.

"Okay," said Neil. Aiden stopped and turned to face the Master Hunter.

"You are naturally good at this, you pick up skills quickly," murmured Neil. "Let's see how quick you are." Without warning, Neil threw his fist forwards, Aiden dodged the knuckle by the skin of his teeth. Falling backwards, Neil turned to face him.

"Let's see what you have learnt. Think fast," said Neil tauntingly.

"What?" said Aiden, startled by the immediate turn of events, avoiding Neil's advances. Aiden bounced to his feet; he knew he didn't stand a chance against the Master Hunter, but he wasn't going to back down. Neil kept taking swings, and Aiden successfully avoided each one. One punch grazed the side of his cheek. With a quick second to think, Aiden realised Neil's feet were unprotected. Remembering what Neil had said, "think fast", and his earlier lesson, Aiden knew this was the moment. Aiden dropped to the floor, spinning his feet round, trying his best to perfect the move he had failed earlier. Neil dodged Aiden's move with ease as if he saw it coming from a mile away.

"Not too bad," said Neil. "I would almost say you performed that move perfect compared to earlier. That's enough for now. Daria will be happy."

Aiden lay on the floor, trying to regain his breath. Neil left him there, and Aiden waited another minute before sprinting towards the male changing room, eager to be home. Aiden felt his cheek, but luckily there was no blood, only a tender mark.

"Hello, Aiden," said a voice. Aiden stopped packing his bag and searched the changing room for the owner of the female voice. Diana appeared from around the corner.

"Hi," said Aiden warily, knowing this to be their first private and direct conversation.

"I've been trying to get to you," she folded her arms. Aiden remained silent, knowing she knew everything. "Why am I talking to you? That's probably what you are wondering." Diana advanced on him, walking circles around him. "I am going to make this quick. The only person I care about is Callie. I've got the VHA right where I want them with regard to her… and Tyler. If you bring any trouble to her—"

"I won't."

"—I will kill you," Diana finished, ignoring Aiden's interruption. Aiden had avoided her eyes, but he couldn't now. He looked deep into them.

"I will not bring any danger to her," said Aiden.

Diana searched his face, seeing if he was telling the truth. "Well, we know what you are, so we shall see. You will not tell Callie of this interaction; she cares for you too much." Diana tapped Aiden on his back and walked off, leaving Aiden alone in the changing rooms to ponder with his thoughts.

It was late at night. Jason had left the VHA in a rush to attend the scene, leaving Aiden in the care of Neil, who seemed to have enjoyed being asked to put Aiden through a fitness and combat session.

Jason stood on the outskirts of Tammonwoods, the neighbouring town to Oakdale, at a horrific scene. Helen and Sofia, two of several cleaners had arrived, dealing with bodies of the dead vampires.

"What do you think this was?" Jason asked. Helen and Sofia paused from examining the scene.

"One could say vampire or even hunter by the way these vampires have been killed. But the impaled vampire is work of a witch," said Helen, dusting off her hands. Jason felt his stomach tense. *Could this possibly be it? Could this be a link, or was this the same witch from all those years ago?*

"Besides, these men were a part of Shun Yun Li's clan. We saw the tattoo which is becoming very apparent at the moment in the dissection room," said Sofia.

"Go and look at the stake. There's some mark on it," said Helen before turning back to examining the closest vampire.

Jason approached the stake, ignoring the overpowering stench as he drew closer. "It's the same," he caught himself whispering. He looked at the sigil that had been burnt onto the stake. It was the same sigil that had been burnt onto the wall of Aiden's bedroom fourteen years ago, when Jason had run home to find the body of a burnt vampire, a smashed window and no sign of his wife. This had been the second time it had occurred. There was no coincidence in Jason's eyes. All the attacks were done by the same being, but why? If this was the same being that killed his wife, why had they returned after fourteen years and started attacking Shun Yun Li's men?

"Shun has something they want," said Jason staring at the sigil.

13
THE ENCOUNTER

Days had passed, which blended into weeks, since Aiden had joined the VHA and his life had changed. He was tired, bruised and sore, which seemed to relax Tyler and Callie to Aiden's astonishment. They had told Aiden that bruising smelt like out-of-date blood to vampires which helped Aiden, as it turned out his scent was growing stronger and remaining in Perfect Blood state longer than his normal blood. He had heard from Callie that over the past couple of days, reports emerged of increased vampires in and around Oakdale and the neighboring towns. From the moment Aiden left his house, attended school and was driven to the VHA, he did not look at people the same way he used to. But that didn't stop Aiden from continuing his day-to-day life. He rarely had any time to himself between school, the VHA and home. From escaping the terror of Mr Burton for it only to be replaced by Neil Gauze, Aiden felt like it was one evil replacing the other. Neil was a hard and draining person, who didn't have time for excuses or "pathetic people". He enjoyed forcing Aiden's class to partake in some horrific HIIT sessions along with muscle-soring combat sessions, but it was a relief when Aiden found out their fitness lesson had been replaced with an induction to the new Vampire Hunter Uniform that Daria had made compulsory for all students to learn.

Aiden sat in the glass cubicle classroom, Gabriella one seat away from where Tobias leant back in his chair at the front. Aiden had quickly come to learn that Tobias was Neil's favourite student.

"Today we will be looking at the analysis of a hunter's uniform," said Neil. He stood at the centre of the classroom and next to a seated Toby, who decided to come and join the lesson. So far, Toby was the kindest person Aiden had come across in the VHA. Despite being stern, he had become one of Aiden's favourites for being fair. He sat silently in a chair listening to the Master Hunter take the lesson. The new VHA uniform hung neatly in front of all the trainees. Aiden studied the uniform carefully. He remembered reading about the VHA uniform in the book his father had given him; however, it was now out of date due to Neil's redesign.

"The VHA uniform is based upon black fitted shirts, black combat trousers, black boots which are sturdy and thick, but there is soft material around the ankle that supports your ankles – this allows for full rotation and flexibility. You also have a black chest rig, vest and backpack with holders for wooden stakes on the front and back, and finally a black waist gun saddle with pockets for extra wooden bullets." Neil pointed towards all the accessories speaking quickly, Aiden struggling to take notes about why all the trainees should be wearing this uniform on missions and, now, around the VHA during training days.

"Why does it not have anything around the neck to protect us from vampire bites?" asked Billy, who had risen his hand in the process.

"Raise your hand first before interrupting my lesson, Tate," said Neil, using Billy's second name. Billy blushed with embarrassment.

"It is because," started Toby, who noted Billy's discomfort, "the VHA believes that if this vulnerable area is exposed, it will force hunters to fight better. Ultimately, making you fight for your life." Aiden sensed the tension in the room suddenly change, and the trainees looked between each other warily.

"Thank you, Toby," said Neil.

"I believe this rule to be foolish, I have lobbied against it," Toby cut in, his elderly voice silencing Neil. The two men exchanged looks of great disrespect.

Aiden's evening finished at the VHA after the tense lesson with Neil and Toby. The journey home and sleep seemed like a blur before Aiden found himself at school the next day.

"I'm beginning to lose time," Aiden had caught himself saying to Callie. They walked down the chaotic hallways of Oakdale Secondary School, students cursing and throwing objects through the crowded hallways, on their way to their next lesson.

"It's okay, you will get used to it," said Callie calmly before they greeted Tyler, who was looking at his phone.

"Sorry, but Mrs Haljo has posted our homework on the forum about the Wall Street Crash," Tyler mumbled. "There are a lot of inconsistencies with the questions." He glared at his phone before walking off and leaving the two. Aiden had heard Tyler talk a few times about how inaccurate some of the history lessons were. But there was no way Tyler could prove he knew about the events.

"What are you doing tonight? Tyler and I are heading out, wanna come?" asked Callie.

"Yes," said Aiden eagerly. "I'm at the VHA though." Aiden felt the sudden happiness evaporate.

"We will wait for you," said Callie blushing. "I want to spend time with you outside of school." Aiden felt his heart skip a beat; it gave him renewed energy knowing Callie wanted to spend time with him, when suddenly someone bumped into the two of them.

"Dyer," a voice screeched. Aiden didn't need to look who it was as girls passed swooning. Tobias's perfectly groomed silver hair stood out. Aiden couldn't help but feel annoyed, thinking he had just missed a perfect opportunity with Callie, who he had noticed slowly moved to stand behind him. "Who's this?" Tobias asked eagerly looking at Callie, taking note of her retreat.

"Callie," said Aiden coldly, knowing he couldn't portray Callie any different, in case Tobias noticed.

"Nice to meet you, Callie. How come we have never spoken before?" said Tobias, looking a bit too interested for Aiden's liking. Callie appeared from behind Aiden, knowing she had to play along.

"I stay away from pretty boys," she said mockingly, keeping her distance and replies short. Aiden stood watching Tobias engage with Callie – if Tobias knew Callie was a vampire, he would kill her without thinking.

"Well, I think we should get to know each other a little bit better, especially if you are hanging out with Dyer." Tobias smirked, putting his charms to good use.

"I think I'm fine, thank you," Callie replied, knowing he was trying to flirt.

"Ouch okay, well I bet I should get going. Guess I will see you later, Dyer."

"Okay," said Aiden, feeling his stomach tense from the awkward atmosphere between Tobias and Callie.

Tobias walked past Callie just as a group of students barged past Tobias, forcing him into Callie, who dropped all her folders and books. Tobias shouted at the younger students who ran off scared.

"I'm sorry about that." Tobias chuckled, kneeling down to help Callie pick all her belongings up, when he quickly graced her hand with his.

"Wow, you're freezing," Tobias spoke with surprise. Callie gulped. "Yes, I'm a cold person." She rose to her feet, quickly gathering the rest of her books.

Aiden attempted to help her up, but without warning, Callie moved quickly. She stood up, pushing Aiden backwards by accident. She quickly moved her hand grabbing his arm before he fell to the floor. Tobias witnessed the incredible action.

"I'm sorry," said Callie worryingly holding Aiden's arm tightly.

"Wow, quick reflexes," Tobias muttered, watching Aiden regain his ground. Aiden found his footing, not sure what to say, but Tobias smiled, walking off before he was submerged within the crowd of students.

"Don't ever leave me with him." Aiden looked towards a frightened Callie. She was looking around the hallways like someone was about jump out and scare her. "He makes me feel uncomfortable. He would do whatever it takes to kill me."

"I will never leave him with you, and if he ever places a finger on you, I will kill him," said Aiden.

Callie smiled at his response; she heard his heart rate increase, showing her that he meant every word.

"Thank you." She grabbed Aiden's hand. Aiden smiled feeling his heart skip a beat once again while the corners of his mouth spiked upwards at her surprisingly soft hands. The two teenagers mumbled innocently as they walked to their next class, continuing to hold hands.

"Interesting," Tobias muttered to himself. He looked towards his hand, rubbing his fingers together. He may be overthinking it. There would be no way a vampire would be in Oakdale Secondary School. However, they were disgusting sneaky creatures which would do anything to get a meal. He turned his head to watch as Callie and Aiden walk off, remembering what he had learnt in vampire anatomy. *I think I will keep my eye on you*, he thought to himself, recalling how chilled Callie felt, her strength and her quick reflexes.

It had been an early finish at the VHA, and Aiden contained his excitement. In record timing, he had arrived home, washed and dressed.

"Okay, Dad, I'm off," Aiden shouted from downstairs. Before Jason could reply, Aiden left the house to be greeted by Tyler who was waiting for Aiden on the opposite side of the road, making sure he stayed clear of the Dyer's household. As far as Aiden knew, there was nothing set up to detect vampires. Though he wouldn't be surprised if there was, given how many secrets his dad had managed to keep from him.

"Good day?" Tyler asked as Aiden crossed the road to meet him.

Aiden shrugged. "Eventful." They walked into Oakdale Shopping Centre where they met Callie at the entrance.

"How was the VHA today?" Tyler queried with Callie approaching the two boys.

"Let's not talk about that tonight. L et's be normal teenagers for one night," pleaded Aiden to which both Callie and Tyler agreed. Aiden locked eyes with Callie, and for the third time, his heart skipped a beat as he knew Callie was going to mean more to him.

"You look beautiful," commentated Aiden.

Callie blushed. "Thank you."

Aiden smiled to himself. He liked being the one to make Callie blush. His dad had always told him to tell a girl when she looked nice. In one of Jason's rare comments about Aiden's mum, he said it's what he missed most about her – not being able to tell her how beautiful she looked. Callie was the first girl Aiden thought was beautiful, and he wanted her to know that.

They fought their way through the shopping centre towards The Local Burger Kitchen for their famous garlic chicken burgers and fusion drinks. Sitting down in a booth, each having ordered large garlic chicken burgers, they finally felt like normal teenagers. They stopped talking about the supernatural world and started gossiping about school.

Leaving the restaurant, Callie insisted she'd walk Aiden home, to which Aiden agreed. Callie and Aiden walked off in a different direction to Tyler, and it wasn't long before Callie and Aiden were alone, walking along a quiet road, the night sky full of dazzling stars.

"That was a lovely evening," said Callie nervously.

"It was. I enjoyed being with you," said Aiden bravely, feeling like this was the perfect opportunity. He stopped and turned to face Callie, and she did the same, moving her hair that covered her face. His brown eyes were warming. She felt her inner core warm up – a feeling she hadn't felt in a long time.

"Aiden." Callie paused, moving closer.

"Callie." Aiden felt her presence. They were inches from one another. If Aiden moved now he would be able to kiss her. His heart raced and his breathing deepened. Aiden knew he would regret this moment if he didn't make a move. This was the first time Aiden had ever felt like this. He had never had a girlfriend before, but he knew that if he felt this way for Callie, he had try something.

Moving closer, Callie closed her eyes. This had been the first time she had felt anything for a boy since she had been transformed. She hadn't had a boyfriend either and didn't know what to do, but she let her body do what it wanted, and waited for the touch of his soft lips on hers, but Aiden stopped.

Something in the corner of his eye, caught his attention. Callie, her eyes still closed, started to purse her lips, but as the seconds went by, she opened her eyes, slightly annoyed. Wondering what could distract Aiden in a moment like this, she turned in the same direction that Aiden was looking in.

In the middle of the road in the distance, underneath a lamppost, was a cloaked floating figure. Aiden and Callie remained silent, watching the figure's clothing billow in the night's breeze.

"What is that?" Aiden glared at the being. He stepped forward imperceptibly, not quite sure what he was seeing. Callie watched Aiden's every move – herself wary of what it was. The figure was floating in the air; their black clothing illuminated by the light of the lamppost. Their face and body were covered, making it almost impossible to identify them. The surrounding area remained quiet; the buzz of the cars in the distance seemed to have disappeared. Aiden and Callie remained still, both sceptical.

There was an unease in the air. When suddenly, a rainbow of colours burst from the hands of the floating figure. A marvelous fire ball erupted and was aimed directly at them.

"Watch out!" Callie shrieked, tackling Aiden to the ground. The fire ball roared over their heads, the immense heat singing the hair on their arms, crashing into the distance, lighting the dark street up. Callie and Aiden jumped back to their feet. The cloaked figure advanced menacingly.

"Aiden, jump on my back!" Callie screeched, reacting quickly.

Aiden didn't hesitate, he leapt on to Callie's back thinking she would fall to the floor with his weight, but she held him as if he were as light as a feather; he had forgotten about her enhanced strength in the panic. The cloaked figure once again rose their hands, but Callie leapt away, following the breeze of the wind.

"What was that?" Aiden yelled into Callie's ears over the powerful wind. Callie didn't reply, she was too preoccupied with dodging trees and cars and focussing on where to take them both. Aiden looked forward, struggling to keep his eyes open. He realised this was the first time he had ever gone at vamp speed, and so far he wasn't impressed. Everything was blurred, and the dust and insects were flying into his face, making it hard for him to see.

Callie came to a stop, skidding across the dusty ground of a building site. Aiden jumped off her back as she spoke. "Follow me." She moved behind a large yellow excavation machine. Aiden followed her footsteps, watching his back for any signs of the cloaked figure.

Pressing themselves against the cold steel of the machine, Aiden took a deep breath in, remembering his training at the VHA, focussing his gaze and calming himself down, before he asked Callie the question he had earlier. "What was that?"

Callie peered round the corner of the machine, gazing at the entrance and her skid marks across the dusty floor, ignoring Aiden.

"Callie," said Aiden in a raised voice through gritted teeth, gaining her attention.

"A witch," Callie replied.

"A witch?" Aiden gulped heavily.

"A dangerous witch."

"What do you mean?"

"There is a powerful vampire named Shun Yun Li. Over the last month or so, his men have been killed by what my mum, and your dad, suspect to be a witch," Callie explained.

"Why?" But before Aiden finished, Callie forced her hand over his mouth, silencing him. Aiden flailed his arms in the air, taken aback by Callie's sudden movement. With an impressive crack of lightning, Callie held her hand stubbornly against Aiden's mouth, twitching from the deafening sound, feeling the warm air leave his mouth. She gulped, chanced a glance, and wished she hadn't. The witch was here. They were floating in the middle of the construction site, looking around.

"Damn," Callie whispered. Aiden frantically tapped her arm before she released her grip, allowing him to speak and breathe. He took a deep breath in before he spoke. "Distract and escape. It's a technique they taught us at the VHA."

But before Callie could respond, a voice shouted, "*Photia Cricia.*" The dark construction site lit up. Crimson flames erupted and circled the area. Aiden and Callie covered their faces, blinded by the light.

"I have an idea," Aiden shouted over the powerful roaring flames.

"What is it?" bellowed Callie, not wanting to waste any more time.

"This machine has petrol in it, right? And we have access to fire?" Callie clicked on to what Aiden was thinking. It was the only idea they had. Aiden quickly pulled his T-shirt off, folding it into a tight roll.

"Throw this," Aiden said, grabbing some gravel from the ground. Callie snatched the stones and threw them to the other side of the site. A metal clanging reverberated throughout the construction site. Callie saw the witch turn immediately, looking for the source of the sound. Aiden quickly took the opportunity and crawled to the closest flame, lighting his rolled-up T-shirt on fire. Returning, he stuffed his shirt inside the petrol tank.

"Get back on," Callie said, kneeling down. Aiden jumped on, and Callie used all her strength to shove the machine towards the witch, before running off.

The yellow machine exploded, sending a fierce shock wave through the grounds, illuminating the entire site. The explosion was so loud it rang in Aiden's ears. The fire which circled them was far more dangerous than Callie anticipated. She screamed horribly which alerted the witch, but before the witch could do anything, they were sent flying backwards by the shock wave.

Running in agony, knowing she had to get as far as she could from the witch, Callie crashed into the ground of a field, unable to run anymore, sending Aiden flying off.

"Are you okay?" said Aiden running over to Callie. Callie bit her tongue, suppressing any screams. Her legs were red raw and blistered from the burns.

"I need it to heal," she cried, slamming her fist against the ground as she let out a loud shriek; she bit her hand so she wouldn't make any more noise. Aiden held her, watching her legs heal quickly. He felt her body relax as he watched her skin slowly turn from red to beige. Callie sighed with relief and looked towards Aiden. Both were covered in dirt and sand, with Aiden sweating profusely. He dragged Callie behind a hay bale, holding her as he sat down, his exposed back against the itchy straw.

"We need to get to Tyler's," Callie murmured.

"I agree, but how did the witch follow us to the building site? And why are they after us?" queried Aiden. Callie sat in between Aiden's legs feeling the cool evening breeze chill her once-burnt legs. She was thinking. The pictures her mother had showed her of the impaled vampires, the conversations she had had with Tyler and what Aiden had just said, and then it hit her like a lightning bolt.

"Sacrifices. You," she said sternly.

"What?" said Aiden, looking around the field, carefully noticing the inhabitance of cows, who barely knew Aiden and Callie were there.

"It's you, Aiden. It's you… it's your blood, the Perfect Blood. Somehow it's able to track you," said Callie in a reedy tone. She leant forwards, turning to face Aiden.

"But I thought only vampires could smell me." Aiden gulped, Callie now witnessing the change in colour of Aiden's skin.

"No, witches have a sixth sense which allow them to identify supernatural creatures. This witch has somehow been able to track you," said Callie. Callie looked round the field. The witch hadn't arrived yet, until a loud thunderous noise erupted through the fields. In the darkness of the night, Callie saw the Dark Witch appear, levitating over the ground.

"I know you're here, I am the Dark Witch," the Dark Witch sung in a high monotone voice. "But it's okay," the witch continued, their speech slow. "It is just us now, Aiden. Your mother isn't here to protect you anymore."

14
RESEARCH

Callie thought she heard someone running, but as she looked at Aiden, she realised it was his heart. He began breathing heavily, and she could sense the rage suddenly appear within him. Never had she heard someone's heart pump this fast.

"Aiden, don't," Callie found herself whispering, grappling Aiden's hands in her own, but Aiden remained silent, in a trance, as the Dark Witch continued to speak.

"That's right, on a night not too dissimilar to this, I came to your house where I found you as a baby. Your mother and I fought, I lost my powers for a few years but she lost her life." A tormenting laugh filled the cool air.

"I am going to kill it," said Aiden, breaking his silence. Callie turned Aiden's head to face hers so he was looking into her eyes.

"Aiden, I'm sorry, but you can't. You jump out, the Dark Witch will capture you, and who knows what will happen.

Please… they are only provoking you." They looked into each other's eyes. Despite his eyes being filled with angry tears, he was able to look past his smeared vision and look Callie in the eyes. She was scared.

"Okay," he whispered weakly, feeling he was doing a great dishonor to his mother. He wanted to jump out and fight the witch – kill it. Was this why his father hadn't told him about his mother's death? Because it was a witch? There were so many questions, but as Aiden looked at Callie who was looking around, all he knew was that he had to get out of there alive with her.

"I have an idea. The Dark Witch is tracking your blood like a vampire, so we just have to overload them." Callie stared at a distraught and speechless Aiden, hoping for a response, but he remained numb. "Just stay here," she murmured before she disappeared.

In the darkness of the night, Aiden saw her appear and disappear, hiding behind hay bales, ready to enact her plan. Running through the field, Callie started to slit the throats of the cows. The cows fell to the ground, blood oozing from their necks. Aiden grimaced. He didn't like a plan that killed innocent animals, but he knew it was their only chance to get away.

The Dark Witch started to move, watching the bodies of the cows drop to the ground. Callie's plan was working. The witch was becoming confused by the overpowering stench of blood. Killing five cows in total, Callie returned to Aiden, her hands and clothes drenched in blood. A foul stench of rotten meat bombarded Aiden, making it almost impossible for him to breath. Callie leant against the hardened hay bale, listening to the Dark Witch move around furiously.

A loud echoing shriek erupted from the Dark Witch, it was as if two sharp pieces of metal were being dragged against one another. Callie and Aiden covered their ears, protecting them against the deafening sound. As it stopped, Callie spoke, "Let's go." Aiden nodded, jumping on her back once again. However, the Dark Witch was able to gain sight of them.

"No!" roared the Dark Witch, flying towards Aiden and Callie, but Callie kicked the hay bale as if it were a football towards the Dark Witch. The Dark Witch easily avoided the bale of hay, but the distraction was just long enough for the witch to lose sight of Aiden and Callie, and they were gone. Suffocating under the heavy aroma and stench of the dead cows, the Dark Witch was unable to track Aiden's scent. Lifting their head into the air, trying to catch any scent, the Dark Witch screamed, consuming the fields in a dazzling fiery inferno, the night sky lighting up as if it were daytime. Frustrated, the Witch disappeared into the darkness of the night, leaving the burnt, smoking field behind.

"I will have you," they murmured.

Tyler opened his front door to a jaw-dropping sight. His two best friends were standing there, both looking tired, bloody and cold. Aiden shirtless and covered in dirt, and Callie, her once pretty white blouse ripped and covered in mud and blood. Tyler pulled them into his house, looking around before he closed the front door.

"We need something to conceal Aiden's scent," said Callie, making her way into the lounge room. Aiden collapsed on Tyler's sofa, taking in the recent events.

"What happened?" Tyler asked, astounded.

Callie took in a deep breath. "The attacks I've been telling you about. It's a witch, the Dark Witch… they attacked us."

"What?" said Tyler timidly, feeling his spine tingle.

"And what's even better is that they were able to track Aiden's blood before we were able to escape and come here."

"You brought the Dark Witch here?" said Tyler worryingly.

"No, I killed enough cows to overpower Aiden's scent. They have no idea where we are," said Callie. "So is there anything we can use to conceal Aiden's scent?" she persisted.

Tyler was struggling to digest the information. He looked towards Aiden who in return was watching both of them talk; he remained still and quiet.

Callie screamed, "Tyler!" demanding his attention.

"I… I… I'm working on it," he stuttered

"Well, how long will it take?" Callie bit back. "I don't want to encounter the Dark Witch again."

"Do you think Cara has an easy job finding the herbs and materials needed to do this bracelet for Aiden? Lydia isn't here, so we have to do it the old-fashioned way," said Tyler raising his voice. The two vampires started to growl at one another.

Aiden's blood pumped in his ears. He couldn't control himself before he bellowed, "That thing killed my mum!" drawing the attention of Callie and Tyler. Callie twitched, listening to the heartbreak in his voice. "Why were they after me? Let them come, I want to kill them!" Aiden finished, his voice reaching new levels which he even didn't know it could reach, while his eyes turned bloodshot with rage. He was breathing heavily, now standing up, facing his two friends. Callie looked into his eyes, shivering, feeling like these were the eyes of a vampire hunter.

"They might be after you because you're the Perfect Blood," said Tyler.

Aiden cursed loudly, running his hands through his hair.

"Who is the Dark Witch?" Aiden snapped, demanding an answer from Tyler and Callie.

"We don't know," said Tyler, allowing Aiden to shout and get his anger out.

"You are going to tell me about these killings and we are going to find out who this Dark Witch is," said Aiden.

"Okay, come with me, I know where we can start," said Tyler. He walked to the far wall and pushed a panel inwards. There was a click, and the panel swung open to reveal a staircase leading downstairs.

Callie and Aiden approached curiously. Aiden followed them down the spiral staircase, and his jaw dropped open when he saw what was hiding underneath Tyler's house.

"This is my library," said Tyler. Aiden looked around at the fabulous candle-lit library. Bookcases touched the ceiling, filled with oddly shaped and colourful books, all dreadfully organised and covered in layers of dust. The threadbare carpet was soft and comfortable, and the walls were decorated with pictures and peculiar markings. Aiden looked high, following the bookshelves. There was bound to be something about the Dark Witch in here.

"Perfect, let's get to work," said Aiden.

The morning mist refused to settle as the spring sun slowly rose. Jason stood inside the construction site, looking at the toppled excavation machine that was charcoaled, the sides blown apart. Diana came walking over, having got off the phone.

"There is another site. I think it's best we go check it out." Reluctant to leave the current scene, Jason followed Diana.

Within minutes, they were in the presence of a farmer who was sobbing at the edge of his field. Jason and Diana looked at the fields from the comfort of the black four-by-four. Black smoke was rising from crisp turf, and crows feasted upon the carcasses.

"She's here," said the driver. Jason looked out his window as another VHA vehicle arrived.

"Who's here?" Diana paused, confused by what the driver meant. A woman exited the vehicle, escorted by two hunters. She was draped in long black clothing. Her lips were black and stood out against the paleness of her skin, and the sun bounced off her eyebrow piercings.

"Why didn't you tell me she was coming?" questioned Diana, who was slightly offended that Jason hadn't told her someone else was arriving. Jason gazed upon the woman who gently pulled forward a black veil covering her face.

"I didn't have time. Stay in the car, that's an order," he said hauntingly, exiting the vehicle and leaving Diana alone, who willingly stayed in the vehicle, glad she didn't have to deal with this particular woman.

"Dyer," said the woman coolly as Jason approached through the smell and smoke of burnt grass and meat.

"Mariam," said Jason.

"I have been studying the pictures you have sent me, and I will tell you this one time only. This is Mayhemic magic, after I have helped you here, I will have nothing to do with this anymore. This witch is powerful and is collecting chi."

"Just do what I have asked you to do, then be off," said Jason through gritted teeth. His entire body felt on edge. Mariam looked towards Jason, who returned a look of utter disdain.

"Fine," said Mariam tersely.

"Take him away." Jason pointed towards the farmer who was still crying. The two hunters left Mariam's side, dragging a wailing farmer away. Mariam walked forwards, scanning the field.

"There is no doubt that this is the same witch who has performed those sacrifices, it looks like this sacrifice managed to escape though," said Mariam. Jason crossed his arms, listened intently.

Mariam lifted her heavily tattooed hands into the air, palms open, facing the scorched field. Closing her eyes, she whispered words under her breath, breathing in deep and slowly. Jason watched her every move, wanting an answer immediately when suddenly, Mariam screeched in pain, falling backwards as if she had been hit in the stomach. Her skin was paler than usual as she covered her face.

"What was it?" Jason pressed as Mariam started cowering, her hands shaking in the air. Standing over the witch, tired of her dramatics, Jason pressed on.

"Mariam, what happened? Tell me now or I will let the council know where you are!" The threat seemed to shake off any lasting fears as Mariam's pure black eyes linked with Jason's.

"Magic is personal. Every witch's magic is different, like DNA. Even though I cannot tell who this witch is, I can tell you one thing for sure," Mariam paused, her voice still shaking. "This is the same witch who killed your wife fourteen years ago."

Working off three hours' sleep was something Aiden never wanted to do again. As the clock struck 3 pm, the school bell rang immediately and students bombarded the hallways, running to the closest exit acting like wild animals.

Aiden was the last student to leave the classroom, dragging his feet behind Callie and Tyler, both of whom were tired as well. He was now up to date with the killings happening around Oakdale, his and Callie's recent encounter confirmed who was responsible. The Dark Witch was a threat. The three had unanimously agreed to stay within crowded areas and from now on and were not to go out at night unless it was an emergency. Aiden could deal with vampires that hunted him, but knowing that an all-powerful witch who had killed his mother was after him was enough to push him to admit himself into a psychiatric ward.

Walking towards the exit, desperate to go home to bed, he knew that wouldn't be possible as it was now time for the VHA. With that thought, he saw the blacked-out four-by-four ahead. Callie was too busy talking when Aiden decided to stop.

"I'm not going," he murmured, his eyes feeling heavy.

"What?" Callie snapped.

"The Dark Witch killed my mum. I don't have time for the VHA. I want to find this witch and kill it."

Callie remained silent, struggling with her tiredness but at the same time not sure what to say.

"We are going to Tyler's, and we are staying in his library until we can find out something about the Dark Witch."

Callie was stunned as she watched Aiden turn back and head towards the back gate, quickly following in his steps, barging her way past students.

Once again, Tyler opened his door in amazement. Aiden and Callie were standing there once again, but this time they were dressed in their school uniform, looking tired.

"I want to kill this witch," said Aiden, revulsion rich in his voice. Callie and Aiden made their way down to Tyler's library, Tyler joining them at the table holding an open book.

"*Tenebris Pythonissam*," said Tyler.

"What?" Callie asked, her face brandishing a look of utter confusion.

"*Tenebris Pythonissam* is 'the Dark Witch' in Latin; it turns out the Dark Witch has been around since the Middle Ages," said Tyler pronouncing 'the Dark Witch' in perfect Latin.

"You've found something," Aiden smiled.

"I have," said Tyler, looking smug.

Callie's face lit up with relief. Tyler read from the book that he had found amongst the hundreds in his disorganised library.

"'The *Tenebris Pythonissam*, also known as the Dark Witch, appeared in 1610, completing three sacrifices by impaling vampires before disappearing by the end of 1620.'"

"It's 400 hundred years old." Aiden gasped.

"It's called a Witch Slumber. It allows a witch to enter a period of slumber for years, it's a powerful spell which only a few witches can do. It explains how they are still alive. It appeared once again in the early eighteenth century before it once again disappeared to not been seen or heard from, and that's it," said Tyler. The three teenagers remained silent as they took the information in. "What now?" Callie asked.

"We wait," said Tyler.

"Wait?" Aiden snapped.

"Yes," Tyler challenged. "Because they hunted you down, you have no idea when this witch will appear again or why is it back. We just have to wait."

Aiden didn't like what Tyler was saying, but the more he thought about it, the more it made sense. Aiden arrived home just before 6 pm, too tired to cook. He ran to his room and collapsed on his bed, falling into a deep sleep within seconds.

Jason, Diana and Hayden sat quietly in Daria's room, once again a thin layer of white smoke hanging in the air from the constant burning of incense in the dark room. Hayden had remained quiet as to why he was present, but his respect for Jason was the reason he remained seated. Jason had placed a beige file on Daria's desk, a file which he had been working on since he had arrived back in England. The vaulted door to Daria's office came swinging in, sending an echo down the hallway and into her office as she came marching in, Neil hanging to her coattail.

"What's the meaning of this?" Daria spat with venom. Jason looked up to the towering figure, who tried their best to intimidate him, but he remained still. Everything he had been working on was now finally coming to light, and he did not have time to deal with intimidation tactics.

"Sit down and open the folder," said Jason pointedly. Daria looked towards the folder that had been thrown onto her desk, breaking the perfect line she had arranged her pens in. Moving round her desk, now noticing Hayden and Diana were present, she sat down in her mahogany chair, opening the folder dubiously.

"What's all this?" she questioned. She pulled picture after picture from the folder, each accompanied with a detailed report written by Jason. The pictures were of the impaled vampires that belonged to Shun Yun Li and one photo of a scorched field and blackened construction site.

"Months ago, you brought me back to England after Exhibit A," Jason began. Daria's eyes flicked between the pieces of paper until her eyes locked on a form titled *Exhibit A*. It was a familiar site – the first of the impaled killings. "When I received your phone call detailing what had happened and that it was one of Shun Yun Li's men, I was excited, but I didn't know what I was getting myself into. When I saw the stake that had impaled the vampire, a similar marking had been brandished onto the wood – a marking I have seen before. I decided to ignore the marking at that time, thinking it was a coincidence, but as my best friend always says"—Jason nodded towards Diana who sat calmly in her chair, looking towards Daria who decided to shoot her a snide look—"there is no such thing as coincidence.

"As time went by, not only were Shun's men slaughtered, but another of his vampires had been impaled, and the mark, now sigil, was the same. Look at Exhibit B." Once again Daria looked at another form titled *Exhibit B*. "And finally, if you look at Exhibit C, you will see a burnt field and singed construction site. Before I made anymore assertions, I quickly did some research into the Scalded Salcomb Sucker, the vampire Arkadian Armstrong killed to see if the vamp had any successors which they didn't, which brings me to this." Jason paused. "This being is after Shun Yun Li. My bet is that Shun Yun Li will be returning to England soon to find out who has been killing his men and interfering in his business. When he does return, the being will go after him to find him."

"Being? Don't you mean vampire?" Daria queried, readjusting herself in her chair, leaning her elbow on her grand desk and covering her mouth.

"This is not a vampire attack. This is a witch attack, and this is the same witch who killed my wife," Jason finished. Diana shivered, remembering that night.

The room went silent. Neil stood by Daria's shoulder, who quickly exchanged a look with Jason, before looking over at the pictures and detailed reports. Daria continued to flick through the pages, briefly scanning what Jason had written, and considered the intense remark about his wife.

"What makes you think these are connected? Fourteen years is a long time for someone to be inactive," Daria challenged.

"Confirmation from a witch, who I privately hired to study the magic that lingered on these fields. Magic that was the same as the magic in my son's room fourteen years ago," answered Jason. Daria gently tapped her knuckle against her wooden desk.

"So, what are you saying?" asked Daria. She placed down the forms, leaning back in her chair, staring at Jason.

"I lost the love of my life to this witch. I know we hunt vampires, but I know that we can achieve two goals here. Revenge for me and, if my theory is correct and if Shun Yun Li comes to England, we get to kill him which will look especially good for you." Daria seemed to smirk with this comment. *Something to help me?* she thought, admiring Jason's intelligence.

"I too have lost someone, and we are a family at the VHA. That means we look out for each other," said Daria. "But what happens if Shun Yun Li doesn't come to England?"

"He will," said Jason with confidence. "They wouldn't put this much effort into killing his men to not gain his attention."

Daria breathed in and out heavily, looking towards Jason who had remained in the same seated position the whole way through.

"You want the witch more than Shun Yun Li? Someone who you have always wanted to catch and kill?"

"Yes," said Jason curtly.

"Promise me Shun Yun Li, and you'll have the witch," said Daria.

"I promise," said Jason immediately. Diana wanted to nudge Jason, to make sure he knew what he was placing on the line, but she resisted. They had fought witches in the past, all they had to do was find some artefacts to help them, but how helpful would they be against a crazed witch who seemed powerful?

"Perfect," said Daria, snapping Diana out of her thoughts. "Let's do this then." Daria rose from her chair, extending an arm to Jason.

"Let the hunt commence."

"*Dracas De Ramores*," said Jason, standing to shake Daria's hand. The two hunters shook hands, both exchanging confident looks. Jason was ready for revenge.

15
ARRIVAL

The last week had been peaceful, something Aiden was sceptical of. Since the encounter, the trio were constantly watching their backs when they left school in case the Dark Witch plucked up enough courage to come after them during daylight. But at the same time, Aiden wanted the Dark Witch to find him so he could go after the witch and avenge his mother. The time the three felt the safest from the VHA, vampires and the witch was when they were walking through the chaotic corridors of the school, students moving to their next lesson, barging past each other with screams and shouts. Teachers trying their best to control the river of students, but their attempts were always futile.

However, it now seemed that Tobias had taken an interest in Callie which Aiden resented. If they ever walked past each other in the hallway Tobias would try to talk to her, but she would shut him down almost instantly. It worried all of them as what they didn't need was a hungry trainee vampire hunter roaming the hallways trying to kill them, especially in what they considered their last safe place. As the clock struck twelve thirty, the bell rung harshly and the students made their way to the cafeteria, grabbing what food they could and making their way to the school field.

Aiden, Tyler and Callie sat down, relieved that the day was almost up. The homework was starting to increase, exams were dawning and the choice for their subjects for Year 10 and 11 were due imminently.

"I think I'm going to take German, French, PE and Business Studies," said Callie, biting her pen, this being the first time since her transformation, that she was actually able to decide what she liked to do. She studied the paper, ticking the boxes for the lessons. "How about you guys?" she asked.

Aiden scanned the piece of paper. PE was a no-brainer; he already knew Tyler was going to take this which would make it even more fun. "I might take the advanced course in science, chemistry is one of my favourite subjects apart from PE, and I can deal with physics and biology."

"What about your language though?" Callie asked, knowing Aiden dreaded the languages.

"Well, if I take German, you better help me in all the exams."

"Of course, I will." Callie smiled, gently placing her hand on Aiden's. Aiden smiled, but he turned to look at Tyler. He and Callie hadn't spoken about the other night when they were moments away from kissing one another, and Aiden didn't know what to say to her about it.

"How about you, Tyler?" Aiden asked feeling his voice break, the feeling never getting old every time Callie touched him. Tyler, on the other hand, wasn't so bothered about his options. He was lying down in the sun absorbing any warmth his cold body could get.

"Probably history. I'll make my mind up in the morning."

"You're a living relic. You don't need to do history," said Callie matter-of-factly, raising her eyebrow, knowing he wasn't taking it as seriously as the other two.

"How's the VHA going?" asked Tyler changing the subject, ignoring Callie.

"It's okay, I am just sore but—"

"I know, we can tell. You have a bruise on the left side near your ribs, am I wrong?" said Callie, interrupting Aiden. Aiden looked at her, remembering when they had told him bruises were like out-of-date blood to vampires.

"Is it that strong?" Aiden asked, slightly embarrassed.

"It doesn't make us vampires want to eat you... which is good," she joked.

"What were you saying before that?" Tyler asked, knowing Aiden was going to say something else before Callie interrupted.

"Only that my dad is acting differently." Aiden shrugged, having noticed how his father was more stern and less caring than usual recently.

"What do you mean?" said Tyler, who was now taking an interest in their conversation turning his head to face Aiden.

"I don't know. Since joining the VHA, I have learnt so much about him. His mum and dad died when he was thirteen, so it makes me wonder if that has damaged him to express his emotions," said Aiden. He felt like he was making an excuse for his dad, something that he would never have done when he lived back in California, but then Aiden felt like his past self was so naïve compared to now.

"That's interesting. Anything happen at the VHA?" Tyler asked Callie.

"No, I haven't seen Mum in a while. She's been on a lot of missions recently, and she doesn't like to text me when she is around the VHA just in case." Callie smiled helplessly.

"Hey, Dyer," a voice roared, breaking the calm lunch that the three were having.

"Bloody Vlad, here we go again," Callie sighed, not needing to look who it was and growing tired of Tobias's advances.

"Hi, Tobias," said Aiden waspishly. Tobias strolled over, drawing the attention of all the girls around him, his bag over his shoulder. Amber stood in the distance, horrified that Tobias would even consider talking to someone as low as Callie.

"You aright, Callie?" Tobias grinned, putting his flirtatious voice on. He graced her shoulder with his hand. "Wow. Cold again, I see," he reacted quickly.

"Don't touch me without asking," said Callie defensively, dismissing Tobias as quickly as he appeared.

"Tyler, what are your reasons for doing history?" she quickly asked, ignoring the looming shadow of Tobias.

"Tobias, just leave it," said Aiden irritable, knowing he was making Callie visibly uncomfortable. Tobias nodded, but he didn't seem annoyed, he seemed content, which worried Aiden as he watched Tobias walk off towards Amber.

"Personal survival. You have learnt the concept of Distract and Escape, but now it is time to learn some basics. I want all you to make these twigs, branches or whatever into a stake with your army knives."

Another afternoon in the VHA meant another day almost over in Aiden's eye.

Neil threw the assortment or twigs and branches into the middle of the class who sat on the gym mats. Grabbing an army knife, having never done this before, Aiden questioned how hard it could be.

"I'll be back in a minute, do your work," said Neil who wandered off. Aiden took this time to look round the group to see they had all started sharpening their twigs and branches, and Aiden followed suit. Despite the noise in the VHA, the circle which the class sat in was quiet and calm, something which Aiden enjoyed, allowing him to focus on his branch. That was until…

"I like Callie," said Tobias, grinning. Aiden looked towards the teenager who seemed to have already sharpened his twig and was now starting on a branch. A sudden eruption of disgust filled Aiden's body after witnessing how uncomfortable Callie was made earlier after Tobias had touched her.

"Well, she doesn't like you," Aiden snapped whilst focussing on sharpening his branch.

"Ouch, that's not nice," Tobias said placing one hand on his knee learning forward.

"Touching girls who don't want to be touched isn't nice either," said Aiden, his eyes now turning to face Tobias.

"You got something to say?" said Tobias with a raised voice. Gabriella and Billy sat in between the two boys, and now found it impossible to focus on making their stakes.

"Yes," said Aiden pointedly, feeling protective over the girl he liked. "She doesn't like you, so stop harassing her."

"And what? You think you're good enough for her? You're just a boy, not a man, like me," said Tobias teasingly.

"Say that again," said Aiden, rising to his feet.

"You're just a boy," Tobias reiterated, now moving to his feet, Tobias centimetres taller from his age.

"Don't do it, guys," said Gabriella calmly, but neither Aiden nor Tobias said anything back to her.

"Looks like they are about to fight," giggled Billy towards Thomas, who returned with a smirk.

"I bet I could put you on your arse," said Aiden, knowing exactly what he would do if he were to fight Tobias.

"Oh really?" The two teenagers stood off to one another. Their eyes, not looking away from the other as the noise in the VHA seemed to elevate.

"Well bring it on then," said Tobias challengingly, moving into his fighting stance.

"Make the first move, beauty boy," Aiden teased, moving into his stance. This comment seemed to agitate Tobias who was about to attack.

"Boys, stop this instant!" Toby roared from the side of the gym mat, which was enough to stop Tobias from advancing on Aiden but not enough to break their stare. Toby shuffled over, bearing a lot of weight on his walking stick. "The enemy is vampires not one another."

Neil came running back over, noticing Toby was in the middle of the two teenagers.

"What's happening?" Neil bellowed, joining Toby. Aiden and Tobias were still in their stance, Aiden ready for a fight. Without an answer, Toby said, "Neil, you take your favourite and I'll take mine." Neil raised an eyebrow, but he did as the elderly man said. Toby guided Aiden off using his weakness to guilt Aiden to come with him as Neil grabbed Tobias by the shoulder, pulling him away.

Now why would he be defending her so much? Tobias thought, glancing round to look at Aiden as they were guided.

An unforgivable storm attacked the coast of England that evening. Everyone in the south-east of England had been put under a weather warning. Flights were either suspended or cancelled. However, this did not stop one plane that was flying under the protection of a witch. The large private aeroplane flew as if nothing was wrong, the long trip from Japan had had no effect on the people aboard. Landing at a private airfield shouted suspicion. The airbus came to a stop amongst the powerful winds as a legion of ground crew worked insanely fast, trying their best to move the precious cargo out of the cargo hold. A staircase was pushed towards the aeroplane door. It opened immediately and a group of suited Asian men ran down the stairs, extending their arms and opening umbrellas.

A tall Asian male walked out last, his expensive blue suit protected by the umbrellas as he wrapped a red scarf around his neck. His hair was jet black and his perfectly chiselled features only enhanced the curl of his lips and hunger in his eyes. Accompanying him was a young Asian woman who followed his every step, keeping her head bowed at all times, knowing who her superior was. Her glamourous sea-grass-coloured kimono stood out amongst the blue and blacks of the men's suits.

"Time to see who's been meddling with my business," said the man irritably. The master and assistant waited at the bottom of the staircase, still protected by the umbrellas, as a black Rolls-Royce came to a stop at their toes. The doors were opened, and they took their seats before speeding off, following the M4 towards London.

16
The Decision

"Why have you called me here?" said Neil with animosity. Daria had pulled him away from one of his torturous HIIT sessions with Aiden's class. Jason, Diana and Hayden stood at the back of Daria's dark office.

"Perfect, you're here," said Daria ignoring the annoyance in Neil's voice. "I have acquired some information that will make you happy, Jason." The three Master Hunters walked towards her desk, a certain eagerness shining in Jason's face as he hoped for what she was going to say.

"Since our last conversation regarding the attacks, the witch and your wife, I placed some of our field agents on high alert for any form of gossip regarding Shun Yun Li based on your theory." Daria paused. She opened a drawer from her oak desk, grabbing some photos within before throwing them over her desktop. "Shun Yun Li has arrived in London," she finished.

Jason took the photo closest to him, squinting due to the darkness of Daria's office.

Perfectly combed hair… a suit from the 1920s… walnut-coloured skin… the face… "This is Shun Yun Li," Jason confirmed.

"You were right, Jason. The witch has successfully brought Shun to England."

His theory was right. His stomach seemed to tense, an odd sensation which never really happened to him. "We need to be ready," he said.

"Of course, but I must say one thing, Jason." Daria paused. "As leader of the VHA, I must tell you to focus on Shun Yun Li, but as someone I respect, plan a mission that will work in order to capture Shun and this witch, otherwise the I-VHA will launch an inquiry as to why we didn't concentrate on capturing Shun." Jason bit his tongue, but he knew she was right, the I-VHA would rain fire on Daria and them if they didn't catch Shun.

"Of course," said Jason.

"What's the plan then? Where is he staying?" asked Diana. Jason held the photo of Shun in his hand before he looked over to her, brandishing a distinct smile which Diana liked to see.

Daria walked away from her desk where three large pieces of rolled-up paper leant against the dark walls of her office. Returning, she unravelled the large pieces of paper on her desk. Several red marks covered the face; it wasn't a piece of paper but a map of a city, a very large, popular, crowded city – London. Two prominent red circles were drawn on the map, one surrounding an ordinary building and the other surrounding a detailed floor plan. When Jason read the building's name, he knew why it looked so large. It was the Natural History Museum.

"This is the Natural History Museum," stated Daria. "Apparently Shun Yun Li donated towards the museum, and ever since, he has been able to use it when and how he wants. It is believed he is currently there with his men and witch, Yuzuki."

"Does the museum say anything about closure?" Jason asked studying the map, already forming a few ideas.

"The museum website says nothing about closure dates, which means we will have someone stake the museum out and, when it closes, we make our move."

"Or we make it close," Jason prompted. Daria tilted her head at Jason's suggestion.

"This would be a perfect training opportunity for some of the new recruits," said Neil, joining in on the conversation. The hunters turned towards Neil, and he didn't let his expression betray his true thoughts.

"What do you mean?" Daria inquired.

"Well, this would be a perfect time to take the new trainees out for a mission, see what they have learnt. I, personally, think Tobias's class is ready for something like this."

Daria remained quiet, thinking about what Neil was saying. It would definitely help her to make sure all trainees had effective training, and this was a perfect opportunity. Jason backtracked. Aiden was in Tobias's class. Jason had witnessed how far Aiden had come and there was no denying that he was a Dyer. He had learnt faster, quicker than others his age, but this mission was different to that of others. For one, this mission for Jason was about capturing the witch. He had already decided he was going to let Diana capture Shun. Despite everything, this was one mission that Jason did not want Aiden on.

"Are you sure?" Diana asked, her eyes playing ping pong between Neil and Daria.

"They are young, but they are some of the most talented trainees we have at the moment," said Hayden in support.

"It's an excellent suggestion, but I will need to look over their files and training in the coming days. I don't want to send them in if they aren't ready," said Daria. Jason looked towards Daria. He had been quiet, trying his best to hide his apprehension of the suggestion by focussing his gaze on the maps.

"Leave Diana and me to the planning," Jason told Daria. "If you want to use the trainees, that must mean Neil will be indisposed till the mission as he will be training them all?"

"Of course," Daria agreed.

"What?" said Neil irritable. Jason knew Neil was the best at training the trainees, but he wasn't the best at planning for missions. *Know your weaknesses*, Jason thought. If Aiden were to be taking part in this mission, he wanted to make sure he could do everything to make sure his son was safe by making an effective plan and getting Neil to put them through the hardest of training sessions.

"He is right, Neil, this is Shun Yun Li. I need you to make sure they are in best condition, and from my observation, I will determine whether they will go into the field. Besides, there is a chance we could be running into the witch as well."

Neil bit his lip.

"Leave the plans to us. We will get it done," said Jason. He rolled the pieces of paper back up, having already constructed a brief plan in his head. He needed to leave before he forgot any important details.

Tobias sat at the back table alone in Religious Education, swinging backwards in his chair. The class had been forced to watch a video, but Tobias's mind was elsewhere. He was too preoccupied by his confrontation the other day which had led to a sour relationship with Aiden. Was he being suspicious? Everything he had learnt at the VHA and the way Aiden defended Callie shouted suspicious, but was this a bit over the top to think a vampire was in the school? But his mother and father always told him to trust his instincts. That is why he had brought a vile of liquid Wild Rose from home. He was planning to open it near Callie to see how she reacted – if she coughed and struggled to breath, then this would confirm his suspicion, but if he was wrong, then he knew he had to punish himself. To be the best hunter in the VHA, he could never be wrong.

He looked forward, catching the eyes of the twin girls in front row, both of whom were swooning over him and giggling. He smirked towards them. They looked away giggling and bickering with one another. *I am the prince of this school*, he thought obnoxiously to himself.

Heading to lunch after the school bell rang, Tobias scanned the cafeteria – no sign of Callie. Walking out to the field, he saw her sitting alone with Aiden; their other friend, Tyler, was not there – perfect opportunity. Quickly unscrewing the lid to the bottle of Wild Rose, Tobias grasped it within his palm. But why would he be approaching them when he had argued with Aiden? A thought popped into his head, a thought he did not like, but if he wanted to get close to Callie, he would have to say sorry. He felt his tongue twist at the thought of the word, but he had to subdue his pride.

Tobias cautiously approached them, the pair in their own little romantic world. Tobias feeling sick to the stomach at their awkward display of affection to one another.

"Hey, Dyer," he shouted, only a few metres away from the two. Aiden whipped his head up to face Tobias when he stopped. Callie kept the back of her head to Tobias.

"I'm sorry," he muttered, standing still. There was a strong breeze to the day and Tobias was wondering if Callie was about to smell the Wild Rose. *Why is it taking so long?* he thought, looking at Aiden who responded with "okay". Tobias turned in the other direction feeling like he had failed, when one strong breeze blew over the bustling field, and that's when the coughing started. Tobias glanced over his shoulder to see Callie's body struggle to deal with her sudden coughing fit. Tobias's eyes illuminated with pride.

Walking further away, he could hear Callie coughing louder and more uncontrollably, her eyes had started to water, and he heard her in the distance saying she struggled to breath. Grinning with content, he screwed the lid back onto the bottle, and Callie stopped instantly, coughing only a couple more times to clear her throat. Vampires were now at Oakdale Secondary School. Tobias was on cloud nine, he had figured it out; a sly smile erupted onto his face.

Revelling in his own excitement and sureness of himself, knowing he would find the right time, only one question remained. *When do I kill her?*

That was weird, Aiden found himself thinking. Tobias, prince of Oakdale Secondary School, had just apologised to him. It caught Aiden off guard when Callie suddenly burst into a spontaneous coughing fit. Her eyes turned red and started watering heavily, luckily it wasn't blood, otherwise she would have been in trouble.

"Are you okay?" Aiden asked, not knowing what to do.

"I-I-I'm stru... struggling to... br... breathe," she splattered, Aiden was ready to perform CPR on her just in case she fainted, but he didn't know if it would work. As quickly as her coughing fit started, it finished. She breathed normally, coughing only a couple of times after.

"What was that?" Aiden asked bewildered.

"That was Wild Rose," said Callie hoarsely, her throat sore from the mild burns; she sounded like she smoked about a hundred cigarettes. Aiden quickly rose to his feet; he saw Tyler in the far distance walking over to them, seemingly unharmed. Worried, Aiden scanned the area to see if he could see any hunters, but there were none. Until he saw him. Tobias. His stomach sank as he watched the smug trainee walk off, now knowing he had apologised to get close enough to Callie.

Now knowing Tobias knew Callie was a vampire, Aiden said, "It was Tobias." She turned to see Tobias in the distance chatting away to Amber.

"I'm going to kill him," she growled from her belly, and Aiden saw her fangs appear.

"Callie don't," Tyler appeared next to her. He dug his hand into her legs, gripping her tightly. The pain distracted her, and her fangs reclined back into her gums.

"You wanted to see me?" said Jason as he stood at the entrance to Daria's office. She sat on her comfy mahogany chair, her desk neatly organised. It had been a few days since Shun's arrival, and Jason had been non-stop planning for the mission.

"I did," said Daria.

Jason walked into the freezing room, for once there was no incense burning, only a faint smell of burnt wood that seemed embedded in the walls. "What was it you wanted?" said Jason, standing adjacent to her. Goosebumps appeared on his skin.

"Aiden," Daria replied. Jason flinched. "He is currently our youngest trainee, yet he is proving to be quite capable." Jason grinned, proud of his son. "So, I want you to know I am agreeing with Neil. Aiden's class will be accompanying you on your mission to kill Shun Yun Li."

Jason's mood was like a rollercoaster. He didn't want his son nor other trainee hunters to come on this mission. It was going to be a bloody one. "Aiden hasn't been here as long as the others, and it is recommended that a vampire hunter trainee must receive at least six months of training in order to partake in their first test," said Jason, seeking solace and protection within the rules of the VHA, hoping this would help his case.

Daria sighed arrogantly, "I agree but rules are made to be broken." She had already made up her mind.

"What happens if one of them is killed?" said Jason dreading her cold response.

She rose from her desk, to meet Jason's gaze. "Well, you won't have to worry about any deaths if your plan is effective. I know Neil has been training the trainees non-stop after seeing their files."

"Fine then," said Jason, lost for words. He knew there was no way to change her mind once it had been made. "I better finish off the plan," he said, walking away from Daria, knowing he had to remove himself from her presence.

"I want the mission to take place soon," said Daria. "Shun won't be here for much longer, I fear. I want this mission to take place this Saturday. The I-VHA are breathing down my neck and want to know why we haven't done anything yet. I have stalled as much as I can, but I cannot do so anymore. This Saturday," Daria reiterated.

Jason gritted his teeth, leaving the frozen office. He slammed the door behind, feeling the pressure mount. Daria, on the other hand, sat back down, moving one of her white pens back into formation.

17
CLUB BÔITE

"Hospital date day." Callie arrived at Tyler's house beaming, her pristine white teeth sparkling. Today was *Hospital Date*, Callie's favourite day of the month. Fresh blood bags had arrived at the hospital, and it was time for Callie and Tyler to stock up. Fresh blood was the best, the closest taste and sensation to feeding off humans.

"Yeah, yeah, I know," said Tyler. He closed the door behind him, feeling the excitement radiate off Callie.

"I want some O negative today. You ready to brainwash people with your Silvertongue?" she asked, remembering Tyler's special ability to control humans which she didn't possess.

"Yes," Tyler replied as he regained his footing.

"It sucks that I don't have that power." Callie sulked as the two vampires left for the hospital.

Aiden sat in the VHA classroom quietly, heaving a sigh of relief, grateful to be sitting down after Neil's horrendous combat lesson, which had been harder than usual – but then so were all his lessons recently. *Why have they been so hard over the last week?* Aiden pondered, or was it because Aiden had now been in the VHA for a while that Neil decided to train them harder? No matter how much Aiden thought about it, he knew he wouldn't think of an answer. He was deep in thought when Tobias walked in.

"Hey, Dyer," said Tobias grinning. "How's Callie? I saw she had a coughing fit when I apologised. Just wanted to make sure she was okay."

You know what you did. Aiden suppressed any sudden urge to jump up from his chair and punch the grin off Tobias's face, but he knew he couldn't. If he did anything, it would only motivate Tobias more.

"Yeah, she said it was something to do with her hay fever?" Aiden lied, accustomed to this feeling after the months he'd had.

It's because she's a vampire, you idiot, Tobias mulled over as he listened to Aiden lie, but he kept his smile. "That's nice to hear."

Tobias took a seat behind Aiden. This was a dangerous game Tobias was playing, if he only knew who her mother was and what Tyler was, he would be running for the hills without looking back. With that, Gabriella and Thomas walked through the door carrying textbooks, handing them out to everyone in the class as Toby followed, frailer than ever. Aiden quickly looked towards the clock, realising he only had another hour left at the VHA before he could go home. Callie and Tyler had already demanded that the three of them were to do something. He watched the clock thinking about their hospital date.

"Good afternoon, everyone," said Toby sighing with relief as he sat down, his goatee swaying in the air as he did.

"Good afternoon, Toby," the six trainees all mumbled at different times.

"This lesson will be based upon history of the VHA between 1900 and 1950. We are continuing our study of the VHA in the twentieth century." Toby stopped before coughing, his eyes bulging out with each cough. Aiden took the initiative, opening the book to the contents page, where he noticed something was wrong.

History of the VHA 1900–2000
By Toby Pearson
1900–1910
1910–1920

THE PERFECT BLOOD SERIES

1920–1930
1936–1940
1940–1950
1950–1960
1960–1970
1970–1980
1980–1990
1990–2000

"Toby," said Aiden raising his hand, puzzled why there were six years of history missing.

"Yes, Aiden," said Toby.

"We have every decade during the twentieth but there are six years missing between 1930 and 1936?"

"That is right, Aiden. Between 1900 and 1940, the headquarters for the VHA was in New York. America was the epicentre of vampires during this period. In 1935, there was a fire that destroyed the VHA headquarters and everything was lost, including its history. All we know is that Sviet the Skull was removed by the I-VHA for failures and banished. You will learn more about this later in life." Toby smiled through his wrinkles.

Tyler and Callie waltzed into the hospital. The censored glass doors slid open into a sweltering waiting room, people sitting on top of one another in the confined room. Callie and Tyler's senses were bombarded with a variety of smells. They were instantly able to smell what was wrong with all the patients: a young man in his mid-twenties was unfortunately suffering from the early stages of appendicitis, a young girl soon-to-be diagnosed asthmatic, and one woman in her early thirties… Callie took a deep breath in, concentrating her sense of smell. What she smelt always brought back dreadful memories. Callie graced one hand over the other, remembering the numerous amounts of injections she'd had to have before each surgery. The woman had cancer. Her toxic blood stood out almost as strong as Aiden's blood.

"Callie, this way," said Tyler. He graced Callie's shoulder as he walked towards a pair of poorly painted green doors. Callie followed, thinking about offering the woman the option of being cured, but was vampirism really a cure? The only way to survive inoperable cancer was to become a vampire, a choice Callie made. Not everyone had a mother and friend like Callie did, who trained and taught her everything she knew. Hopefully modern science would be the woman's saviour.

Leaving the waiting room and walking through the green doors, the two turned a corner, making their way to the second floor. It wasn't long before the blood donations department lay ahead, the queue line busy as ever.

"Okay, where is the closest nurse?" said Tyler. Callie peeped her head around the corner as they searched the hallway.

"There." Callie pointed. It was a young nurse, new. Tyler and Callie made sure they knew all the nurses who worked on the second floor.

"Sweet. She is even helping us out." Tyler smirked. The nurse walked towards the storeroom.

"Quickly," Callie whispered.

The pair moved round the corner as they watched the nurse enter the code to the storeroom. The door buzzed open, and she walked in. Tyler sped up, the door was about to close, but luckily Tyler manoeuvred his fingers into the gap, stopping the door from closing. The two vampires slipped into the storeroom.

The storeroom was relatively empty; a light hum filled the stuffy room as the lights flickered on. The nurse was at the back filling an empty box with supplies. Tyler looked at Callie winking, she chortled knowing he was about to Silvertongue the nurse. Tyler approached the nurse slowly, readying his hands so he could grab her head before she could scream.

The young nurse turned, meeting Tyler's gaze as his pupils turned into snake slits. Before she could scream, Tyler moved at vamp speed, placing his hands on her forehead.

"Remain calm," said Tyler quickly. He felt every muscle in the young nurse's body relax. Her olive-coloured skin was warm, his fingers a little moist. Callie cackled in the corner.

"You are going to take us to the blood bank. We are here to collect some blood bags for a patient in another hospital," said Tyler slowly. The nurse's face started to drop; she was not in control of her own body. She repeated everything Tyler said with a monotone voice, her eyes glazed, as Tyler moved his hands by her ears gently.

"Now, take me and my friend to the blood bank."

"I will take you and your friend to the blood bank now," the nurse repeated, her eyes still glazed, but as Tyler removed his hands from her head, she looked at both Tyler and Callie. Her face returned to its previous perky nature and her eyes went back to normal.

"Come with me," she spoke, placing the box of bandages to the side. Tyler sighed, and Callie smiled as the nurse walked past her.

Following the nurse down the hallways, Tyler and Callie kept their heads low to avoid any unwanted attention. It wasn't long before they were a corner away from the blood bank. Tyler did a quick look down the hallway and then pushed Callie into the adjacent room. Callie cursed from the sudden force of movement.

"What was that about?" she hissed as Tyler closed the door. He ignored her and peered through the closed shutters that covered the window.

"Hunters," he whispered.

Callie's eyes widened. "Where?"

Tyler tapped his ears, signalling Callie to focus her hearing. Callie moved her hair that covered her ears and took a deep breath in – focussing on the voices and footsteps, ignoring the beeping of machines.

"This is an easy shift." Callie heard one of the hunters speak.

"I agree," responded the other hunter. Even without the difference in their voices, Callie could tell one was a man and the other a woman based on their footsteps. She quickly glanced at Tyler who snapped his fingers, snapping the nurse out of his control. He peered through the blind, noticing the bewildered look on her face as to how she ended up in the other side of the hospital, before she headed back to the storeroom.

"Have you heard the rumours about the mission?" the female spoke. Tyler and Callie listened in carefully.

"The one to London?"

"Yeah, that one."

"What about it?" the male hunter asked.

"Apparently they are taking the new lot of trainees with them and I heard that Jason Dyer's kid is in that class." Tyler and Callie exchanged a worrisome look.

"Let's do a quick sweep of the rooms," the female ordered.

Callie and Tyler looked at one another, their eyes scrambled around the room they were in, but there was nothing for them to hide behind. Doors opened and closed; Callie twitched with every door slam. Then before they knew it, the hunters stood at the door, ready to open it.

Tyler pulled Callie backwards until their backs were against the wall behind the door. The hunter opened the door, pressing Callie and Tyler in between. Tyler grasped Callie's hand. She was shaking. The door kept them against the wall, the only thing keeping them safe from the hunter.

"Nobody in here," said the hunter, after a quick scan of the room. He closed the door. Tyler and Callie crouched down, feeling a tsunami of relief pulse through their bodies.

"What's going on in London?" Callie whispered. Tyler was thinking about what they had just heard; he looked over to Callie, knowing there was only one person they could go to who knew the answer.

"No," Callie hissed knowing that look, but Tyler had made up his mind. They waited another ten minutes, hearing the hunters move down the hallways until there were gone. They left the hospital without any blood, stopping off at Callie's on the way back to Tyler's for her to change as they were off to see Frederico, owner of Club Bôite.

Aiden was barely home for ten minutes before he was summoned by Callie and Tyler, who seemed vocal about Aiden coming out with them tonight. Unsurprisingly, Jason wasn't in, so Aiden slipped into some clean clothes before leaving his house. Callie and Tyler met Aiden outside, Aiden noticing Callie's trepidation as they filled Aiden in on what they had overheard.

"But why are we going to a club?" questioned Aiden.

"Because the owner, Frederico, will have the answers we want," said Tyler.

They were standing at the entrance to the opulent club. The thick black carpet was impeccably clean despite the vast amount of people in the confined room. Despite all the walls being smoothly painted white, the opposite wall to the entrance was panelled. A magnificent chandelier dangled from above, illuminating every corner. Aiden could not see any entrance to the club, the room was filled with people holding plastic champagne flutes, drinking and laughing away. A young woman stood in the middle, holding an iPad.

"How can I help?" she said cheerfully.

"Here to see Frederico. Name is Tyler Steede."

The women froze. Her crystal blue eyes shot a piercing look towards the three teenagers. "I will be back," she said with sudden repugnance, walking off in her tight black dress and towering high heels. Aiden looked around the room; several workers were now staring at the trio. Aiden's scent was currently subtle but strong enough for vampires to question what he was. So far no one had noticed Aiden was different.

"Two vampires and a…" the woman returned looking Aiden up and down, unable to grasp an indication as to what his scent was.

"Is Fred expecting us?" said Tyler irritably, moving in front of Aiden, avoiding the question.

"Yes, he is. Follow me please."

The three followed her towards the paneled wall at the back. Callie quickly seized Aiden's hand not wanting to be separated from him but at the same time wanting to feel his warmth and comfort hoping it would relax her. Aiden gulped. It was nice feeling her soft hand, but it wasn't long before Tyler said, "Watch this."

The young woman stepped forward pushing two of the several white panels inwards. An air-conditioned breeze attacked Aiden's face. Thundering music filled the quiet entrance as strobe lighting illuminated the club within. The panels rotated sideways as lasers pierced the smoke-filled air. Aiden, whose mouth had now fallen open, saw the club emerge from behind the white panels.

"Welcome to Club Bôite," the women yelled against the loud music.

The three levels of the club were overflowing with people, each floor separated by a thick glass sheet. The young woman walked into the club, and they followed. Aiden looked down, noticing the different levels of the club – people were dancing to different genres of music on each floor. Avoiding the crowded dance floor, the woman guided them through the VIP booth section. One group was celebrating a birthday, another looked like an office night out from the shouting and amount of drinks on one table, and one group of women was celebrating a divorce party. Aiden was taken aback; he never knew Oakdale had a night life like this. It was a contrast to Oakdale during the day.

As they were guided to the back of the club, a large white box under the DJ, caught Aiden's attention. It was privatised using thick drawn black curtains, and Aiden could only guess that this was where Frederico was.

The woman extended her arm as they reached the glass cube. People passing by looked the three up and down, knowing they were not over the age of eighteen. Tyler and Callie hadn't used their Vamporosium ability. Aiden was the youngest one in the club. The woman rapped her knuckles against the glass door. Aiden could hear the knock amongst the music. The door opened immediately, and the woman walked in, moving through the gold embroidered curtains.

"Be prepared for what's inside," Callie shouted into Aiden's ear who struggled to comprehend what she meant. Aiden walked in last, feeling the weight of the curtains restrict his movement as they separated the club to the room. When Aiden reached the other side, he understood why the curtains were so thick and why Callie had warned him.

The room was filled with a muffled echo of music, and there was a strong smell of alcohol and blood that filled the air, but Aiden couldn't understand where the smell of blood was coming from until he saw a woman lying in a corner dead. Blood stained the white walls as she sat in her own puddle.

A black man stood in the centre of the white-tiled room, grinning callously. Feeling slightly nauseated from the scene, it didn't help when Aiden was able to taste a rich whiskey in the air. The door behind closed and plunged the room into an eerie silence. Aiden stood in the middle, behind Tyler and Callie who seemed to be adjusting to the blood in the room.

"Well hello, Perfect Blood," said the man sardonically. He took a sip of whiskey that he held in his right hand. He was a towering figure, almost six foot five, his muscular physique magnified by his fitted light blue shirt and decorative waistcoat.

"Can we get someone to clean this up, please?" the man shouted, snapping his fingers. Two bodyguards standing in the corner of the room nodded to his demand. For the meantime, the woman was covered with a white sheet.

"I'm guessing you are Frederico?" Aiden said bravely, trying not to be distracted by the scene which had unfolded in front the three of them.

"Depends who's guessing," teased the man. "But yes, I am. Please call my Fred though." He turned to face the teenagers. His clothing was impeccably clean – he was not the one to have killed the women earlier, merely a spectator.

"Redecorating, are we?" said Tyler sarcastically, ignoring the strong aroma of blood.

"She was a bad business partner if I may say so." Fred sighed. "Your scent isn't as strong as I thought it would be," said Fred, directing his attention to Aiden before he drank the remains of his whiskey, licking his lips.

"I have it under control," Aiden lied.

Fred chortled. "Nice to see you guys again, it has been a while. Take a seat, please." Fred pointed towards the handsome dark oak table.

"How's the plan for world domination going?" said Callie. Aiden sat down as Tyler and Callie placed themselves either side.

"Had to put it on pause; too many pieces on the chessboard at the current moment. So how may I be of service today to my dear vampire friends?" Fred said pompously, sitting down on the opposite side.

"I know you have a contact inside the VHA," said Tyler.

"Why not ask your mother?" asked Fred.

"I cannot compromise her," Callie replied with Aiden listening carefully.

"As if she isn't compromised enough having a vampire daughter?" Fred laughed.

"We don't have time to waste, we are here to ask about a mission the VHA seems to be conducting to London, and it turns out Aiden is on it. What can you tell us about it?" said Tyler, radiating a demeanour that Aiden had never seen before. Tyler was sterner, like he didn't have time for fun or jokes. Fred curled his lips looking at Aiden. An unease followed as the bodyguards returned for the woman covered under the white cloth. "And anything else you know," Tyler added.

"What do you mean?" Fred retorted feeling offended that he asked such a question like this.

"'Too many pieces on the chest board'?" Tyler quoted. "You are the most selfish person I know. You would never stop your operations if you knew your business was in trouble. I know that first-hand."

Aiden was watching the interaction between Tyler and Fred; it seemed to him that they knew each other well.

"I forgot how smart you are, but yes, as it so happens something is killing vampires out there using the power of chi absorption, and I want to know who it is. While I don't, my business is on pause."

"We know who it is, and what's chi absorption?" said Aiden joining the conversation.

"Chi absorption is Mayhemic magic, in other words dark magic. Where a witch absorbs the life force or energy of another being. It can only be cast by witches who have entered a certain room in the Library of Wickery. My guess is they are absorbing chi to use it against Shun Yun Li."

"Shun Yun Li?" said Callie, hoping she had heard wrong, but she knew she hadn't.

"Yes, Shun Yun Li, that's the mission the VHA will be sending you on, Aiden. Now who is the witch?" Fred pushed.

"Those vampires who were killed," said Callie, looking at Tyler.

"They must have been Shun's men," Tyler replied.

"Yes, that is why he came to England because he wants to know who has been killing and interfering with his business. Now please tell Fred who this witch is," said Fred mockingly, looking at the trio.

"The Dark Witch," Callie snapped.

"Oh," said Fred.

"Oh?" Tyler questioned.

"How do you kill a witch?" Aiden queried. The question gained Fred's attention.

"Just like a human, but it's harder because they have magic. Why?"

"Because the Dark Witch killed my mum, and I want it dead," said Aiden. Fred looked at Aiden with a sort of admiration before it disappeared into a laugh.

"I'm sorry your mum was killed by this witch, but if a vampire can't stand up to them, what makes you think you will?" said Fred pointedly as he looked deep into Aiden's eyes. "Stop being so naïve, this is a dangerous world." The statement seemed to resonate with Aiden. He hadn't thought of it like that before. Fred waited for Aiden to say something back, but when Aiden did not oblige, he continued. "Everything I have learnt I have gathered from the books from the Library of Wickery and what I have pieced together."

"Library of Wickery?" Aiden questioned gingerly with Fred's pause.

"Magical library that holds books and more published by witches," said Callie in the briefest of words just as Fred continued.

"*Witches of the Middles Ages* by Harriet Stockholm, to be precise, was the book I found. The Dark Witch is believed to have originated from the same era as the Sisterhood of

Witches, during the 1500s. This was at the time of the third Perfect Blood."

Rowan Drukheim, Aiden found himself thinking, referring back to the table of Perfect Bloods that he had come to memorise.

"Since the Middle Ages, there have been another three entries regarding the Dark Witch. They have obviously been using a Witch Slumber to stay alive, but the laws of nature and magic state a witch can only use the witch slumber spell a maximum of three times. This being their last possible Witch Slumber. Since the Dark Witch has returned for the third and, presumably, last time, they now want to finish their plan."

"What makes you think they have a plan?" said Aiden.

"Are you dumb?" said Fred before a distinct growl came from Callie. "Someone like that who casts chi absorption sacrifices suggests they have a plan," Fred explained.

"But who's this vampire? Shun Yun Li?" asked Aiden.

"Shun Yun Li is a notorious bloody, dangerous and merciless killer. He is famous in the vampire world because he eradicated the VHA from Japan. Killing him would allow the VHA back in. The man has been round for hundreds of years. Obviously, he has something the Dark Witch wants," said Fred.

"So that's why the VHA are launching a mission against him?" Aiden asked.

"Yes."

"But why take trainees on such a dangerous mission?" Callie asked.

"Does anyone at the VHA know you are the Perfect Blood?" asked Fred. Aiden shook his head. The only person who knew was Diana, but she would never tell anyone.

"I don't trust the leader… Daria." Fred paused. "And you shouldn't either. There is something off about her. It feels like the stars are aligning for something, so make sure you stay safe and do not bring me into it."

"Why have you happily told us about this?" Aiden queried.

"You have to play both sides in order to win. Besides, as I've willingly told you all this information, I hope this is enough to settle our debt." Fred shot a sharp look towards Tyler, smiling faintly.

"It's not a life for a life," said Tyler. *Life for life?* Despite thinking he knew all about his friend, there was still a cavernous depth of knowledge which Aiden did not know, and it made Aiden realise how long Tyler had lived for.

Fred's once-confident faint smile had now disappeared. "May I add something." Fred moved forward, leaning on the table.

"What?" said Callie wary. Fred directed his eyes to Aiden. "What do you know about the Perfect Blood?" The question took the three off guard.

"What do you mean?" said Tyler speculating.

"I want to dominate the world. I cannot have competition from the strongest vampire in existence. So I want to add that I understand your desire to know more, but maybe not knowing will be better for this world." Fred made a persuasive argument. Despite Aiden's desire to know more about the power that circulated through his body, knowing less was the best way to protect the world and those he cared about.

"Well, if we ever need your help to protect Aiden, I'm sure you would be happy to help out then," Callie teased, taking advantage of what Fred had just said. Fred ignored her comment.

"I'm afraid I have more business to attend to. I enjoyed our talk, and I will have a taxi take you back to your houses." Fred rose from his chair abruptly. The three teenagers did the same, turning to face the young female who had miraculously returned, two bodyguards standing beside her.

"Hopefully, I will see you soon, Perfect Blood," said Fred fervently. Aiden ignored him.

The three teenagers were escorted out of the club and into one of Fred's personal taxis as it started their route home.

"How do you know him so well?" Aiden asked as he sat in the middle of his two friends.

"Remember when I told you I was the one who turned Callie?" said Tyler, turning to face Aiden. "The VHA had hunted down Fred, and I saw he needed help. I saved his life, but Diana found me. Instead of killing me she told me to transform Callie. Life for a life, I saved his and I have that debt over his head." Tyler finished abruptly.

It wasn't long until Aiden was dropped off home and was in bed, alone with his thoughts. Tyler had lived a long life, and it made Aiden realise he hardly knew his friend. As he fell asleep, he began thinking about Tyler's life and what else he had been through.

18
LONDON

It was the morning after Club Bôite, and Aiden felt particularly tired. His eyes were heavy as he walked to school alongside Callie who was yapping away. He was happy enough to listen to her, but his mind was still trying to remember everything from the night before, everything that Fred had told them about the Dark Witch and Shun Yun Li.

"Are you listening to me?" Callie snapped. She nudged the teenage boy harder than she thought, pushing him further than intended.

"Woah," Aiden muttered. The sudden fright of falling into the road was enough to wake Aiden up before he regained his footing.

"Sorry," Callie apologised, forgetting her own strength. "How are you feeling about everything?" she added.

"Tired. I'm surprised my dad hasn't told me about a mission yet. I thought he would have given me a warning by now," said Aiden. Since he joined the VHA, their relationship had improved: his dad was now calmer and more understanding, but his recent mood change suggested otherwise.

Joining the throng of students, heading towards the school, Callie tried her best to relax Aiden with little effect; it was hard when it felt like threats were coming from every direction. They met Tyler at towering school gates before making their way to tutor.

"Here you go, Aid, this is for you." Sitting down in tutor amongst the wild noises of students, Tyler presented Aiden with a bracelet in a gloved hand.

"What's this?" Aiden studied the black leather bracelet.

"Cara finished it last night. It's your concealment bracelet. It will hopefully cover your scent long enough till Lydia returns, then she can make you an official witch one," said Tyler hopefully. Aiden admired Cara's handy work. The bracelet was made of black leather strips plaited together and finished with a drawstring close.

"Tell her I said thank you," said Aiden. He tied the bracelet round his wrist, witnessing the burning effect it had on a vampire if one touched it after Callie's attempt to help him.

"Does it work?" he asked.

"It does, I can't smell you," said Callie astounded. *One less thing to worry about*, Aiden caught himself thinking. Tyler nodded in agreement just as Mr Burton stormed into the classroom, once again taking aim at Tyler and Aiden for their messy uniforms, despite the entire class looking worse. If anything, Aiden welcomed the condescending statement from his teacher. With tutor finished, Aiden, Tyler and Callie left the class, heading towards their first lesson.

Callie walked towards to the girl's bathroom, rubbing her belly, still full from indulging on too many blood bags after returning from Club Bôite. She passed the assembly hall which was empty at this time. Every Tuesday morning, she would sit in that hall listening to lectures from either the head teacher or the head of year about the coming choices they had to make relevant to their Year 10 and 11 exams and modules. Oh, how she hated it. She was only a couple years older than the others in her year, and she felt like she didn't have time to focus on something that had become so petty now, especially with the climate she, Aiden and Tyler were in. But her mother wanted her to have as normal a life as possible which included going to school. Her mind was constantly thinking about what was going to happen if something went wrong, or if one of them was attacked by the Dark Witch, or if she had an unpleasant meeting with Tobias.

She turned the corner showing her hall pass to a passing teacher, who nodded in recognition. She rolled her eyes as he passed. It was pathetic that to follow through on a biological process that your body needed to do, a student needed to gain a hall pass. Callie thought it was only a way for teachers to have any power in their life.

She passed the windows that looked out onto the school field and tried looking out for Tyler and Aiden, knowing that they both had PE right now. She thought she saw a teenager who looked like Aiden run past, but she couldn't be sure as the sunlight pierced through the windows making it harder for her to see. She was too preoccupied that she had unconsciously walked into the back of another student.

"Oh... sorry," Callie stuttered. She dropped the hall pass without knowing. The boy turned around, and Callie felt her throat tighten.

"Wow, for such a little girl, you pack a punch," said Tobias tauntingly. The silver-haired boy crossed his arms. Callie forgot about needing the toilet. She didn't trust being alone with Tobias. Even though they were at school, she still wouldn't put it past him to do something.

"You've never felt one of my punches. What do you want?" said Callie sternly. Tobias advanced forwards menacingly as Callie resisted the urge to move backwards.

"What do you mean?" he said deviously. "Am I not allowed to be out of lesson? I'm just wandering the halls making sure the school stays safe."

"Safe from what?" said Callie, refusing to let her voice break. Tobias squinted, raising one eyebrow, looking Callie up and down. For once in her life, Callie wanted a teacher to be present.

"I wonder what the VHA would do if it found out one of their Master Hunter's children was friends with a vampire," said Tobias threateningly. A sudden eruption of pins started to jab Callie in her stomach. She thought about ripping Tobias's throat out, stamping on it while he watched, then draining his body of blood. But she couldn't. Instead, Callie decided to play him at his own game. Taking a deep breath, she said, "I honestly don't know what you are talking about, you psycho."

Tobias twitched his head. He had thought he hit a pressure point, but obviously, Callie had more to her than just her looks.

"It has been so lovely talking to you, Tobias, but I really must go." Callie paused as she knelt down to grab the hall pass that was on the floor. "And as a good student, I can't allow you to miss out on your important education, especially as you are in Year 11 with exams coming up soon," said Callie righteously. She walked slowly to the closest door. Tobias watched her every step, wary of her movements. "Come at me again and I may not be so merciful," Callie put simply before she knocked on the door. A silver plate screwed to the door read *Deputy Head, Mrs Wilson*. Mrs. Wilson answered the door displaying a face of thunder, not enjoying the fact that she had been disturbed. "Sorry, Mrs Wilson, but I was on my way to the toilet, and Tobias here is out of lesson. I would hate for him to miss anything important," said Callie softly, acting innocent. She quickly brandished her hall pass in front of the deputy head, who nodded before she turned to Tobias, looking him straight in the eyes.

"Thank you, Miss Shaw. Tobias, will you return to your lesson, please? Unacceptable behaviour from a model student." Tobias stood still; Callie had played him well.

"Of course, Mrs Wilson," he replied cheerfully, smiling and using his charms. Callie left and continued to the toilet, taking a deep breath as she left the two behind. If her heart was alive, it would be pounding.

Ready to enter the girl's toilet, the world suddenly went slow as Callie heard Tobias. "Well played, Callie, I give you that, but that doesn't excuse the fact that I know what you are! You vampire scum." Callie quivered, that was the first time he had called her a vampire, and Callie could hear the revulsion in his voice. "Be safe, I would hate to see you lying on the floor with a stake in your back," Tobias finished.

Callie turned her head to see Tobias turning the corner. He turned his head and exchanged a smirk, knowing that she had heard his little message. Slamming the door behind her, blood tears forming in her eyes and she became short of breath. Callie digested the fact that she, Tyler and even Aiden had threats inside the school where she thought they were safe.

Callie remained silent on her way to her last lesson. Aiden and Tyler were talking away next to her. She hadn't forgotten what Tobias had said and was now reacting to every little noise around the school. At lunch, she jumped when she heard the football hit the wooden board which lay behind the goal, bearing in mind she was at the other side of the school.

"Callie." Tyler nudged her trying to gain her attention, but she took it the wrong way. She looked towards him and Aiden, pushing him back with power, propelling the two boys against the cracked cream walls.

"Woah," said Aiden. It was the second time she had almost knocked Aiden over in the same day.

"Oh my god, I'm sorry." Callie snapped out of her funny mood and walked towards them. "What's up with you?" said Tyler under his breath. Callie looked around. Groups of students were walking by, and she wiggled her way in between Tyler and Aiden, making them walk again.

"Callie, what's up?" said Aiden. He touched her hand, which she had put through his arm.

"Tobias. He basically told me to watch my back," she spoke quickly, looking at Aiden knowing that Tyler would hear what she had said.

"What do you mean?" Tyler asked, pulling her attention his way.

"He knows I am a vampire and that I need to be careful as I may end up with a stake in my back," she whispered as students walked past towards their classrooms.

"Right," said Aiden. Hearing his heart rate increase, he attempted to escape Callie's grip to go and confront Tobias, but she pulled him back in.

"Aiden, no! We have to play this carefully," said Callie, not wanting to mention Tobias's comment about Jason.

"Well, that is easy for you to say, but I have training with him later at the VHA," said Aiden.

"Do nothing," said Tyler, cautiously. "For all we know, he may be bluffing, but do nothing. Go to the VHA tonight and act natural – if you were to cause a scene, he would probably tell them all then, and if he tells anyone, you will all be killed."

Aiden sighed deeply without truly understanding the consequences.

"Please, Aiden, don't do anything stupid. Just go to the VHA, and see if they tell you anything about the mission; this is something we cannot be dealing with. I can look after myself."

Aiden agreed reluctantly when a teacher came down the hallway, ushering them towards their lessons.

One moment, Aiden was standing on the training mats, ready for his personal survival lesson, and the next, Neil had come over ushering the class into the closest teaching room. Bewildered by the sudden change of events, taking their seats and wondering why they were in a class, Aiden noticed a towering figure walking towards their class. That's when Aiden knew this wasn't going to be a normal lesson. Daria walked in, followed by her four Master Hunters. Her black hair illuminated her pale features.

"Good evening, everyone," said Daria in an uncharacteristically soft tone. "I imagine you are all wondering why you have been gathered? I am here to tell you all that you will be partaking in your first field mission tomorrow."

"Tomorrow?" Tobias spluttered out. He slammed his hands against his wooden desk excitedly as his face shone with anticipation.

"Yes, tomorrow. You will be heading to London with Jason and Diana on a spectacular mission that will surely help in your development and advancement in the VHA." Aiden looked towards Tobias. He had never seen the boy smile so much. He was acting like he had just received the best Christmas gift in history. Whereas Aiden remained reserved, he knew why they were going to London, and he speculated if Daria was going to tell them the aim of the mission.

"Neil has spoken fondly of all your development, and he thinks you are all personally ready for this mission. And after careful consideration, I agreed."

"This is amazing," chirped up Thomas, one of the last people Aiden thought to be on board with this mission.

"Now I must tell you all. This mission is not a game, and you will be representing the VHA and what the VHA stands for. So, if I hear of any stupid behaviour"—Daria quickly shot a sharp look towards Tobias and even Aiden—"you will be dealing with me. The cars will be around to your individual houses tomorrow to pick you up. Safe journeys and let the hunt commence. *Dracas De Ramores*," finished Daria, returning to her usual intimidating tone before bowing.

"*Dracas De Ramores*," the class responded before she left the room, taking her menacing presence with her. She was followed by Diana and Neil, Jason shooting a quick wink in Aiden's direction.

"Damn, your dad is so cool," said Tobias, this being the first time they had communicated since they arrived. Aiden smiled back in his direction not sure what to make of the comment, but he was too preoccupied with how Daria had not told them who they were hunting. It seemed the visit to Fred last night now paid off.

"That's the calmest I have ever heard her voice before," Aiden mumbled, joining in on the class conversation.

"I agree," spoke Gabriella. The six trainees chatted away realising that no one was coming back until Neil barged back in, catching them off guard. Edward who was sitting on the tables fell off backwards with shock.

"What are you still doing in here? You have a mission tomorrow! Let's go, let's go! Let's get training!" Neil clapped his hands, spurring Aiden and the others from their seats and back to the training mats as he chased them all out.

19
Mission A

"Aiden, wake up."

It was the following morning. Jason was storming around his son's room making as much noise as possible. Aiden groaned feeling tired; his body was refusing to wake up, but Jason didn't stop.

"Aiden!" Jason shouted, opening the curtains and letting in a piercing shaft of light.

"Agh," Aiden groaned. The sun's beams illuminated the messy room, forcing Aiden to retreat under the covers. "What is it?" Aiden demanded, unwilling to leave the warm cocoon he had made himself.

"It's Saturday. Today is the mission in London, remember?" Jason stopped moving and pulled the covers off his son.

"Dad," Aiden cried, feeling the cold air attack his warm body.

"Be ready in fifteen, we are being picked up."

Aiden groaned.

"Come on, Aiden!" Jason clapped his hands, trying to get his son moving before leaving his room.

Aiden remained in bed for a couple of minutes, thinking about what the day held for him. One thing which settled his mind was the fact that he now had his concealment bracelet.

Aiden walked down his stairs in his black VHA uniform, suffering from horrendous bed head. He could hear his dad throwing bags around the house and locking the door which led to the basement under the house.

"Finally ready, I see," said Jason contemptuously, he passed Aiden carrying two large black bags.

"Unfortunately, whether you like it or not, you will become a vampire hunter. Vampires are evil creatures of the devil." Jason placed the heavy bags on the kitchen units. Aiden was unsure why his dad was in such a mood and beginning a tangent. "There aren't enough of us. Like I said, I was going to tell you once you turned sixteen but—"

"Yes, I know, Dad. I got attacked by a vampire so you had to take me to the VHA to protect me."

"Don't use that tone with me," Jason snarled.

A knock came from the front door, breaking the scornful staring contest between father and son. Jason walked to answer the door, and when his dad opened the front door, a soft voice followed.

"Oh hello. I'm Callie, and this is my friend Tyler, we are friends of Aiden's from school."

"Oh, I know you guys. Aiden speaks about you all the time."

Aiden gulped. He was about to go on a mission to kill a vampire, but for now he had to make sure his dad didn't kill his two best friends.

"Hey." Aiden appeared behind Jason, his heart pumping in his throat.

"Here's the champ of the house," said Jason turning to face his son, completely different to a minute ago, his persona and attitude having completely changed. However, that didn't surprise Aiden; he had been acting well for the past fourteen years, so why stop now. "Well, I will leave you guys to it." Jason walked away and back into the kitchen. Aiden didn't leave it to chance: he stepped outside to join his friends, pulling the front door closed.

"What are you guys doing here?" Aiden hissed, making sure his dad couldn't hear them.

"I was worried about you, and I wanted to come and check on you," Callie replied, while Tyler watched the windows. "I can't stop myself thinking that this might be a trap," she continued.

"What do you mean?" said Aiden, trying to speed up the conversation.

"Well, Fred says the stars are aligning for something, and I just can't stop myself from thinking that this may be a trap. What happens if the Dark Witch turns up? They will have you there, the Perfect Blood and Shun Yun Li, the vampire they brought to England." The words hung in the air, and it took a moment for them to make sense. What Callie said made a lot of sense, the Dark Witch would know the VHA would launch an attack on Shun.

"It's a bit late now the cars are on their way," said Aiden worryingly.

"Just don't get separated from your father or my mother, they will protect you from the vampires," said Callie apprehensively. Tyler nodded in agreement. "Have you got your bracelet on?" Callie paused as she grabbed Aiden's wrist, like a mother.

"Yes, I have, I haven't taken it off. It is working though? It doesn't feel like it's working." Aiden needed their reassurance. Both Callie and Tyler took a deep breath in through their noses.

"Yes, it's working," Tyler whispered, finally breaking his silence. But before Aiden could reply, Jason appeared at the door.

"Nice meeting you guys," said Jason tersely, almost dismissing Callie and Tyler, both of whom were caught off guard by Jason's sudden appearance and shortness.

"Well, have a nice family trip," said Tyler, when roaring car engines turned the corner at the top of Aiden's road, drawing the attention of the friends to the squad of black VHA vehicles.

"Go. I'll message you when I get home." Callie and Tyler needn't be told twice. In a minute, they would have been sitting ducks if the VHA found out what they were. They walked away quickly, leaving Aiden's front garden and heading down the street.

The three black cars pulled up in front of Aiden's house. Almost immediately, Diana exited the back of one of the pristine cars. She was followed by two other hunters as they walked up the pathway to the house. She winked as she passed Aiden. Aiden turned, watching her enter his house along with the others. The two hunters re-emerged carrying the bags Jason had prepared. Diana and Jason followed laughing.

"Come on, Aiden, you are riding with me and your dad today," said Diana, pulling Aiden into her. They headed towards the black vehicle. Aiden followed Diana noticing Tobias was holding the door open, both exchanging a cold unpleasant look at one another. Aiden knew that Tobias knew about Callie, but for once that wasn't the issue. Jason followed and Tobias jumped into the car, closing the door behind.

Aiden sat opposite Tobias for the journey. This VHA vehicle was different to the one which Aiden was picked up from school in. The inwards-facing seats allowed for Jason and Diana to talk throughout the trip, and Diana had told the boys the extended boot was house to an engine booster, helpful in escaping from tight situations.

Aiden distracted himself by looking out the window, watching the world go by without anyone knowing what they were up to. *This is my first mission.* The sudden, dreaded thought flashed through Aiden's mind without him even thinking about it. This was the first time Aiden had worked with his father, and he didn't know what to expect. What was his dad going to be like? Aiden's eyes were darting around the vehicle as he tried to distract himself, but as he looked over at Diana, Callie flashed through his mind. *What if this was a trap and the Dark Witch was waiting?* Aiden turned away from the others and back to the window knowing he wasn't able to talk to anyone. All he hoped was that this mission would be easy. They find Shun and bring him back to the VHA. That's all Aiden wanted.

Aiden watched as they drove deeper into the heart of London, and it wasn't long before the driver broke the silence. "We are here," he said.

Tobias and Aiden looked out their windows noticing they had arrived in front of a row of cheap chain souvenir shops. Exiting the cars on Harrington Street, Aiden looked down the street and saw the distinct architecture of the Natural History Museum through the trees.

As they walked into a souvenir shop, the shop owner nodded at Jason and Diana. The shelves on the walls were full of teapots with British flags and little figurines of the royal family. The hunters and trainees ascended stairs quickly at the back of the shop and arrived in a privately owned room. The sleek modern door was nothing like what sat behind it. Inside, the room was barely lit by the open ceiling bulbs, and large curtains on the windows only allowed in a fraction of light. The room smelled musty and unused, and dust puffed from the threadbare carpet with every footstep. The peeling walls were filled with weapons, maps, and VHA diagrams.

"It looks like it hasn't been decorated since the war", said Edward observantly.

"That's because it hasn't," said a hunter named Jamie, the other hunters joining in laughing. Aiden made his way to the cobwebbed curtains, peering through a gap to look down onto the busy street of Queensberry Place. In the distance, Aiden saw the museum had been fenced off with towering metal walls.

"They've been enchanted," said Jason looming over his son looking out the window. Initially caught off guard, Aiden asked "Why? Who did the enchantment?"

"You'd be surprised, we have a few connections with witches in London who are always after their next payday. It just allows us to make sure the public stay safe. No one will enter the protected circle the witches drew around the museum," said Jason before he was pulled away by the other hunters.

Having grown accustomed to the smell of the room, it wasn't long until Jason had gathered everyone round the frail table in the middle. Three maps covered the face. Jason bravely leant on the table that made an unconvincing squeaking noise, but somehow it didn't collapse under his weight. With every passing minute, Aiden felt more and more anxious, almost ready to throw up.

"Now, there are four of us and six of you. You have to listen to us extremely carefully because if you don't, you will die," Jason began. Aiden looked around the room; several of the trainees either gulped heavily or turned pale like a ghost. Aiden looked to his right, noticing Gabriella, who looked like she wanted to cry and run away. "There are two ways into this museum. One way is through the front entrance here." Jason pointed down to the maps highlighting the building prints of the museum. "But we need to go in without being seen. That is why we will be going down the sewers." Jason pulled a map from underneath, the table once again making a creaking noise that suggested it would be breaking any second now.

"The sewers will give us a direct route to the museum. We will be able to come up in the basement of the museum, and we should have a clear path to Shun Yun Li." Jason glided his finger over the route of the London sewers beneath the ground. Internally hoping that the Dark Witch would be making an appearance today, Aiden took note of the route they had to take. A muttering broke out amongst the trainees. This was the first time they had learnt of their mission objective.

"Stop bickering," Jason snapped. "You trainees have been chosen for this mission. Daria believes you are ready. If this goes successfully, all our names will go down in history as the ones to bring down Shun Yun Li." *And to kill the witch who killed my wife*, Jason thought.

"Awesome," said Tobias, his smile almost reaching both his ears.

"What's the plan then?" said Aiden. His father turned to face him, smirking.

"When I go into a mission, I always make sure I have a Plan B. So firstly, Plan A is to go underneath in the sewers and make our way to the basement of the museum. If no one here listens to me or does as I say, I will kick you off this mission without evening thinking," said Jason threateningly.

"Now onto Plan B," said Diana entering the musty room. The trainees turned to face the female Master Hunter as she closed the door behind her. "Nice to see we have one person in here with a brain," she muttered as she walked past Gabriella, making the young girl smile.

"Plan B is the plan I want everyone to memorise. The plan that may just save your life." Diana squeezed in between Jason and a hunter, making her presence known.

"Now," Jason started. "Plan B is in case something goes wrong. If we are attacked in the sewers, there are three exits, one will bring us up in front of a building, the second in the middle of the road and the third will be in front of the museum – try your best to avoid the one at the entrance to the museum because then Shun Yun Li will be notified and could leave before we have finished fighting our way through his guards. Memorise these three exits, and then we can get going."

With the speeches finished, the group began their revision of the exits, each taking it in turns to study the maps and gather their weapons of choice. Tobias spent more time choosing his weapon than revising the plan. Aiden, on the other hand, grabbed the first handgun he saw, saddling it up and making sure he had enough wooden bullets. The action felt so natural now after his training, and he wasn't sure how to feel about that.

With the help of his dad, Aiden attached two wooden stakes to his back so he was ready to pull one out whenever he needed them and attached a knife to his calf. Jason tightened his straps around Aiden's shoulder and smiled at his son.

"You can do this," said Jason. Aiden nodded back, feeling the sickening feeling in his stomach grow.

Leaving the somewhat comfort of the historic room, the group of hunters made their way to the basement of the building, heading towards the entrance of the sewers, Aiden and the others trailing behind. The chemically fumed basement made it hard for Aiden to breathe – that was until a hunter grappled the manhole cover pulling it from its place. The aroma of sewage erupted from below as it filled the basement. The odour was a mixture of rotten eggs and stagnant water at its best. The smell mixed with nerves didn't help – Aiden already wanted to throw up. He'd rather be suffocating amongst the fumes of the machinery and chemicals than the sewage stench. In the background, Aiden heard a couple of trainees throw up, but he wouldn't allow himself to do that, he didn't want to disappoint his father.

"Are you done yet?" said Jason disdainfully looking towards Thomas and Billy who were wiping their mouths clean. Looking down into the sewers, Jason dropped several glow sticks, helping to illuminate the path downwards into the dark abyss. One by one, the group started to descend, Aiden was the last trainee to go down followed by Diana. He looked down, hearing the churning sounds of water as the faint glowing green guided his way down.

Making a small splash, Aiden felt his feet submerge beneath the water where a soft layer of human waste cushioned his landing. He grimaced as he felt his socks absorb the discoloured water through his *apparent* waterproof boots.

Diana and Jason, along with the other hunters, divided the trainees into three groups of two. Aiden was paired with Gabriella who was shivering with fear, her teeth clattered away. The others still looked pale, all but Tobias who bore a malevolent grin. Each hunter crouched, holding their guns or crossbows. Moving forwards, Aiden eventually dismissed the smell, concentrating on the route ahead. Despite it being such a large group, they were as quiet as mice, working their way through the water silently. Droplets falling from the ceiling saw to the group being sodden within five minutes of their journey. Every few steps, something within the water would bump into their legs, but Aiden refused to look down, having a strong idea of what it may be.

The green glow sticks lighting the way forwards revealed the oil texture of the sewers. All Aiden knew was that he never wanted to do this again.

"Stop here for two." Jason signalled. The group huddled and remained in silence as Jason spoke with the other hunters, quickly examining the map. "We should have another five minutes to go, and then we should be beneath the museum," said Jason returning to the trainees who all nodded back; none of them daring to make a sound.

The group started to disburse when suddenly… *grrr*… Aiden turned to face the darkness behind the group. He strained his eyes, looking into the darkness beyond, wondering if he was imagining noises. Diana remained glaring at Aiden, who looked towards her pointing at his ears. She held back from the group listening carefully. Aiden graced his wrist to see if his concealment bracelet was still there, and it was.

GRRRRR... The growling noise reverberated throughout the sewers.

Diana nudged Aiden, signalling him to stay low and move behind. Aiden did as she commanded and moved behind as Diana moved forwards. She pressed a button on her wrist sending a signal to Jason. Within seconds, the group in front stopped with Jason receiving Diana's signal. Holding his fist in the air, the sewers remained quiet.

Then screeches erupted through the sewers. Aiden's stomach sunk.

"Ru—" but before Diana could finish, an Asian man jumped out of the shadows, pouncing towards her. His cloudy white eyes stared Diana down, but Aiden pressed the trigger to his gun, killing the pouncing man, who fell to the floor dead. Aiden took note of the bloody scars that covered the man's body as he floated in the sewer's stream.

"In a circle, now!" Jason roared. Diana grabbed Aiden by his collar, dragging him back. Diana placed Aiden in between Tobias and Gabriella, Gabriella shaking as she drew her gun slowly. Another vampire jumped out, this time aiming itself for Gabriella. She screamed, firing bullets into the head of the creature, killing it instantly. Aiden was confused, he had never seen a vampire look like this before. From what he had seen in the past, their eyes were red, so why were theirs white?

"Throw a flare," Jason said towards a hunter, who lit one as soon as Jason finished. He threw it down the confined sewage pipe, illuminating the deadly hoard in front of them. The vampires screeched as they climbed the walls attempting to avoid the light of the flare. Aiden looked into the sea of white eyes and noticed how they stood out in the darkness. These vamps were acting like wild animals, crawling on all fours moving menacingly towards the group.

"Open fire!" shouted Jason. Within seconds, the sewer went from silence to a warzone. The sounds of gunshots reverberated off the sewer walls, making them louder than usual. Wooden bullets plopped into the water from the heavy machine gun one of the hunters were carrying. The irregular flashing of guns continued to illuminate the sewers, enough to notice that the cursed vampires had begun to scale the ceiling in an attempt to avoid the bullets. Their hollow shrieks were drowned out by the firing of bullets. Unzipping one of many pockets in his cargo trousers, Jason pulled a metallic ball out and pulled a pin out with his mouth. He threw the grenade at the monsters, and it exploded immediately. The sewers turned into a fiery inferno, Aiden covering his eyes as the bewitched vampires howled in agony. Fire clung to the sewers walls and danced on the water, stopping the vampires in their tracks.

"Go to Plan B!" bellowed Jason, as the demented vampires started to pluck up the courage and leap through the fire, controlled by their hunger.

Arthur, one of the hunters, retreated behind the line of defence, as the group continued firing at the vampires. He lit another flare, and finally with a bit of luck, he saw the exit. A ladder was directly next to them, leading to the surface. He quickly climbed the ladder just as a vampire pounced for his ankles, but Diana saw the move a mile away and fired several wooden bullets into the vampire, killing it instantly. Arthur climbed quickly and pushed the steel cover off, and light illuminated the tunnel. The vampires screeched as they stepped into the sunlight, and then their bodies went up in a display of amber and orange flames.

"They don't have sunlight protection, everyone, move towards the sunlight," ordered Jason.

"Hunters, trainees, climb now!" shouted Diana. The group did as she commanded and climbed the ladder. Tobias climbed first followed by Gabriella and Thomas… when an unexpected human scream reverberated through the sewers. A vampire had leapt into the air, fangs bearing towards the three trainees on the ladder. Gabriella screamed and tucked her feet in, and the vampire missed her. But Thomas was not lucky enough. The vampire tackled the young teenage boy off the ladder. They slammed into the darkness, and the poor boy screamed horrendously as every vampire jumped onto his body. Aiden looked away quickly.

"Now!" Jason roared. He pulled Aiden away, pushing him towards the ladder. Climbing quickly, Jason left Thomas knowing the young teenager would now be dead. Dropping a Wild Rose grenade behind, making sure everyone was out the sewer, Jason catapulted himself out of the manhole as the grenade exploded, the vampires down below screaming in agony as Diana shoved the steel cover back on.

20
Plan B

"What were those?" Aiden shouted, collapsing on the ground, gasping for air.

"Rabids," said a hunter fighting for breath.

"What are rabids?" Aiden howled.

"That's one gone," Jason muttered, cursing loudly. Aiden rewound the events like a videotape in his head, remembering Thomas's being set upon by the merciless horde of rabids.

"Rabid vampires are crazy vampires," Billy cried.

"Rabid vamps are vampires who are cursed by a witch. The witch sires them to either a witch or vampire and they will do whatever their master commands." Gabriella recited as if she were reading it out of a book. Aiden noticed her cheeks glistening with tears.

"Shun's witch is powerful," said Diana hoarsely looking towards Jason.

"It seems so," he replied. "We need to get moving, we can't stay here out in the open."

Aiden was so dazed he didn't even know where they were. Looking around, he saw they were standing behind trees on the outskirts of the Natural History Museum. Thanks to the barriers that surrounded the museum, no one on the outside knew they were in the grounds. The architecture took Aiden's breath away. It was designed so intricately it could have been a cathedral with its rounded windows and spires. Two wooden doors at the top of the entrance stairs seemed to be unlocked and unguarded.

Jason pulled Aiden to his feet along with other trainees, signalling the group to move forwards. They made their way up the stairs, reeking of sewage, under the shadows of the historic building. Pushing the wooden doors inwards slowly, the group moved into the reception as a stomach-churning sight greeted the group.

Tens of bodies lay on the white marble floor drenched in their own bloody puddles, the ruby liquid seeping into the crevices. The smell of blood bombarded Aiden's sinuses, overwhelming him. The silence of the museum was eerie, whatever had done this to the group of people was surely gone by now as the stillness suggested no one had been here for a few hours.

"Stay calm, don't look at the bodies," Jason whispered to the trainees, who were unable to take their eyes off the floor.

Ushering them forwards, along with the help of the other hunters, Aiden kicked something that felt like a football. He looked down, covering his mouth as he gasped. A female's head lay several feet away from her body as it rolled to a stop. Aiden looked around, and the floor was littered with several others. *They are monsters*, Aiden thought, understanding the reason for creating the VHA. Gingerly, the group passed through the war-torn reception, finding it almost impossible to avoid the streams of blood, when a faint cry sounded from behind the group.

"Help me." The group turned to face a young ginger-haired female, her hair sodden in what seemed like her own blood. She massaged her throat, searching for the cause of her bloody appearance.

"Follow me," whispered Arthur, the trainees were forced to follow, leaving Jason alone with the girl.

"What's happening to me? My body is burning," Aiden heard her say.

"It's okay, everything will be fine," said Jason as he reached for a wooden stake. Aiden turned the corner before he could see what happened.

A moment later, Jason appeared bearing the same disdainful look as before. Aiden looked at his father's back where he'd had two clean wooden steaks, only this time, one was crimson stained.

Aiden took a step back as he felt some invisible force clench his windpipe. *The girl could have been saved. She could have been taught.* Aiden forced himself to breathe. He had never imagined what it truly meant for his father to be a hunter. He had never thought about all the lives he must have taken and terrible decisions he had made. If there was ever any hope of Aiden telling him about Callie and Tyler, it was certainly gone now.

Jason returned to the front of the pack, treading bloody footprints. The group followed, making their way through the museum. Aiden struggled to concentrate, his chest tight with mingled fear and anger, but Diana gently pushed him to continue. He never thought he would have to see his father kill. Aiden knew the symptoms of a panic attack from what he had learnt in his personal survival lessons. He must continue, he could not stop, otherwise he would be a sitting duck right for plucking.

Readjusting his gaze and concentrating on his breathing, focussing on following the other trainees, Aiden continued on, clenching his handgun. It wasn't long before Jason stopped the pack, shoving the trainees into a small events room, the hunters following.

"Take five," Jason whispered. The lecture room was the calming influence Aiden needed. Despite the baskets of biscuits teasing him and the other hunters, Jason and Diana strictly said no in case they had been poisoned, remembering a mission when that had happened. Taking a seat on the blue plastic chairs that reminded him of school, he ran his hands through his wild, curly hair, feeling slightly better after he had successfully fended off the impending panic attack. He watched the room of hunters, seeing how they acted, and none of them seemed to be bothered by what Aiden's father had done. Was this life destined for Aiden? Did Aiden want to become like his father? A cold-hearted man, killing people without a second thought.

"You okay, Aid?" said Jason, approaching his troubled son.

Before Aiden could even think, he spoke. "You killed that girl."

Jason frowned, glaring at his son. "That thing was not a girl but a vampire," Jason spat. "Within the hour she would have been consumed with a hunger that could only be fed by killing tens of humans. Better her than us," Jason finished annoyed, unable to understand why his son couldn't see it. If anything, he gave the girl a merciful death. Aiden couldn't reply; this man was not his father.

Jason turned to the rest of the group. "We have made it into the museum. We must be careful. If there were rabids in the sewers, then we can assume rabids are here. We move with caution and make sure we cover our backs. We use their hunger to our strength; rabids are sloppy, so they will make mistakes."

"Yes, sir," said Tobias, who had watched the exchange between father and son in the corner of the room, quickly exchanging a look of *I'm the son your father wanted* to Aiden, which Aiden believed in that moment.

The icy hallways remained eerily silent. Bodies continued to cover the floor as the coldness of Jason and the other hunters was truly revealed. Another four humans had awoken in the process of transforming into vampires, Jason and the hunters killed them before they could seek out their master and make their transformation permanent. Tobias had muttered that he was going to kill the next transforming human, but Diana objected. It was a burden to take a life like that; therefore, only a trained hunter or Master Hunter was allowed to kill them.

Reaching the end of the hallway, past the Egyptian exhibit, a grand stone staircase presented itself in front of the group. Keeping their backs against the pillars, Diana relayed a message from Jason to Aiden and the hunters in front of her.

"Up the stairs," said Jason in the briefest of terms. Counting down from three, in sync with Jason, the group made their way towards the marble steps. Aiden felt the cold stone penetrate the souls of his shoes as they climbed the staircase. Their footsteps seemed loud in the silence and made Aiden's heart beat wildly as he wondered if there was going to be another attack.

Suddenly, screeches erupted from the grand hall. The hair on Aiden's arms stood on end as he swallowed his nerves. Turning their heads in the direction of the sound, a herd of galloping rabids descended from the opposite grand staircase on the other side, making their way towards the hunters like mindless zombies.

"Get to the landing and make a circle!" Jason roared, knowing there was no point in being quiet now. Tobias yelped with excitement as he started to shoot the vampires who had made it to the foot of the stairs, whereas Gabriella once again looked as if she was about to faint. The group ran up the stairs as the sound of gunfire erupted. As they formed a circle in the central landing, the rabids scaled the walls of the ancient museum, ferociously digging their hands into the multi-coloured stone walls, not flinching at the knuckle-breaking pain.

"I think it's fair to say Shun knows we are here," Diana roared towards Jason, who grunted in return, taking aim at the mindless wall-climbing rabids.

"Gabriella… Edward… shoot at the ceiling," Diana ordered sharply. The overpowering herd of rabids grew. More and more scaled the walls before rabids began swinging themselves from the ceiling towards the group of hunters, blinded by their hunger. The hunters responded by shooting them dead in the air, who fell to the floor like droplets of rain, helping take out the rabids that ascended the staircase. With grenades now detonating and filling the air with stone flooring and bodies, it wasn't long before a nearby sound attracted the attention of the pack – Arthur screaming horrifically. A rabid had successfully landed on top of him, sinking their razor-sharp fangs and claws into his skin, ripping him apart. Aiden quickly unloaded several rounds of wooden bullets into the vampire, but it was too late. The rabids moved on, and Jason appeared beside Arthur's body. "Sorry, buddy," he panted, throwing the body over the balcony. The rabids bounced towards the dead body with interest.

"Follow me!" Diana screamed running up the staircase towards the next floor.

"That will only hold them for a few seconds," said Jason, pulling Aiden and Tobias away. The two trainees followed the hunter. The quick distraction had diverted all the rabids' attention to the body, allowing the group to reach to third floor, but before Aiden could even breathe a sigh of relief, he ripped himself free of his father's grip, pushing Jason backwards and out of the way of the rabid herd that had burst through the door at the top of the staircase. The blind monsters crawled up the staircase, separating Aiden and Billy from the group. Billy shot the monsters before his gun locked and a rabid pounced onto him. He fell to the floor, reaching out to Aiden for help, but there was nothing Aiden could do as more and more rabids jumped on top, draining the boy's body of blood within seconds. The rabids had blocked Aiden from the rest of the group, and he backed away, searching for a way past them.

"Aiden... Run!" shouted Jason hoarsely, fighting several rabids at once. Aiden needn't be told twice; there was no way through the herd to his father and the others. Leaving the group and rabids behind, Aiden ran down the hallway, taking the first corner. The sudden realisation of being alone in this rabid-filled museum was terrifying. In this moment, more than ever, he wished he had Tyler and Callie by his side. No doubt they were worrying about him at home, but if anything, this mission had shown Aiden what he was capable of. The VHA training had paid off.

Sprinting through the museum hallways, the sounds of gunshots and screams bouncing off the walls behind and rabids' roars in front, Aiden decided to hide. Running towards the only door in the long hallway, Aiden shuffled into the large, dark room, quickly closing the door behind, heaving a great sigh of relief.

For just a moment, he felt safe.

"I find it outstanding that a Dyer has become the Perfect Blood." A sudden voice penetrated the silence of the dark room. The chandelier lights were miraculously switched on, blinding Aiden who had turned round. Out of fear, he pulled his handgun out as he felt his heart pound in his throat. He opened his eyes only to lock them with an Asian man standing in the centre of the room, smirking. The man spoke with a refined British accent, "Hello, Aiden Dyer, I am Shun Yun Li."

21
THE SLAUGHTER

"How do you know who I am?" Aiden demanded, peering down the gun's barrel pointed at Shun's chest. Shun stood in the middle of the room delighted; he had not taken any notice of the gun that Aiden had clenched in his hands. The marble flooring squeaked under Aiden's dried shoes as he shifted his weight. His eyes flicked away from Shun, and he noticed that the ancient vampire was not alone. A female stood next to him, dressed in an emerald green kimono tightly wrapped around her tiny waist. She was utterly mesmerised by the door that Aiden had come through, staring at them through her protuberant eyes, suggesting to Aiden that she was not present in the conversation.

"She won't hear us." Shun paused, staring back at his witch, who had not moved. "I have relinquished control of the rabids to her for now. She is concentrating on making sure we don't get interrupted."

"How do you know who I am?" Aiden pressed, ignoring what Shun had just said.

"This is baffling. The Perfect Blood happens to be the son of one of the most renowned hunters in the VHA and a Dyer." Shun spoke unhurriedly. The man in a blue silk suit advanced on Aiden, leaving the woman behind and disregarding Aiden's question. Aiden continued to aim his gun at Shun's chest, knowing that if he fired now, the Wild Rose bullet would pierce his heart, but Aiden resisted. Why hadn't Shun killed him if he knew he was the Perfect Blood?

"Aiden, if I was going to kill you, you'd already be dead. Lower that gun," Shun ordered, finally paying attention to the gun Aiden held. His soft walnut-coloured skin and black eyes seemed calming, which terrified Aiden as this was supposed to be one of the most dangerous vampires the VHA wanted. Aiden didn't immediately lower his gun, but the more he thought about it, he realised that Shun was right; he'd had plenty of chances to kill him.

"How do you know who I am?" said Aiden cautiously, placing the gun back in his holster.

"Unfortunately, we don't have time for questions like that." His accent sounded like he was a part of the royal family. He closed his eyes, taking a deep, dramatic breath in.

"You won't be able to smell me," said Aiden knowing what Shun was trying to do.

"Are you sure?" Shun grimaced with his eyes still closed. Aiden quickly grabbed his wrist with his other hand and felt his heart sink to the bottom of his stomach.

"My bracelet," gasped Aiden with the sudden horrifying realisation that he was now unprotected in a museum full of vampires, a majority of which couldn't control their hunger.

Shun opened his eyes. "Don't worry, I will not hurt you. I need you. And besides, I've already ordered Yuzuki to start rounding up my dear rabids," he said.

"What do you need me for?" said Aiden, still shell-shocked that he had lost his bracelet.

"To save the vampire race and to destroy the Dark Witch."

"Oh, I plan to kill the Dark Witch," Aiden snapped, this being a strong enough reaction to push the worry about his bracelet to the back of his mind. Shun raised an eyebrow at Aiden's sudden display of emotion.

"What has the Dark Witch ever done to you?" queried Shun.

"The Dark Witch killed my mum," said Aiden.

Shun looked at him, almost sympathetically. "I understand your vendetta against them, but it must wait. Because if the Dark Witch gets their hands on the Scrolls of Decimation, then there will be more people out there who lose their mothers to this wicked being."

"The Scrolls of Decimation?" repeated Aiden making sure he heard correctly.

"Yes," said Shun. "The Dark Witch is after me because I know the whereabouts of a set of scrolls which have the power to, quite frankly, destroy the vampire race," said Shun abruptly. Aiden's eyes widened. "Therefore, I have a task for you."

"What do you mean?" asked Aiden, sensing the severity in Shun's voice.

"Follow me," said Shun, turning his back on Aiden. Aiden followed the man hesitantly, quite taken aback by the sudden turn of events; Shun was not what Aiden thought he would be. He expected an evil man, who was impossible to negotiate or talk to, choosing death over surrender.

Making their way to the back of the large room, where floor-to-ceiling windows looked out onto the grounds of the museum and the bustling life beyond the fence, Shun continued, "In my early years as a vampire, when I learnt of witches, I was fascinated by magic. The power they had, the respect for nature. For a period of time, I lived in the Library of Wickery, learning about magic until I came across a group called the Sisterhood of Witches. I became captivated by them. The research they had conducted and how they helped advance the witch community from under the radar was amazing. My witch friend and I travelled to where they lived, that's where she sensed it. We found a box buried and inside that box was a map to a set of scrolls and a map to an artefact so powerful that it could wipe out the entire vampire race. I knew then I had to keep it safe. Unfortunately, in that moment of time, I sensed a change in my partner and killed her before we left. I then returned to England and aided in the development and construction of the museum and sealed the scrolls away here. Decades went by, and I became anxious having left the scrolls here for too long, and at the time, I was on the VHA's radar. The headquarters were in Oakdale, and I knew that Oakdale would have been heavily protected and guarded. I decided to come to England and move the scrolls to the Oakdale Library. These scrolls also contain knowledge of the Perfect Blood."

"What knowledge?" said Aiden incredulously. There was a screech from the hallway as if rabids were standing outside. Aiden glanced over his shoulder, knowing they wouldn't hurt him, then back at Shun, who went on.

"If I am correct, there have been four Perfect Bloods before you, one named Rowan Drukheim?" Shun sounded as if he doubted himself before he continued. "This previous Perfect Blood allowed himself to be studied by the Sisterhood, who apparently were able to extract and use the power of the Perfect Blood."

"They extracted the power?" said Aiden, flabbergasted. "Why didn't you destroy the scrolls then?" Aiden pressed.

"A witch's curse. Only a Perfect Blood can destroy them," said Shun.

"That's why you wanted to meet me."

"Bingo," said Shun, flexing his perfect eyebrows.

"Why didn't you just go get the scroll and bring it here where I could destroy it?" asked Aiden, thinking this would have been the most logical thing to do.

Shun spread his hands arrogantly. "I am Shun Yun Li, top ten most hunted vampire in VHA history. As soon as I landed in England, the VHA knew. I couldn't walk into Oakdale, the headquarters of the VHA, and grab the scrolls." Shun made a convincing argument. "This is why I need you. I need you to find these scrolls in Oakdale Library and destroy them. I am sorry this feels so rushed, you must be under quite the pressure, but I fear the Dark Witch may be approaching soon. I needed to share this knowledge so I can erase it from my mind, then the Dark Witch will never be able to carry out their plan."

"Where are the scrolls in the library then?" asked Aiden.

"All I know is that they are hidden… where old meets new. GAS20." Aiden looked at the vampire with the most confounded look. *Where old meets new? GAS20?* It made no sense to Aiden, what did Shun mean? "All I know is the scrolls are hidden there. Remember, where old meets new. GAS20," Shun repeated. "I had a witch erase my mind so I only knew the bare minimum but enough to be able to tell the next person the location of them. I leave it to you, Aiden Dyer. Get the scrolls and destroy them before the Dark Witch finds them," said Shun, walking back to his witch. He tapped the woman on her shoulder, and she seemed to snap out of her trance.

"Good luck, Aiden Dyer, you'll need it." Shun nodded towards his witch, who placed her hands beside his head, chanting in a language that Aiden had never heard before. Her hands began to glow with a magnificent sapphire blue mist surrounding them. Before Aiden could ask another question, the witch removed her hands and the magnificent sapphire blue mist disappeared. Shun reopened his eyes and looked towards the witch. They exchanged brief words in Japanese before he turned his glaring gaze back to Aiden. Without another word, Shun and the female witch bowed and left the room.

Aiden took a moment before he left the room; his legs were weak as he stumbled through the museum. His mind was spinning, and he couldn't tell if he was shaking from nerves or trepidation. It was odd to think that barely a day ago, he was concerned about avenging his mother, but now to top it off, he had to protect the vampire race from the Dark Witch, especially Callie and Tyler.

Aiden started to follow the breadcrumb trail of bullets on the floor, which took him back towards the grand stone staircase from where he was separated from the group earlier.

"Dad... Dad!" Aiden shouted, now knowing that none of the rabids would harm him. He continued shouting until he heard noises which came from ahead. "Dad!" he shouted, turning the corner, back to the stairs.

"Aiden!" Jason shouted from down below, alarmed at the current situation. Aiden's face dropped as he felt the hairs on the back of his neck stand up – hardly daring to breathe out of fear that the Dark Witch might spot him at the top of the staircase. *It was a trap all along*, he thought, noticing the all-too-familiar outfit of the being that had come for him and Callie that night.

"Open fire!" Jason shouted. Aiden twitched. The hunters pointed their guns at the witch and opened fire. The Dark Witch danced in the air, avoiding all the bullets. Aiden stepped back, somewhat mesmerised by the agility of the Dark Witch, but a sudden unease erupted in Aiden when the Dark Witch straightened out and started flying towards him. Aiden felt as though he'd been glued to the floor, unable to move.

And then a voice whispered in his ear. "Run, boy."

Aiden was pulled backwards, and he watched the man in the silk suit run past him. Shun jumped for the witch, tackling them mid-air. Aiden crouched to the ground as he watched Shun mount the witch, climbing all around them like he was a spider. Looking back to where Shun came from, Aiden noticed the emerald green kimono of Yuzuki as she came striding into the room.

"Liiykufureous," she roared, and jets of blue lightning exited her fingers, aimed directly at the Dark Witch. Aiden covered his head as he felt the searing heat of the lightning bypass him. Peeping through his fingers, he watched Shun jump from the Dark Witch as the lightning bolts collided with the flying being.

The Dark Witch roared with pain before turning towards Aiden and Yuzuki. In a muffled screech, gale force winds erupted from the body of the witch, wiping the hunters beneath away like rag dolls. Jason and the others slamming against marble pillars before the Dark Witch took aim at Aiden. But before he was sent flying back by the winds, he was quickly pulled back around the corner.

"I have him, get out of here!" Diana roared through her earpiece to Jason over the winds as they broke the windows in front of them. Aiden imagined how he would have been blown backwards and through those very windows. He looked to his side, watching Yuzuki run off, most likely back to Shun who had disappeared.

"I owe you," Aiden heard from Diana's earpiece realising it was his father's voice. Diana pulled Aiden by his collar. He followed Diana towards the back of the museum, hoping not to have another encounter with the Dark Witch. Following the vibrant green *Fire Exit* signs, it wasn't long before Aiden and Diana were on the outskirts of the museum running towards the barriers.

"Is Dad okay?" Aiden shouted to Diana, worried about his father, wondering if he was still on the inside or not.

"Yes, he's fine," said Diana, separating the barriers just enough for her and Aiden to slip through. "He and the others slipped out and are being picked up by vehicles now." Aiden stepped through the gap into what felt like another world. The two hunters stood covered in blood and smelling of sewage on the bustling streets of London. Aiden immediately noticed the attention they were gaining from shocked tourists and passers, but luckily it wasn't long before a VHA vehicle screeched to a stop at the kerb. The door was opened, and the two jumped inside.

"How are you feeling?" said Diana. Aiden sat in the back, massaging his hands against the black leather interior whilst Diana stared at him. He remained silent, constantly replaying the meeting with Shun in his head all the way back—"Scrolls of Decimation" constantly on repeat in Shun's voice. He only briefly exchanged looks with Diana when they passed Jason on the M4. They had overtaken Jason on the way back and were now the leading vehicle, minutes away from Oakdale back towards headquarters. Aiden had not said a word since they left the museum in London.

"Where were you when we got separated?" Diana pressed, trying to break Aiden's silence.

"With Shun," he said quite casually, knowing he would have to break his silence at any moment.

"*Who?*" Diana shouted louder than expected. Aiden looked towards Diana, she quickly glanced between Aiden and the driver.

"He told me there are scrolls… scrolls that I have to find before the Dark Witch," said Aiden as he began to divulge everything to Diana. But before he could continue, Diana pressed her finger against her lips, using her other hand to point towards the driver. Aiden looked forwards taking notice of the driver's eyes looking directly at them through the rear mirror.

"I think you have done exceptionally well today, and I think you will pass with flying colours, Aiden," said Diana, changing the subject to avoid the eavesdropping driver.

"Ms Shaw, there are people in the road ahead," the driver spoke, gaining Diana's attention. She looked in between the driver's and passenger's seats, noticing two people in the distance standing side by side in the middle of the road dressed in regular clothing.

"Don't stop," said Diana curtly. The driver kept his foot on the accelerator. That's when Aiden once again graced his wrist with his free hand, remembering that he had lost his bracelet. Feeling like his heart was about to burst out of his chest, Aiden barely spoke the words, "Diana, it's me." Diana looked towards him. She turned back round to look at the people ahead noticing the distinctive red eyes.

"Vampires," she spat. She returned to her seat as the group of individuals refused to move with the impending threat of the car. But as they inched closer, Diana felt the car slow.

"What are you doing?" Diana shouted towards the driver.

"They are people. I'm not going to hit them."

"They're vampires. Speed up!" Diana shouted. She withdrew her gun, holding it against the driver's head. The driver feeling the cold steel of the gun against his scalp, pressed down on the accelerator.

"Open the door now, Aiden," said Diana. Aiden did as she said, but without warning, a car came from the bushes crashing into the VHA vehicle, sending it tumbling. Aiden was sucked from the car as Diana screamed his name. The car flipped several times until it finally came to a stop on its side.

Diana pulled herself from the wreckage, moaning, feeling every muscle in her body scream with pain. Two men exited the car that had hit Diana and Aiden and advanced menacingly towards her. Just in time, another VHA vehicle arrived, heading straight for the two men, Diana scanned her surroundings looking for Aiden.

Groaning, she forced herself to her feet and sprinted towards the boy who was lying on the floor. A trail of skin and blood led the way as a flashing image of Aiden being sucked from the car door returned. She climbed over his body, gasping at his injuries. Aiden's right arm was broken, the bone piercing his skin.

She looked back to the toppled car, seeing the vampires crawl from the wreckage. She quickly withdrew her gun, firing several bullets into the chest of the vampires before they could stand up. The bodies fell to the floor with a thud as she frantically tried to stop Aiden's blood from pumping out. She looked around the open fields apprehensively, expecting a herd of vampires to jump out in lust for the Perfect Blood.

"Diana," a friendly voice shouted behind her. She turned back to see Jason running over to her

"Be prepared!" Diana cried back.

Jason approached his best friend and his son, and his face twisted at the sight. He stepped back from the initial shock. His son lay still, barely breathing and pale; his puddle of blood had soaked Diana.

"We have to get him to the VHA now," said Diana as Jason collapsed to his knees, barely able to breathe. Diana let Jason scoop Aiden up, and she continued to watch her surroundings in fear of more vampires arriving at the highway battle scene, praying the Ultimatum wouldn't be born today.

22
RECOVERY

Aiden slept restlessly. The images of bodies being ripped apart, Shun standing under a light murmuring the "Scrolls of Decimation" and the soulless white eyes of rabids wreaked havoc in Aiden's dreams. A sudden fiery, burning sensation erupted in his arm, the same pain he had felt the night he was attacked by the vampire and Tyler had forced Aiden to drink his blood to heal his broken leg. However, after what felt like forever, the pain eventually subsided with a faint stinging sensation remaining. Aiden's eyes remained closed, and he drifted into unconsciousness. He began dreaming of the night he went out into Oakdale with Callie and Tyler—before life became complicated, when he didn't know about Perfect Bloods, vampires, hunters, the VHA and especially the Dark Witch. The feeling of normality returned and Aiden welcomed it, but it wasn't long before he felt a tug pulling him away from a lovely dream and eventually into a blinding white light as he awoke.

Am I alive or dead? The sudden thought popped into Aiden's head. He had heard stories of people going towards the light when they died, but as he focussed his vision, expecting to see someone almighty, he was pretty sure he wouldn't begin his journey in a hospital bed. Aiden's blurred vision returned to normal as he realised he was in the infirmary at the VHA. He remembered being shown this room on his tour of the VHA, remembering the blinding lightness of the room compared to the rest of the VHA. Here was the only room in the entire complex that wasn't painted black; it was all white.

Continuing his dreamy gaze around the large room with a soft beeping of a monitor in the background, Aiden eyes followed the white wooden beams that led up towards the hollow ceiling of the infirmary, reminding Aiden very much of a church. Aiden counted nineteen empty beds confined within their own glass box.

A sudden wet sensation gained Aiden's attention. He looked down the bed hoping he hadn't wet himself but heaved a sigh of relief when he observed a wet, gooey bandage that had been wound around his right arm, across his shoulder and on half of his chest. A slight stinging sensation remained, but with every passing second, it seemed to disappear. A half-empty red bag of liquid stood out against the legion of white. Aiden followed the little stream of blood, taking note of the needle in his hand, before he suddenly remembered everything – the mission to London, his encounter with Shun and the Dark Witch, and then everything went blurry after he was sucked out the car door. But he couldn't forget about the Scrolls of Decimation. Knowing that the vampire race now depended on him made it almost impossible for him to forget these words. He needed to leave the infirmary and get to Oakdale Museum, but how? The VHA wasn't exactly going to let him waltz out after what had happened, but that's when a short, plump nurse came striding towards Aiden's glass box, carrying a white tray, distracting him from his thoughts. At first, she seemed preoccupied before she looked towards Aiden, noticing he was now awake. Her mouth dropped open, making Aiden think there was something wrong with his face, but when she began mouthing words he could not hear, thinking he was now deaf, another nurse came running over instantly. Both of them watching and muttering to one another with the most profound looks.

Eventually, after their short deliberation and speaking through a walkie-talkie, Cambal, the Master Healer, appeared, taking the tray from the nurse and entering Aiden's private glass box.

"Hello, Aiden," he muttered, gliding the glass door open. His soft voice matched the calmness of the room. "It's nice to see you're awake."

"Hi," said Aiden hoarsely, his voice limiting the happiness in knowing he wasn't deaf.

"Don't talk," said Cambal calmly, gently sliding his hands into a pair of rubber blue gloves. "You arrived here on Saturday after your mission. After you were sucked out the car, vampires came running towards the battle. Your father and the other hunters fought for at least ten minutes before Diana and your father got you into a car, bringing you here," Cambal finished.

Aiden couldn't help but gulp knowing his scent must have been active. He hoped no one else had been killed – apart from Tobias – and that he wouldn't be responsible for anyone else's death, remembering the horrific murders of some of the hunters during the mission.

Cambal moved towards Aiden's bandaged shoulder, slowly peeling the moist material away. In a moment of intense trepidation, expecting to feel his skin being pulled from his bones, Aiden was pleasantly surprised when he felt the fresh air caress his vulnerable flesh.

"Well, I must say that is perfect," said Cambal, peering through his glasses admiring his work. "Your wounds seem to be healing exceptionally well. Just bruising remains." Cambal slowly removed the winding, slimy bandage, revealing the mixture of purple, black and off-brown colours from underneath. Aiden was slightly repulsed by the petroleum-like gel and not the bruising.

"What is that?" asked Aiden, taking aim at the gooey substance, feeling the clean air almost rejuvenate his bare skin.

"It's special serum made by a herbalist."

"Herbalist?" Aiden interrupted, feeling his voice slowly return to normal.

"A herbalist is a witch who possesses no magical ability but is able to extract the power of flowers, plants and more in order to create potions, serums, et cetera," Cambal explained. "This serum helps in the process of healing the outer body but for the more severe injuries, for example, your broken arm, we use special blood that has been enhanced. The only downside is you feel the pain when you heal, but you were unconscious so you didn't feel a thing."

Aiden looked towards Cambal. *Vampire Venom*, he found himself thinking. The way Cambal had just explained it was exactly the way Tyler had explained it. Aiden was all too familiar with the experience of vampire venom, especially after Tyler, when he had forced his venom into Aiden to help heal him after the attack at Jasper's party.

"It's good stuff then," said Aiden, feeling sick to the stomach at the hypocrisy of the VHA. Happy to kill the creatures that have most likely been the saviour of thousands of hunters over the decades. Cambal continued his assessment on Aiden as Jason came running into the infirmary, appearing at the door of Aiden's cubicle.

"Ah, Jason," said Cambal. Aiden's dad made his way hastily into the cubicle, but before Cambal could finish, Jason embraced Aiden in the tightest hug he had ever given him. Aiden was gobsmacked by the sudden affection, never having felt a hug like this from his father before.

"Hi, Dad," Aiden coughed, unsure how to react.

"Don't do that to me again," said Jason who began to tear up as he continued to embrace his son.

"Dad, I'm okay," Aiden pleaded. Jason released his grip, leaning back. His eyes were bloodshot with tears threatening to make an appearance. Aiden was lost for words, never knowing his father to cry, not even on the anniversary of losing Aiden's mother.

"I am happy with his condition, and once your day is up, you are more than welcome to take him home," said Cambal, taking pride in his work.

"Thank you, Cambal, I owe you one," said Jason. He rose from Aiden's bed, shaking the hand of the Master Healer.

"For old times," replied Cambal before leaving the glass cubicle.

"Right, I have a few things to do, but once they are done, we are off home for a pizza and movie night," said Jason, turning his attention to his son. Aiden felt his stomach growl. When was the last time he ate? But the sound of pizza was heavenly. Jason left Aiden, once again hugging his son. To his word, Jason didn't let Aiden down: within the hour, he had returned from his office, ready to take Aiden home. Cambal handed Jason a bag of bandages, medicine and pills for Aiden's injuries and a note detailing Aiden's absence from the VHA for the following week. Shaking hands, and after several thanks to Cambal and the nurses, Jason wheeled Aiden out, with an escort from Cambal, to a VHA vehicle.

The thought of getting home and messaging Callie and Tyler about everything that had happened was a pressing issue, but Aiden knew Diana would have kept them up to date with recent events. They left the darkness of the VHA, passing the Guardians of the Palace who remained hidden in the shrubbery, and out into the rather beautiful Tuesday afternoon. Aiden had been anxious to get into the car after what had happened, but he relaxed as soon as he felt the warm breeze blow through the car on their way home. Breathing in the smell of freshly cut grass, Aiden couldn't help but feel the tension release. That was until Jason suddenly broke the silence of the car with some words that Aiden had been dying to hear since he could remember.

"Your mother..." Jason paused.

Aiden whipped his head round to look at his father, wondering if he had heard correct, but he could sense the fragility in his father's voice. Aiden knew this was a moment that was going to change his life.

"Your mother was killed by a witch. The witch that appeared in London is who killed her," said Jason, his tone taking a dark turn towards the end. Aiden felt his stomach shrivel and his throat tighten. The pain which Aiden was witnessing in his father's voice was heartbreaking, but what hurt Aiden even further was that he already knew this; he had found it out from the Dark Witch the night they tried to capture Callie and him.

As much as Aiden wanted to tell his father everything he knew, he couldn't. Otherwise it would end up in Aiden telling the truth about Callie, Tyler and what he was. For once, he wished he didn't have to lie, but feeling like it was his duty, Aiden replied, lying, forcing himself to be responsible for hindering any advancements in his father finding the witch in order to protect his friends.

"What?" he said.

"Barely a month after you were born, I had to return to the VHA to capture a vampire named Giovanni." His dad's voice was thick with grief. "One day, after a meeting, a hunter came to me saying Giovanni had had his fun, but tonight was the night he was going to end it. In that moment I ran home, knowing he was coming for you and your mum, but when I arrived home, I found a burnt corpse and a sigil burnt into the wall of your room. The body was Giovanni's, and your mother was gone.

I searched for your mum night and day, but I couldn't find her. In the end, I resorted to hiring a witch who had told me a witch had killed Giovanni and your mother. A day later, we moved, and I vowed never to come back to Oakdale… until recently when a witch killed one of Shun Yun Li's men, leaving the same sigil as the one in your bedroom."

Aiden had never felt so whole in his life. He finally knew what happened to his mother. But now, more than ever, he wanted to find the Scrolls of Decimation, destroy them and any hope the Dark Witch had of erasing the vampire race. After he had done that, he would then search for the Witch and kill them himself.

"Thank you for telling me, Dad," said Aiden, holding back his tears. Jason turned to his son, his eyes watery. He nodded before he turned back to look out the window, hoping Aiden wouldn't ask any more questions.

It wasn't long after the two had arrived home and indulged in a large pizza that Aiden headed to bed. Thinking it would be impossible to sleep that night, having divulged everything about the Dark Witch and his mother to Callie and Tyler, who said they would be coming round the next morning, Aiden found that he fell asleep peacefully, feeling like an unknown hole in his heart had been filled—a hole that offered an immense sense of closure.

Having made breakfast for Aiden, Jason left for work later than usual. Aiden studied his bruising in the mirror in his room. The multitude of colours decorated Aiden's olive skin as he began taking the pills Cambal had recommended. Having struggled to dress himself, Aiden moved downstairs slowly, awaiting a knock at the door. Eventually a loud bang came, and without hesitation, Aiden opened it to see a relieved Callie and even Tyler. Half expecting Callie to pounce on him, grateful he was fine, she resisted after taking note of his bruising which she could smell before Aiden even answered the door. Once again, everything Aiden had seen on his trip to London—the rabids, the Dark Witch, nearly everything Shun Yun Li had told him – he had now shared Callie and Tyler.

"Yikes," said Tyler incredulously. "So we need to go to the library then?"

"Yes. Today. Now," said Aiden as the three sat in the safety of his room. Aiden had had to invite them in officially, like he had done for the vampire who'd attacked him.

"Well, let's get going then if the vampire race depends on it," said Tyler jumping to his feet.

"Yes, but first, your mum, Aiden. How does it feel hearing it from your father?" said Callie. Aiden looked towards her, in some way hoping she hadn't asked.

"The Dark Witch killed my mother; I can't tell my dad what I know so I just need to make sure we kill it after we have destroyed the scrolls," he said.

Having helped Aiden with his shoes, the three teenagers left the house, Aiden struggling to keep up.

"By the way, Cara is making you another bracelet with alterations," said Tyler, as he slowed his pace to accommodate Aiden.

"Alterations?" queried Aiden.

"Well, it seemed rather than hinder you scent, it withheld it, so when your bracelet was torn off, a massive surge of your scent was sent around the UK, even reaching Europe."

"Our friend Lydia was even able to pick it up," Callie added.

"That explains the highway attack," said Aiden, remembering how Cambal had said vampires didn't stop coming.

Within the hour, the three teenagers arrived at the outdated library on the outskirts of Oakdale shopping centre. A frail woman at the front behind a swaying desk slowly stamped the pile of books that had been returned. The smell of old people hung in the air.

"What did Shun say again?" asked Tyler, walking past the old woman through a pair of frosted glass doors and into the suddenly large library.

"Where the old meets the new, GAS20," said Aiden, surprised by the multiple levels within the library, each accommodating rows and rows of bookshelves, filled to the max with books.

"What does G-A-S even mean though?" Tyler asked.

"The coding normally means the first initial of the author," said Callie matter-of-factly.

"Let's begin then," said Aiden. The three teenagers separated, dividing the floor into sections, agreeing to text once they had found something. Splitting off, Aiden began searching the first floor as Tyler and Callie moved to the upper floors.

The History of Castle Nort: Disappearance of the Builders – Aiden read the title in his head, looking at the fine leather book which seemed like it hadn't seen daylight in years before gently placing it back, starting to think that the precious and dangerous scrolls wouldn't be left on the shelf for anyone to find.

Hours had gone by and no scrolls had been found. Callie was watching her watch carefully; the library had started to empty out slowly. She was becoming bored. Aiden and Tyler had gone to the other two floors, once again, searching for the scrolls.

"Bored, bored, bored, bored, bored," she whispered to herself, walking down another row of shelving. "Where the old meets the new, GAS20," she repeated for the thousandth time, scrambling her brain for an answer to what it meant. She hovered her hand over the books that lay in front of her, reminding her of her first visit to the Library of Wickery with Tyler and

Lydia. She felt her phone buzz which bought her attention away from the books, but before she looked at her phone, something had caught her attention. On the floor, right beside the bookcase was the letter S. Her brows furrowed. She looked at the bookcase, comparing it to the others. The bookcase compared to the others was richer in colour, standing out amongst the old darker ones.

"Where the old meets the new," Callie whispered, her eyes widening and her mouth dropping open, realising the riddle meant the bookcase. Scurrying to the other side of the bookshelf, Callie looked on the floor, where the letter G had been engraved. Looking at the configuration of the bookshelf row, she realized it sideways would only make the shelf topple and push all the others down causing a catastrophic scene. She walked back to face the golden oak of the bookshelf, where she saw G and S either side of the case. Pushing the bookcase forward using her strength, the shelf started creaking, shattering the silence of the quiet library, but it didn't stop Callie. She continued to push the bookshelf. Eventually, the bookshelf glided over the last letter A.

"Where the old meets the new, GAS20," said Callie, heaving a sigh of relief as the number 20 appeared. There was a small metal handle on top of the imprinted tile. Kneeling down, Callie pulled the handle, and the tile came off easily. She placed the lid to one side, and underneath was a box wrapped in leather. She pulled the box out, unwrapping it like a Christmas present. *The Scrolls of Decimation* had been brandished in a crimson ink on the ancient box.

"The scrolls," Callie whispered, her eyes gleaming. She was overjoyed to have found them and pleased for beating Aiden and Tyler to it, when by surprise, Callie felt a hand grip on her shoulder.

"Guys, it's the scrolls," she said, not paying attention to the hand on her shoulder.

"Callie." Callie looked up smiling, but her smile was bought to an end quickly. Tyler and Aiden were standing in front of her, both looking alarmed. Her stomach sank immediately. If the two boys were in front of her, who had their hand on her shoulder? The hand removed itself as Callie turned her head slowly, gripping the box of scrolls tightly.

The Dark Witch, draped in their hooded black cloak, floated just behind Callie. Unconsciously pulling the box into her chest, the Dark Witch struck Callie with an almighty blow. Callie was sent flying, crashing into a bookshelf, accidentally having let go of the box as it fell to the feet of the Dark Witch. Tyler and Aiden ran towards the Dark Witch. The adrenaline which pumped through Aiden's body hindered any pain he felt from his injuries. Running for the scrolls, the Dark Witch easily grabbed the ancient black box, moving backwards and into the air. Hovering in the centre of the library, Aiden looked below, the few remaining people left in the library were all frozen, like there were statues.

"Freezing spell," said Tyler, but Aiden was more preoccupied with the fact that the witch had the Scrolls of Decimation and not about what spell they had used to enter the library unannounced without causing any commotion.

"I'm going to kill you," Aiden spat, looking deep into the hood of the Dark Witch, hoping to see a face through the darkness they were shrouded in. Callie appeared next to Aiden, bearing her fangs at the Dark Witch.

"You all have your part to play, Mother Nature demands what's fair is fair," said the Dark Witch conspiratorially, not revealing any sense of who they might be, before a raucous laugh erupted from their hood. Clapping their hands together with the box tightly squeezed between their arms, a bright black flame illuminated the air, sending a powerful energy outwards. The three teenagers were propelled backwards as the Dark Witch disappeared.

"Are you okay?" Aiden asked. "Did you get anything from the scrolls?"

"I'm fine," said Callie, irritable, slightly annoyed that Aiden was more worried about the scrolls than her.

"Come on, guys, we can't stay," said Tyler anxiously. The three teenagers left the library in a hurry before the freezing spell could wear off, and made their way to Tyler's house.

"I can't believe that was the Dark Witch again," said Callie shaking. The second time Callie had come into contact with the Dark Witch, a second time she had made it out alive compared to the other vampires. Cara joined the three teenagers, wearing a silk sapphire-coloured night gown, her hair held back by her large pink hairband.

"If only Lydia was around," she added, making her presence known. Aiden stood, still thinking about the situation while struggling to hinder the thoughts about wanting to meet Lydia.

"Is there anything you can remember from the scrolls?" asked Aiden. He was becoming impatient for answers. They were so close yet had done the one thing Shun had asked him not to do and that was to give the Dark Witch the scrolls.

"No," said Callie.

"Great," said Aiden. "The one thing Shun asked me to do was not to give the scrolls to the Dark Witch, and we led them straight to it and basically gave it to them." Aiden was unable to contain his annoyance.

Callie noticed the tone in his voice and couldn't help but feel disappointed in herself.

"Why did the Sisterhood of Witches have to put a spell on these scrolls?" said Aiden.

"Sisterhood of Witches?" snapped Cara. The three teenagers all turned to look at the elderly woman who downed her large glass of red wine.

"What do you know?" said Tyler. Cara gasped for air after, filling her glass once again before answering Tyler's questions. She made her way towards a bookshelf, remaining silent, skimming her finger over the spines of the multitude of books.

"Here we go," she said, pulling a thin book from the shelf. She walked towards the dining room table, slamming the book down.

"The Sisterhood of Witches were a group of witches in sixteenth and seventeenth century devoted to learning about the supernatural world. There were four of them until one was killed by a fire. Their work was revolutionary."

"So they have something to do with the Perfect Blood then?" asked Callie.

"Yes," said Aiden remembering. "Shun said they worked with Rowan Drukheim. They extracted the power of the Perfect Blood from him."

"So these scrolls have something to do with the Perfect Blood's power then," said Cara.

"Fred was right," said Tyler. "The Dark Witch has a plan."

"Damn," said Callie suddenly. "Aiden, your dad is on his way home." Callie was looking at her phone at a text from her mum. Without a moment to lose, Callie and Aiden left Tyler's house, Callie once again giving Aiden a piggyback ride home, but this time Aiden kept his eyes closed, a lesson learnt from the previous time.

Aiden jumped off her back, barely having any time to say goodbye before Callie had left out of fear of being caught. Rushing into his house, thinking he had heard the familiar roar of a VHA vehicle at the top of the street, Aiden quickly undressed and jumped into his bed, twitching from the sudden pain of his bruising. Having waited five minutes, Jason still hadn't arrived home.

This was now the first time Aiden was left to his thoughts. *What has the Dark Witch got planned? Why do they need us?* These were all the questions circling Aiden's head. But at the same time, he couldn't help but feel guilty for leading his friends to the library for them to fail in securing the scrolls and encounter the Dark Witch. On edge and unsure how he was going to fall asleep, it wasn't long before he dozed off. If only he had stayed awake longer he may have noticed the Dark Witch floating in the shadows of the house, watching him sleep like they had done when he was a baby – when they came to his house fourteen years ago.

23
IMPLODED

It was the following Friday and, despite their failed attempt to get the Scrolls of Decimation, Aiden couldn't help but feel stronger. The bruising had finally subsided, and any pains which remained were just a memory. The pills Cambal had given Aiden had definitely helped, but Aiden thought his break from the VHA was the main cause. It was his first day back at school, and he had ended up with a detention from Mr Burton – although this time he was to be joined by Callie and Tyler – for accidentally talking over the teacher when he read from the register. Despite all this, the three friends sat on the field during lunch, enjoying the heat from the sun, when a dreaded thought arose in Aiden's mind which he couldn't shake.

"I have a question to ask you guys," he said.

"What's that?" Callie asked.

"Well after what happened on the mission, at one point I thought I was going to die. So what happens when we die?" The heavy question seemed to upset Callie who began to tear up. She never liked to think about death after how close she had come to it herself, and she had to stop herself before the blood left the corner of her eyes. Tyler answered, allowing Callie time to grab her mirror from her bag.

"There are two places that you can go, one is called the Realm and the other is called the Oscuro Realm. From what I have learnt, once we die we, go to this place called the waiting room where we wait for our souls to be judged by the gods."

"Gods?" Aiden interrupted, thinking there was something else to worry about now.

"All fictional, I think."

"Just like vampires?" Aiden joked. Callie snorted, and Tyler grinned before he continued.

"The Realm is kinda like heaven whereas the Oscuro Realm is like hell, the place where the worst of the worst go. The gods judge our souls based on whether we have lived a good life or not. Until we have been judged, our souls remain in the waiting room. However, souls can remain in the waiting room until our loved one joins us."

"Is that only for supernatural beings or humans as well?" questioned Aiden.

"According to the books I have read, it is for both," answered Tyler. Aiden couldn't help but be surprised that there was another version of heaven and hell. It made him wonder if the VHA knew about the Realms, but Aiden didn't have time to dwell on it as someone in his peripheral caught his attention.

"Anything happen with Tobias?" said Aiden as the prince of Oakdale Secondary School strode arrogantly onto the field, yet again drawing the attention of all the girls.

"No, he wasn't in till Wednesday, recovering we guess, but he's remained silent still," said Callie.

"Well, Dad, let it slip that he has his check-up today, and I have mine on Monday," Aiden added, as they began to eat their lunch.

Neil left Daria's office as Jason arrived. Jason nodded at his coworker, but Neil ignored him as if he had something more important on his mind than to exchange pleasantries with Jason. Walking into the incensed, dimly lit office, he saw Daria staring out her window, watching the hunters as they moved between training rooms below.

"We need to have a chat," said Jason. Daria sighed, listening to the Master Hunter.

"Did you manage to capture Shun Yun Li?" said Daria woefully, already knowing the answer but wanting to hear it again.

"No," said Jason.

"Then what do we need to talk about?" said Daria, remaining in the shadows of her office.

"I believe the witch is up to something. They had the chance to kill me and the others in the museum but they didn't."

"What happens if the witch is on our side? Maybe we should let these events unfold and see what happens. Besides, I doubt this witch will kill any more humans when all they have done is kill vampires," said Daria. She turned to face Jason. Her hair was messy, and she had heavy, black bags under her eyes, which were illuminated due to her pale skin.

"It killed my wife," Jason said with venom.

"Fourteen years ago," said Daria, cradling her arms in one another. "The I-VHA is breathing down my neck and is not happy that we failed to catch Shun Yun Li, and now they want compensation."

"Compensation?" said Jason.

"They want someone to take the blame for this failure," said Daria.

BOOM!

An eardrum-rupturing explosion erupted from outside Daria's office. Her windows came shattering inwards, and the two hunters crouched, covering their faces, the ground beneath them shaking. Black smoke billowed into Daria's office, filling the air as horrific screams followed.

Jason's ears rang, filling his head with a loud buzzing.

"What was that?" Daria shouted coughing. Jason moved towards the shattered window looking out into the VHA.

"It looks like it was bomb," he muttered bewildered. Another explosion erupted in the VHA, this time the bomb far closer to Daria's office.

Jason was thrown backwards from the shockwave, slamming against Daria's desk. Groaning with pain, dazed, Daria grabbed Jason by the scruff of his shirt pulling the Master Hunter to his feet, then they made their way from her office and down into the chaos of the VHA.

Tobias sat in the infirmary watching the nurses attend to the newcomers. A group of hunters had just returned from their mission and, from what Tobias could see, it seemed to have been a deadly one. Several hunters lay unconscious in the beds, but the nurses remained calm, injecting needles into their arms and wrapping their wounds with bandages.

Tobias watched one nurse who stood at the door. She held a folder, asking the hunters for their names, a portable fridge that contained blood pouches had been moved next to her. Opening the container, she handed the hunters a blood pouch each as she ushered them onwards to the next nurse. This must have been the special serum that Tobias had heard so much about; he knew that it was a way to speed up recovery.

After watching the nurse, Tobias saw the young girl from his class, Gabriella, walking from the back of the room. She had just finished her check-up after the mission, and it was now Tobias's turn.

Rising to his feet, Tobias felt a sudden shockwave which made the earth beneath his feet move. The infirmary erupted into screams. The glass cubicles cracked. When the vibration stopped, Tobias gulped as a nervous and wary silence fell upon the infirmary. Nurses held onto the hunters who lay in the beds… when suddenly an explosion erupted in the infirmary.

Tobias was thrown through the air, along with others, by the shockwave. Slamming against the floor, he looked into the ceiling as the white wooden beams cracked. His eyes widened as the ceiling began to collapse, instantly killing the nurses and hunters beneath. Tobias jumped to his feet and by, the skin of his teeth, was able to jump out of the infirmary door as it closed shut with the security system going into action.

Tobias crawled on the floor, panting and squinting as his eyesight was blurry from the dust in the hallway. He coughed heavily before he was picked up by someone and slammed against the wall.

"Don't move! I'll be back!" the voice shouted. Tobias readjusted his gaze, watching Neil run off.

"Daria, we have a serious problem." Neil arrived, panting. Jason and Daria had begun the evacuation process. Rubble littered the flooring with hunters listening intently to Jason and Daria as they quickly pointed to the exit.

"Go on," said Daria hastily before she focussed on Neil, coughing, struggling to breathe amongst the thick black smoke.

"The infirmary was hit. All the doors went into lockdown so nothing can get out," said Neil apprehensively.

"What do you mean 'get out'?" Jason snapped, fear jabbing the insides of his stomach. He knew a group of hunters had been sent there from their mission.

Daria cursed hoarsely. "Hunters will begin the transformation any moment."

"Transformation!" Jason snapped, wondering what Daria had done.

"We've been using the vampire venom in the blood pouches to heal the patients quicker."

"So, they are all potentially vampires," said Jason, interrupting Daria. "You used that on my son!" Jason roared against a blaring siren. He felt betrayed, he had never thought before about what he would do if Aiden became a vampire.

"I don't want them getting out and causing more havoc. Neil, exterminate them now," Daria commanded ruthlessly. Neil nodded and ran off back to the infirmary.

"How is it Neil knows about this and I don't?" said Jason furiously, feeling the anger build up inside him. He felt like he was ready to burst, sick of Daria's secrets.

"There is no time to talk about this. We have to help the others," said Daria. The wails and screams of people in the background were enough to stop Jason from challenging her right now. Besides, he needed to save the other hunters. Another deafening explosion erupted inside the VHA.

Jason and Daria looked up as rubble from the ceiling fell to the floor. They both jumped backwards, separating from one another; the rubble piled high, knocking Jason backwards and Daria out of sight.

Jason coughed furiously as he rose to his feet, the taste of dust on his mouth making it almost impossible to swallow.

"Daria!" Jason shouted, his ears ringing from the explosion.

"I'm okay, I'm on the other side!" Daria shouted back, her voice piercing through the rubble as a surge of relief pulsed through Jason's body. "I can't get around! We need to split up. I have a lot of people injured on this side."

"Okay!" Jason replied, covering his mouth with his arm, attempting to block any more dust from entering his mouth.

Gabriella was hiding behind rubble, resisting the urge to cry. She was holding her side, trying to stop the blood from pouring out from the scrap metal that had pierced her. The screams had all stopped, but the scratching hadn't. Two hunters had transformed into vampires, and so far, they had killed the infirmary team and the patients who tried to escape. Their senses had been overwhelmed by the amount of blood, allowing Gabriella to remain unnoticed. She was thinking what to do, but nothing came to her. She just wanted to stay alive.

"Ouch," a body moaned. Gabriella twisted her neck to face the hunter. A steel bar had penetrated his abdomen. Moments ago, Gabriella watched him die, and now he had transformed into a vampire.

Knowing she didn't have much time, Gabriella quickly looked around. Noticing the storeroom door ajar, she winced hard knowing she had to get there. The two hunters continued scratching the doors, growling with hunger, either wanting to find their master or feed on the frenzy of humans in the VHA. She knew she had to move soon before the other newly born vampire was able to detach himself from the steel bar.

Gabriella moved her stone-like limbs towards the storeroom, her broken ribs taking their toll as she limped. Avoiding the rubble and the bodies, the door was still agape, a chink of light illuminating her route to safety. *Another ten metres*, Gabriella thought as she manoeuvred her way around the rubble, keeping a watchful eye on the three vampires, feeling like she was going to make it, when... *Crack!*

The world stopped. Gabriella looked down, staring at the broken glass under her feet. Her lips started to tremble as the noises behind her stopped. She dared to look back. "Hello, young one," he spoke. But before Gabriella even turned round, the vampire pounced on her, and her horrific wails filled the infirmary. The vamp inserted his freshly carved fangs into her neck, draining her of her life.

"Now!" Neil shouted as he watched the vampires around Gabriella. Tobias stood next to Neil, clenching a shotgun. Enraged, Tobias unleased every pellet into the vampires.

Neil stood back, not firing a single bullet. Tobias advanced menacingly until only one vampire remained feasting on Gabriella. The vamp pounced towards Tobias, who fired his last pellet into its head. The vampire collapsed to the floor. Tobias proceeded to beat the dead corpse with the end of his shotgun.

Neil watched on, silently assessing the young hunter. Then he stepped forward.

"I have an important mission. Something that will change this world," he said.

Tobias turned to face his teacher. "Where do I sign up?" he spoke hoarsely with a cold, venomous voice.

The final bomb went off less than an hour ago. Jason had met up with Diana and Hayden and they had been able to evacuate the VHA. Hunters were on the floor crying as others looked for family or friends – not everyone was lucky enough to get out. Jason, Diana and Hayden, were busy helping Cambal and Alicia with the wounded, bandaging up anyone who was bleeding while the two Master Healers were dealing with the severe cases. He hadn't heard from Daria nor Neil; the only thing that was rushing through his mind was that he was grateful that Aiden was at home.

Jason continued to help amongst the mayhem when two hunters approached him. He turned to face them, and his heart sank when he saw their grim expressions. They looked desperate, and he wondered for a moment what terrible news they had for them.

At last, one of them found their voice and muttered words that made Jason's blood run cold. "Daria is dead."

24
THE ANNOUNCEMENT

"A dark day has come over the VHA," said Jason, as he read from the cards he had prepared the night before. He was standing on a podium, addressing the entire VHA, looking out at hundreds of vampire hunters and trainees. Hunters had travelled from all over the world to be in attendance for this funeral. Even the seven members of the I-VHA were attending.

"It also saddens me to say that we have lost one of our own Master Hunters, Neil Gauze and trainee hunter, Tobias Tate, who were killed saving the lives of hunters when rubble collapsed on them," Jason read with an overwhelming feeling of grief. It was devastating to Jason to have lost Neil, someone who was so talented.

In the front row of the audience was Diana, Hayden, Cambal and Alicia. All four of them sat in frozen shock, their brows furrowed, their eyes on the ground. Every so often, Alicia would reach for a tissue to blow her nose and wipe her tears, and Cambal beside her would mumble comforting words.

It turned out Daria's body was almost unidentifiable; it had taken Alicia and Cambal a whole day to produce a report that they were one-hundred percent certain it was the leader of the VHA.

"Daria has gone by many names over the years," Jason continued. "Daria the Great, Daria the Fierce, Daria the Warrior. She was someone with exceptional talent, someone who was taken too soon. Her goal in life was to protect the world and to gain the title every VHA leader wanted – Daria the Extinguisher. She always believed she would be the one to rid the world of vile, deathly vampires." Jason paused looking down the aisle, staring at the four hunters who had entered the room carrying a shiny black coffin.

Aiden sat in his designated class row, alone, the last of his class. Learning that Tobias and Gabriella had been killed in the explosion made him feel older than he had ever felt in his lifetime. The girls at Oakdale Secondary School had entered a state of mourning, knowing that they would never get to see the prince of Oakdale Secondary School again. However, Aiden thought about Gabriella; everyone had been so preoccupied with remembering Tobias that no one paid attention to her.

With the black coffin making its way down the aisle, Aiden heard the scuffling of hunters rising from their chairs to pay their respects. Aiden didn't bother looking. Jason had let it slip that the coffin was empty as her body was unsalvageable.

The four hunters marched past, the coffin balancing on their shoulders, walking up the stairs slowly, heading towards Jason. They placed Daria's coffin in front of the podium. The four hunters removed their hats, bowing in respect before they walked backwards down the steps to sit in their designated seats.

"However, Daria wasn't the only one we lost. We lost Toby Pearson, one of the greatest minds in our generation and some of our first-year students, who were sadly training when the bomb went off. They will forever be remembered and forever loved," said Jason as a cry echoed in the eerily silent hall. "Daria once said to me. 'Hope is for the young, but in a world so dark with creature likes vampires, it's all we have.' We will continue this fight and hope to eradicate vampires for the good of mankind. They have spilt far too much blood, and we will have our vengeance," Jason finished. Aiden could hear the darkness in his father's voice. "And now, Cambal has a few words to say," Jason finished. Nodding to the audience, he walked away from the podium, taking a seat next to Diana.

Cambal approached the coffin, gently positioning two swords in an 'X' symbol.

"Daria was one of the finest leaders the VHA has ever had," he said from the podium. "When we learnt that she was the next in line to become the VHA Leader, I couldn't think of anyone better." Cambal paused. Jason had asked him to speak as he was the only one who knew her long enough. Despite their fractious relationship, Jason could tell Cambal was saying everything to please the audience rather than what he truly thought of her. "She revived the VHA to a new life. I heard she fought with elegance and grace, and I am truly thankful she was able to encourage every vampire hunter that we have in this room, new or old. I always counted myself lucky that I never had to face her in a fight. So, as I say my final words, may Daria have a good afterlife, Daria the Great will always be remembered." People started clapping as Cambal walked away from the podium and back to his seat, once again comforting a hysterical Alicia.

"Thank you, everyone," said Diana, appearing at the podium. "Now, Daria, may her soul rest in peace."

The four hunters appeared once again on the podium, lifting Daria's coffin above their shoulders, proceeding to walk down the staircase. No one spoke, whispered or mumbled as they walked back down the aisle before disappearing through a pair of black doors.

"So, she is dead then?" Tyler said, walking side by side with Callie, a little joyous from recent events.

"Yeah, she is," Callie replied. They were out walking, feeling the need to celebrate Daria's death. Despite it only having happened a few days ago, Cara had told them the vampire community already knew. For a few weeks, they were allowed to relax; when a leader died, it always took time for the new one to be elected, but from what Aiden had told them, Jason had been made temporary leader by the I-VHA until a replacement could be found.

"So, what happens now then, Tyler?" Callie asked.

"I guess… we can have a bit of fun without any repercussions." Callie snorted at Tyler's statement. Tyler was always by the book, always telling her to blend in and not to be noticed, and now he seemed to have relaxed.

"Well, we can't relax yet," Callie said, starting to sound like Tyler. For once, since knowing each other, they had swapped personalities.

"We still have the Dark Witch to deal with, and they have been radio silent recently."

"True, but until then, we just make sure we watch each other's backs," said Tyler. "Besides, how's your mum after the bombs?"

"She's okay, been complaining about some headaches since that day, but I'm not surprised after what happened," said Callie, slightly concerned for her mum.

"Well, it should pass. Besides, I have some of your favourite blood at mine." Tyler nudged Callie grinning.

"Race you there," said Callie teasingly, but before Tyler could even reply, Callie had zoomed off leaving him in her dirt tracks.

"Such a cheat," Tyler laughed as he zoomed off after her, racing back to his for a night of celebration.

Diana returned home after the funeral, her head still sore from the headaches she had been suffering from since the bombs.

"Callie," Diana moaned softly as she started to feel dizzy.

"Hey, Mum," Callie appeared at the top of the stairs wearing her florescent pink pyjamas, having only recently returned from Tyler's. "Mum, do you feel okay?" Callie questioned. Diana placed her keys on the side table, massaging her head.

"I... I..." but before Diana could finish, she collapsed. Callie let out a yelp. She sprinted towards her mother, making it down the stairs, cradling her mother's head in her arms before it slammed against their stone flooring.

"Mum!" Callie screamed.

The small Russian town was facing a blistering cold snowstorm, when it came to an abrupt end. The snow settled, covering the earth in a fresh pristine layer of white, the ancient buildings suddenly becoming more visible. The primeval town had been erased from the memory of humans, the wooden houses remained weak – any of the next storms had the power to blow them away, but the houses remained stubborn, refusing to give in to the power of Mother Nature. Everything seemed natural and in place, that was apart from the black, floating figure. The cloaked figure levitated over the snow at a slow pace, without making a footstep, allowing the snow to maintain its purity.

The Dark Witch had travelled long and far according to the instructions of The Scrolls of Decimation… returning to a suppressed time of their own.

The graveyard remained calm as the Dark Witch entered. Floating past the graves, the Dark Witch moved towards the back of the graveyard where an ancient angel oak tree hung, frozen with spectacular stalactites – a beautiful masterpiece. Underneath the tree was a gravestone. *Rowan Drukheim* was faintly engraved on the stone.

Looming over the grave, the Dark Witch extended their arms, chanting. The ground shuddered, cracking instantly as the snow seeped into the cracks. Eventually, with a final thrust, the grave caved inwards, disappearing as a wooden coffin was revealed six feet below. A frail skeleton remained inside the eroded coffin. For the first time ever, the Dark Witch showed a piece of remorse, bowing before entering the grave.

The Dark Witch levitated downwards into the ground until they were face to face with the human remains, staring into the oblivion of the skull's eye sockets. The Dark Witch seemed to examine the face before they turned their gaze towards the skeleton's chest.

A square object, which had once been wrapped tightly, now tasted its first gaze of the world in almost four hundred years. The Dark Witch grappled the object without remorse, murmuring some ancient words before bowing their head and returning to the frozen wasteland.

Touching down on the ground, massaging their feet into the soft snow, the Dark Witch held the item in their hand – a small wooden box that looked as though it had not suffered the consequences of time.

Overjoyed with their finding, after hundreds of years of searching, planning, the Dark Witch expelled a ravenous wind from their body, causing a hurricane of snow. The winds were far more powerful than anything that came through this town before. As the Dark Witch laughed, the hurricane expanded, consuming the graveyard and forgotten town. The gravestones were de-rooted from the ground, the frail houses which had stood the test of time were blown away by the winds. After almost four hundred years of waiting and scheming, the Dark Witch finally had the items they need for their master plan.

The snowy hurricane subsided, the once-stubborn town now having been removed from the earth along with the graveyard. The only thing which remained was the angel oak tree.

As the snow sprinkled down, the Dark Witch removed their overly boisterous clothing to reveal a more refined cloak which hugged the figure of the person within, showing a more feminine figure. Through the darkness which concealed the face, the Dark Witch was grinning. The sacrifices and gathering of chi were now complete, and only two things remained to obtain. One was a vampire and the other, the Perfect Blood.

25
NIGHT OF DARKNESS

The last couple of days had been non-stop for Callie. Diana was now in hospital, having been induced into a coma – meaning Callie was in between the hospital, school and Tyler's house. Despite hers and Tyler's best efforts, their vampire venom was unable to heal Diana, something that confused and concerned Cara, who was now brewing her best natural remedy, thinking something more sinister was behind this. On top of all this, the three friends researched the Sisterhood of Witches which proved more difficult as the books in Tyler's library didn't provide anything useful. With everything piling up, Callie needed a moment to focus on herself.

She sat outside her favourite coffee shop, sipping on her oat latte, her phone placed on the silver metallic table in front of her. She was watching it patiently, hoping to receive a phone call from the hospital to tell her that her mother was okay and that she was walking around, but she was doubtful. The horrible image of her mother collapsing still haunted her memory. She remained seated watching the throngs of people pass by. Families, couples and teenagers, all having fun… unaware of what the world was truly like. In the distance, Callie saw a group of girls from school in the year below. They all looked identical – straight hair, blue jeans and white blouses that showed off their poorly fake tanned bodies. They were thirteen going on sixteen, the way they were acting.

However, behind the group of girls was a man. A man that caught Callie's attention. Diana had always taught Callie to be aware of her surroundings and how to identity a vampire hunter. An average built man, wearing black sports gear and a pair of white running shoes spoke into the phone, now and then glancing towards Callie. Callie hid her searching eyes behind her sunglasses. Diana had taught Callie hunters would normally choose tight clothing, allowing them to run and fight effectively. Sports clothing being the best choice for a new hunter.

Listen to their heart rate, it will always tell you more, said Diana's voice in Callie's head. Callie remembered the lessons Tyler had taught her about focussing her hearing.

Zoning out from the world and closing her eyes behind her sunglasses, she knew the general direction in which to focus her hearing. Firstly, it felt like there was a hummingbird in her head, the dozens of heartbeats all pumping at their usual rate, but as she slowly removed each heartbeat to focus on the man's, she caught wind of his conversation.

"She is just sitting there, looking around… She has been sitting outside the café for at least an hour… It's hard to tell… Okay, bye."

Callie opened her eyes. He had disappeared from where he was once standing. She gulped, but she knew to keep calm.

If you ever come across a hunter, run. If they attack you, knock them out. If they go to kill you, you kill them first, Diana's final teaching drifted into Callie's head.

Callie rose from her seat, picking up her phone and moving away. She walked into the throng of people heading towards the alleyway, a shortcut out of the centre. Leaving the crowd of people and walking into the shaded alleyway full of over-flowing bins, Callie turned the corner to see the fence which led to a car park. Alone, she removed her sunglasses, turning round to make sure no one had followed her. Softly, she leapt from the ground and into the air, gliding over the eight-foot fence that blocked her exit. Landing gently on her knees, she heard a haughty laugh. Callie gasped, thinking she had avoided detection, but she was wrong. She looked at the man, who leant casually against the alleyway wall.

"This will be fun," he said.

"What makes you think that?" said Callie, rising to her feet, ready for a fight. The man shrugged his shoulders. He opened the palm of his hand, and a silver ball fell out and rolled towards Callie.

"It's cute," she said, curling her lips mockingly. She looked at the man, her eyes turning crimson red as thick red veins appeared under her face. Her precise, razor-sharp fangs appeared from her gums. She leapt for the man, but before she even made it halfway, the man pressed a button.

The silver ball exploded, spraying a white mist into the air. Callie howled with pain as the fine mist attacked her skin. She collapsed to the floor, her skin blistering and her eyes burning from the Wild Rose poison. Through her distorted vision, she watched as a black blur approached, dealing an almighty punch which dislocated her jaw immediately. Struggling to breath, her lungs burning, she awaited the wooden stake to pierce her heart, ending her life. But another punch landed in her stomach. Lying on the floor helpless, the hunter continued his attack, kicking her stomach, but despite every kick and punch, the effects of the silver ball wore off, and Callie regained her vision.

The hunter readied himself to kick her in the head. Callie focussed her vision and grabbed his foot before it touched her, the man's shoe centimetres from her eyes. Callie screamed, letting her rage free. Her senses returned. Despite feeling dizzy, she would not stop fighting for her life. The hunter fell backwards as Callie shoved her jaw back into place, moaning when it clicked. She rose to her feet, feeling her body regain its power.

She growled menacingly, sounding like a raging tiger as she tied her hair back in a ponytail.

"That's it," she said, venom in her voice. Callie ran at vamp speed, tackling the man into the wall. In a blur, she turned her back to the man, grabbing his arm and dislocating his shoulder. She pulled the man forwards, hurtling him towards the ground. Revelling in the pain she had caused him; she muffled his scream before she knocked him out cold. The hunter's body remained lifeless.

She placed her sunglasses back on her face, covering her bloodshot eyes. Withdrawing her phone from her pocket, Callie quickly typed a message to Tyler and Aiden. Following the route of the alley, leaving the body of the man behind, she turned the final corner, busy sending her message before she stopped in her tracks. Callie looked up to be greeted by a blacked-out VHA vehicle with three masked figures waiting for her.

For once in what seemed like forever, Tyler was able to enjoy his run. Aiden was at the VHA and Callie wanted some alone time, allowing Tyler to escape the clutches of Cara and enjoy the sunny afternoon. Running through Oakdale Monument Park at normal human speed, he was indulging in the chorus of the birds and sounds of the tree leaves singing amongst the wind.

Kids were playing on the silver sphere monument in the centre of the park. The skeletal metal eyesore monument had been erected to mark the history of Oakdale in 1990. Tyler had been present at the event, remembering the evening well – the night which ended Lesa's control over him and her life.

Distancing himself from the monument and the memories, Tyler carried on down his normal route. Any minute now, he would be approaching the beautiful stream that came down from the nearby hills. It always glistened in the sun. Disappearing deep into the woods, where only certain adventurous teenagers or adults would go, Tyler was able to relax and speed up. But as he turned, following the stream, he stopped running, frozen in his tracks.

A body lay mutilated in the stream. The sickening sight made Tyler's stomach turn, but he ignored it. This wouldn't have been the first time he had seen a body like this. Cautiously approaching the body, Tyler looked around. Nobody else was here. He was alone. The clearness of the stream had now been polluted with the man's blood, like poison.

Tyler knelt down timidly, studying the corpse. The body swayed in the stream, their back to Tyler. The man's hair was singed in places, leaving sore blisters on his skin.

Continuing to sniff round like a dog looking for treats, to make sure he was the only being around, Tyler couldn't shake a daunting feeling that this body had been purposely left here for him to find.

The forest remained tranquil, but Tyler decided to move the man as the blood continued to seep from the front of the body.

Tyler rolled the man over and jumped back when he saw the long scar down the front of his body, as though he'd been sliced as easily as a piece of paper. "It's beautiful, isn't it?" said a voice behind. Tyler jumped to his feet, he gazed towards a black hooded figure levitating over the ground on the opposite side of the stream. Tyler felt his stomach sink, at the presence of the Dark Witch.

Callie growled with pain as she dropped her phone. A syringe, shot by a hunter, pierced her skin as she felt the frozen liquid enter her body.

"What was that?" said Callie, pulling the syringe from her arm. She felt the immediate effect of the unknown liquid. She tumbled backwards falling to one knee, her arm going numb as the odd sensation travelled through her body.

"You really think we would take a vampire on without ammunition?" a tall, unmasked figure spoke as they approached Callie. Callie's skin started to turn pasty white; she felt her lungs begin to restrict her ability to breath.

"Who are you?" she asked, her vison starting to blur. She felt like her blood and muscles were turning to stone. Her limbs started to turn numb. She strained her vision to keep her eyes focussed, trying for a mere second to see who she was talking to.

"Well, I did warn you to watch your back now, didn't I? Unfortunately, I can't put a stake in it today."

Fear vibrated throughout her body. She recognised the voice but how was it possible? She glanced up at Tobias.

"You're supposed to be dead," said Callie hoarsely, shivering from the serum. Tobias knelt down, watching Callie's body turn to ice.

"Like Daria?" he grinned. Callie felt her eyelids grow heavy as her body slowly stopped moving, her head now touching the solid ground. "I guess the school has entered days of mourning for their prince, but this was an opportunity I couldn't miss. All I needed to do for them was to bring them a vampire, and I had the perfect candidate," said Tobias disdainfully. "I'll see you later." He chuckled.

The last scene Callie saw were the hunters scurrying around and back into the VHA vehicle, before she shut her eyes and was greeted by a never-ending darkness, dreading to wake up.

Aiden looked at his phone. The words of the text message from Callie staring back at him:

Hunter tried to capture me. Run.

Aiden stood still, his hands grasping his phone as he stood at his open locker. He couldn't go and get Diana, she was in hospital and in a coma, but why had hunters gone after Callie? As far as Aiden knew, all missions had been suspended for the week following Daria's death, unless these were rouge hunters. But even then, Aiden was sure he would have heard through the grapevine of hunters going rogue to capture vampires. The only thing Aiden was able to think about was asking his father to help, but then that would lead to further complications.

Quickly messaging Tyler, who hadn't already replied to Aiden's spam of texting, he asked him what they should do. Aiden waited in the locker room, his heart racing with every second they were wasting. Yet an unease came over Aiden. It was taking Tyler longer than usual to reply – never had Aiden known Tyler to take longer than five minutes to reply.

The locker room remained quiet with the dirty and muddy footprints plastered over the flooring. This was supposed to be Aiden's first day back, except Aiden was already getting ready to leave. He was ready to take on some rogue vampire hunters if it meant saving Callie and, at this moment Tyler if they had captured him as well.

The locker room door burst opened. Aiden flinched, his breath catching in his throat. The door slammed shut, and Aiden heard the distinct click of the lock being turned. Goosebumps spread over his body, and he wondered if something more sinister was at play. "Hello?" Aiden called, not expecting a reply, yet there were no hollowing footsteps. He moved his back to the lockers, walking slowly to the edge. He peeped his head round… No one was there. Aiden continued to walk slowly while looking around the changing rooms.

"Did you learn anything?" said the voice. Aiden turned to where the voice was before he was greeted by the end of a black gun, knocking him unconscious immediately.

The girl's body lay still. Her arms and face were white in colour; the para-coma serum had forced her into a deep sleep.

"What's the next step?" asked the female hunter. She sat next to Callie watching her intently, making sure she didn't move or twitch.

"We are off to meet them," said Tobias, cautiously watching the road. The sun was setting over the hills, the night rapidly approaching. "The months of planning are about to pay off. I am glad I can be a part of this."

"When does it begin?" asked a male hunter. Tobias turned to face him, taking his eyes away from the road. The sun had disappeared behind the hills, leaving a daunting shadow over the town of Oakdale.

"It begins at the peak of moonlight."

The car exited the forest and was driving down a damaged and overgrown road, heading towards a deserted church in the distance. The night sky was slowly appearing. By this time tomorrow, the world would be cleansed, and a new era would begin. As the car drove closer to the forgotten church, Tobias saw a figure standing by the entrance.

The car engine was turned off; Tobias exited the car commanding the other hunter to take Callie's body inside.

"I never doubted you," said a shadowy figure. Tobias walked up to the man with perfectly combed hair. "Faking our deaths was the best thing we could have done. I am so glad you joined this mission," said Neil Gauze in the shadows of the church.

"I am grateful that you choose me, and I will not let you down. If only Daria was here," said Tobias bowing.

Neil smirked. "Get them inside, we still have work to do." He waved everyone in. The hunters peeled off to their separate duties as though this moment had been well rehearsed.

Neil turned pointedly to Tobias. "The time has come, and we have the Perfect Blood."

26
REVELATIONS

"What do you want?" Tyler shouted, trying to inject some confidence into his voice. This wouldn't be the first time Tyler had fought and killed a plagued witch. The images of Lesa came flooding into his head. So, why would this be any different?

He stared at the cloaked figure, trying to look into the black oblivion of where the face should be. The Dark Witch remained still, continuing to watch the vampire, tilting their head slightly.

The forest chorus had been driven away by an eerie silence that seemed to make time go slower. Daring to wait another minute, fear stabbing at his insides, Tyler tensed all his muscles and ran at vamp speed, towards the Dark Witch, bearing his bleached white fangs.

The Dark Witch dodged the failed tackle attempt, but Tyler rebounded. Using the momentum, he kicked off the ground, jumping from tree to tree like a spider monkey, before once again aiming himself at the Dark Witch. In a blur, Tyler tackled the Dark Witch towards the ground, forcing his shoulder into their stomach. However, just as Tyler expected the Dark Witch to slam against the ground, his grip around their body disappeared and the vampire hit the ground holding a pile of black robes in his arms. He groaned from the rude awakening of slamming into the ground alone and, an ominous laugh echoed throughout the forest.

Rising to his feet, Tyler hissed, bearing his fangs, throwing the pile of black robes to one side. "Where are you?" said Tyler malevolently, his scarlet eyes full of indignation. The spine-tingling laughter continued, then a powerful gust moved through the silent trees, ruffling the branches and leaves against one another. The Dark Witch appeared from a puff of smoke, accompanied by a seven-foot staff with a pale gem glistening at the apex.

"Enough," said the Dark Witch tersely, holding their newly acquired staff, pointing it towards Tyler, who felt his body freeze. "Mother Nature demands what's fair is fair."

Every muscle in Tyler's body now belonged to the Dark Witch. He strained against their magic but couldn't move.

Raising their staff into the air, the Dark Witch launched Tyler into the air and levitated him.

"When the sacrifice has begun," the Dark Witch started to chant in a tongue-twisting language.

Tyler screamed, filling the silent woodland with a torturous tune, feeling the unimaginable pain of Mayhemic magic flow through his body.

"As soon as the sacrifice has been completed, may the vampire wake up. Until then, he shall lie in an eternal sleep, haunted by his worst fears, immobilized and unable to move," the Dark Witch finished. The Dark Witch, snapped their fingers, plunging Tyler's into an instant deep sleep, silencing his screams. Tyler's body fell within a charred circle of grass, and the Dark Witch floated away.

The dark, charred church was eerily silent. The jarring floorboards creaked, and the wind whistled through the crumbling walls. Two metal poles recently erected stood out against the charred wood. Aiden was slumped to one side, hands tied to a pole behind his back. Opposite him, Callie was ghostly white and chained to the pole, the chains the only thing strong enough against her vampiric strength.

Aiden jarred his head backwards, dreaming he had fallen off a kerb. Looking around at his surroundings, wondering where he was, he glanced at the roofless building, the moon shining brightly against the legion of stars in the sky. The moonlight reflected off the glass shards across the floor, and Aiden realised where he was this. This was the same church he had stumbled upon after arriving in Oakdale.

Trying to remember what happened, the faint images slowly returned to his head – the message from Callie and then being knocked out by someone he didn't see. The memory made Aiden wince as he realised how sore his head was. He wanted to rub his head but realised his hands were tied up against the pole. He noticed Callie opposite him.

"Callie," Aiden whispered across the desolate church. Her body appeared lifeless to Aiden, and for a dreaded moment, Aiden wondered if she was dead. "Callie," Aiden whispered once more, but still she remained unresponsive.

"They're here," shouted a voice from the outside. Aiden cracked his head round to see several shadows standing outside the church. They hadn't noticed he was awake yet.

"Callie!" Aiden hissed through clenched teeth.

"Get inside now," an all-too-familiar voice commanded.

Aiden started to fidget, seeing if he could escape or move, but the rope round his wrists were bound tight. The ancient gothic church doors which grasped to their hinges came flying inwards as three hunters walked in.

"Oh, you are awake then," said a hunter. It was Stephanie, a hunter Aiden never had the pleasure of meeting or talking to until now. She was followed by two other hunters who Aiden recognised as Max and Connor, but two figures entered last, grabbing Aiden's immediate attention. Gasping with bewilderment, Aiden had to double-take. Neil and Tobias walked in, unharmed and alive.

"You're alive?" Aiden gasped, surprised he had been able to form these words. The two hunters looked at him just as Aiden heard a moan come from Callie.

"Seems like she is coming to," said Tobias observantly.

"Callie," said Aiden. Callie jolted to life like she had been electrocuted, frantically looking around, locking eyes with Aiden.

"Aiden… where… where are we?" said Callie, alarmed.

"You are in this forbidden church," said Neil. Both Callie and Aiden turned to face him.

"How was I allowed to enter the church?" said Callie cautiously. Neil took a seat upon the creaking floorboards of the podium.

"In 1990, a witch was killed here. Mayhemic magic is embedded within these walls from her death, plus the cross has fallen off, meaning this is not sacred ground anymore," said Neil.

"Why are we here?" said Aiden, turning his attention to Tobias, who came striding over arrogantly.

"You know why you are here." Tobias grinned, glancing down at Aiden.

"You are quite special, aren't you, Aiden." Neil stared at him knowingly.

"What do you mean?" Aiden bluffed.

"Well, you are the Perfect Blood, the most hunted being in the vampire world. I should have seen it. Ever since you joined the VHA, there was an increase in vampire sightings in and around Oakdale. It wasn't until—" Neil stopped before he said too much.

"Until what?" said Callie scornfully. Tobias moved towards Neil.

"You will understand soon. Everything will make sense when they arrive," said Neil.

Callie and Aiden both exchanged a worrisome look with one another.

"I can't wait for your father to find out you were friends with vampires. What a disappointment you must be," Tobias said tauntingly.

"Well, why don't you untie me, and we will see who the disappointment is," Aiden challenged. Neil held Tobias back who attempted to advance on Aiden. The other three vampire hunters were walking around the church, their heavy black boots making the fragile floorboards squeak, disturbing the tension.

Aiden glanced at Callie who looked at him in return. *Are you okay?* he mouthed. She nodded back, looking wary. Then a sudden gust of wind blew the two gothic church doors off their hinges, taking the group by surprise.

"They're here. Well, nice knowing ya, kid," said Neil, waving as he walked past.

"Who's here?" said Callie waspishly.

"I am," said the Dark Witch standing at the doorframe of the church. Aiden fought for breath, sensing the darkness radiate off the powerful being.

"Hello, my love," said Neil bowing. The Dark Witch admired his faithfulness and continued forwards towards the podium, their staff slamming against the feeble floorboards.

"Who are you?" Aiden roared, feeling a monster born into his stomach as the one responsible for his mother's death was metres away.

"You should know who I am, Aiden Dyer."

Aiden frowned. Did he know them? Before he could respond, the Dark Witch grabbed their hood and threw it back, exposing their pale face. The air left Aiden's lungs like he'd been punched.

"Yes, Aiden Dyer. I, Daria, leader of the VHA, am the Dark Witch." Daria turned to face the crowd. She slammed her staff against the wood.

"You're supposed to dead," howled Aiden in disbelief, before he continued. "You're the one who killed my mum!"

Daria mimicked Aiden as if she were making fun of him, laughing as he finished, a total contrast to the Daria Aiden knew at the VHA.

"I cast a spell and blew up the VHA. It was always my plan to fake my death once I had everything ready. And as for your mother, well that's a story." Daria paused, taking a dramatic breath in.

"What do you mean?" Aiden was now trying his best to escape the bounds that kept him still.

"Stop acting like a petulant child, and I'll tell you," Daria teased, but this didn't make Aiden stop; he felt his wrist rubbing against the rope. Daria observed Aiden as he struggled, knowing it was hopeless.

"It began when I awoke from my final witch slumber," Daria started, hoping this would now silence Aiden, which it had as he stopped moving. "As soon as I awoke, I sensed you, I smelt you, I craved you. You were not even a month old, and your blood became the Perfect Blood. I followed the scent, and it bought me to you. Unfortunately, your mother was in the way, a formidable witch—"

"My mother wasn't a witch," Aiden stated.

"How do you know? You never met her." Daria laughed, the sound reaching the corners of the church before she continued. "Your mother had no idea what you were at that moment, so I enlightened her. Before we were about to fight, a vampire entered, and your mother exchanged words with him quickly while I placed a concealment spell on you, subduing your scent so no other vampire or witch could find you. I then killed the vampire.

"That night, which should have been easy, turned out to be quite a disaster. After killing the vampire, your mother and

I fought. She became Mayhemic, and she almost killed me but failed. I escaped and left her to die under the starry sky." Daria paused for a moment. "The thing about Mayhemic magic is it's unpredictable. Magic at its purest is pure mayhem; it's not meant to be controlled. But the Supreme Witches channelled magic and used spells to control it, but when a witch becomes Mayhemic, the spell they cast can be interpreted in any way. The incarceration spell your mother cast on me sealed my powers away instead of killing me. It was only when you were due to return that the spell broke."

Aiden was still. He now knew his mother died protecting him. All along, he thought his mother was human, but finding out she was a witch led to so many more questions, questions which he didn't have time to ask.

The hunters, Tobias and Neil all seemed in awe of Daria. Callie, on the other hand, was looking at Aiden, sensing his broken heart.

"We are going to kill you," she promised.

"Good luck, but back to the main story. I must thank you. You made my life a hell of a lot easier when you found the Scrolls of Decimation. Shun played me at my own game, but now I have everything that I need to conduct the forbidden spell." Daria walked towards the podium. Standing tall at the top, she pulled her black pendant necklace from her neck, breaking the black crystal within her palm. Concealed in the shards of the crystal was a small sapphire diamond. Daria threw the diamond into the air. Callie, and now Aiden, watched, half expecting it to fall back down and smash, but it didn't. It remained and hovered over her head.

"What's that?" asked Callie.

"This is the Stone of Life. The Stone of Life was made by the four great witches using the blood from the Perfect Blood. These four witches were known as the Sisterhood of Witch—"

"Three witches," said Callie, correcting Daria. Daria glanced over to the vampire with a grimace.

"Four Witches. Those weak women believed they killed the fourth witch, but she was intelligent and cunning. After the creation of the Stone of Life, the fourth witch discovered a plot to kill her because she was the only one who saw the power that it held and what it could do with the Perfect Blood. So one night, the fourth witch placed a powerful spell on herself, that if she were hit with a killing spell she would enter a deep slumber. As the fourth witch predicted, that evening, the three witches came and killed her. Well, they thought they killed me." The church was silent, the sudden realisation set in. Neil, on the other hand, crossed his arms smugly, knowing all along Daria was the fourth witch of the Sisterhood of Witches.

"You're the fourth witch?" said Aiden for clarification. Daria ignored him, thinking she had made herself perfectly clear.

"Obviously, they tried to destroy the Stone of Life, but were unsuccessful as it can only be destroyed once it has been activated. They buried the Stone of Life with the Perfect Blood, Rowan Drukheim. One of the scrolls held the spell to use the stone. Ever since I awoke from the Witch's Slumber, I have been searching the earth for Scrolls of Decimation to rid the world of vampires."

"But why do you want to rid the world of vampires?" Callie screeched.

"Because they did this to me!" Daria yelled at Callie. The blackened church went silent as Daria moved her staff through the air, the gem wrapped within the top glowed magnificently, drawing Aiden's attention, but as it stopped glowing, Aiden was drawn to the monstrous, true face of Daria. The initial shock made both he and Callie look away. Daria's true form was horrifying. Her face was long and disjointed, a long scar replaced her right eye, and her head was balding, the remaining hair like straw. She cackled, almost whistling through the gaps in her teeth.

"A vampire killed my entire family and showed no mercy to me. This is how they left me, deformed and hideous," she cried. "I will be the one to erase the vampire race and complete the prophecy."

"What prophecy?" asked Aiden, still looking away.

"In the Library of Wickery, in the Chamber of the Darkol. The Darkol prophecy predicts that 'the fifth Perfect Blood shall change the world.' You are the fifth Perfect Blood, Aiden Dyer, so let's change the world," said Daria fervently.

"There's a prophecy about me?" Aiden asked, moving his head furtively.

"Yes, but less about you. It's time to complete the spell," said Daria.

Aiden was shell-shocked. He didn't know what to say. Why was there a prophecy about him? What did this mean? Aiden repeated the prophecy in his head. *The fifth Perfect Blood shall change the world.* Change the world? Yes, because no matter what Aiden knew, he was going to kill Daria.

"What's needed to complete the spell then?" said Tobias inquisitively. All the heads in the church turned to face the young hunter at Neil's side.

"Good question, my curious hunter. For the Stone of Life to work, we need two objects. One which is extremely common in this world and the other extremely rare. One which appears almost once every two to three hundred years." Daria paused. She began to pour a white sand around her, concealing her in a large circle. "These are the two substances which offer structure to the circle that I have just drawn." Daria finished drawing the circle, starting to draw a triangle shape concealing the circle within. "One is the heart of a vampire and the other the blood of the Perfect Blood – the most powerful type of chi. With these two combined, I will be able to rid the world of vampires once and for all."

Callie and Aiden looked at one another terrified, both understanding why they were now needed for the ritual. Daria turned her disfigured head and looked at Callie menacingly. "Bring me the girl." Aiden pulled against the rope, but there was no way for him to escape.

Stephanie, Max and Connor released Callie from the metal pole, the chains remaining, keeping her captive.

"Aiden!" said Callie hysterically. Her strength was still weak from the serum. Daria chanted, her body convulsing suddenly until it stopped. Daria moved her finger, signalling the hunter to bring her the vampire. Within moments, Daria and Callie were eye to eye.

"Pretty," said Daria, studying Callie's face before she forced her arm into her chest. The metal chains which restrained Callie now dissipated into a silver dust. Callie's eyes widened as she screamed, feeling Daria's hand around her heart. Max and Connor continued to restrain Callie.

"Callie!" Aiden cried.

Daria withdrew her hand from Callie's chest, holding Callie's heart in her bloodied hand. Aiden wrestled against his bonds, the rope burning and rubbing his wrists raw.

And then Callie dropped to the floor, dead.

27
THE FORBIDDEN SPELL

Tyler lay peacefully under the moonlight. Animals had retreated into their burrows and nests as the wind blew across a nocturnal land. A seared circle of grass that surrounded Tyler had slowly faded as the events of the night unfolded. Tyler's calm exterior didn't reveal the trauma he was reliving on the inside. He dreamt of the night he was transformed, remembering the glowing scarlet eyes from the bush in Central Park, then waking up in the coffin that he had been buried alive in… the dream was on constant repeat. Then suddenly, Tyler bolted upright, gasping deeply. Alone in the forest clearing, Tyler rose to his feet looking down at the charred grass.

You can only awake when the sacrifice has taken place. The words of the Dark Witch echoed in Tyler's head.

"Callie," said Tyler in disbelief, feeling his dead heart sting with pain. Tyler lifted his nose into the evenfall air, sniffing the insatiable scent that only belonged to one person... Aiden. "Desperate times call for desperate measures, Tyler whispered as he bolted towards Oakdale hospital knowing he needed Diana Shaw and Jason Dyer's help.

Callie's body lay at the bottom of Daria's feet. Aiden, now exhausted from trying to escape, felt a warm trickle down his hands; the friction from the ropes had burnt the skin from his wrists, leaving them raw and bloodied. Callie's body was still and lifeless.

"Callie," Aiden whimpered, tears falling from his eyes.

"Now, now, no time for tears," said Daria in a sly manner, holding Callie's heart. Aiden turned to face the witch. Callie's heart started to defy gravity, rising from Daria's hand upwards, towards the stone. Daria bonded the two together. The blue stone absorbed the heart. A surge of power vibrated outwards, the hunters fighting the force to remain standing. Aiden detected a slight hum from the stone. Daria looked towards Aiden. The stench of his blood infected the room. She took a deep breath in, her body shivering with the need for his blood. Pointing towards Aiden, she spoke, "Now it's your turn."

Jason sat quietly by Diana's bedside. Her breathing was slow and feeble, the doctors still unable to explain what had happened to her. Jason checked his phone, looking for any messages or missed calls from Aiden. His screen was blank. Aiden hadn't been in contact with Jason all evening. He would normally have sent a text to say he was home… but there was nothing.

"Jason," said a voice that shattered the silence of the hospital room. Catching Jason off guard, he leapt to his feet, turning round to face the door of Diana's private room.

"Tyler?" said Jason astonished, wondering why he was standing at the door and how he knew where they were.

"We need to talk," said Tyler cautiously. He raised both his arms in the air, surrendering. Jason had to double take, slightly lost for words at what was happening.

"About what? Why are you raising your hands?" Jason laughed, not sure what to think or do.

Tyler paused for a heartbeat, his expression serious. "You're a vampire hunter. I am a vampire. Aiden is in trouble, and he needs our help," he said, feeling the words tumble out. There was no time to waste, and Tyler needed Jason to grasp the situation at hand.

Jason's face turned stone cold. Tyler was surely lying. This was a joke. Aiden must have told Tyler what he did, and Tyler wanted a piece of the action or he wanted to see what Jason would do. Jason kept his eyes on Tyler, who had now closed the door behind him, yet Jason hadn't got to where he was in life by not being cautious. In a swift movement, Jason withdrew a gun from his back, not wanting to take any chances after his short deliberation.

"Good joke, Tyler," said Jason curtly, snorting towards the end.

"I'm not joking," said Tyler, and in the moment Jason blinked, Tyler moved fast. He had taken Jason's gun and was now pointing it back at the Master Hunter, but Jason was fast too. He spun round, kicking Tyler square in the chest. Tyler dropped the gun as he fell backwards against the wall.

"Then you shall die," said Jason, pulling a wooden stake from his back pocket. He advanced forwards, pushing Tyler against the wall, aiming the stake for Tyler's heart.

"Aiden is in trouble," coughed Tyler, surprised with Jason's strength, whilst concentrating on making sure the stake didn't pierce his skin. "And so is her daughter." Tyler's eyes pointed towards Diana.

"She doesn't have a daughter. She died years ago from cancer," said Jason matter-of-factly, who continued to use all his strength to push the wooden stake closer to Tyler's heart. "My son wouldn't be friends with vampires," said Jason. Yet as he looked at Tyler, a slight itch in the back of Jason's mind said otherwise. Aiden would never be friends with vampires. Aiden obviously didn't know who his friends were. That's what vampires did.

Tyler kept his arms against Jason's, now feeling uncomfortable at how close the wooden stake was to his chest. Tyler knew that if he wanted to he could push Jason back, but if he wanted Jason to believe him, he had to appear weak.

"The Dark Witch has them," said Tyler, and with those words, the pressure which Jason was applying seemed to lift. "We don't have long. I can heal Diana."

Jason studied Tyler carefully, his face etched with the utmost loathing and hatred for Tyler and his kind. "She doesn't have a daughter, and my son isn't friends with vampires," Jason echoed, Tyler sensing the anger in Jason's voice towards the end, seemingly unable to deal with the information in which Tyler had just offered.

"Diana may be a vampire hunter, but she would do anything to make sure that her daughter was safe. Aiden will be dead if we don't leave now. Let me heal Diana," said Tyler carefully. Jason deliberated for a moment. His eyes full of anguish and betrayal.

"How can you heal her?" he asked, and once again reapplied the pressure. The wooden stake inched closer and closer to Tyler's heart.

"I have a natural remedy. Infused with my venom, it will remove any witch's curse and allow me to heal Diana."

"Witch's curse?" Jason's eyes narrowed.

"Let me go and I'll explain," said Tyler.

Jason resisted at first but did so carefully. Tyler released a deep sigh, happy he hadn't been killed. Pulling away from Tyler and back to Diana's bedside, Jason kept a keen eye on Tyler.

Reaching for his pockets, Tyler withdrew a tiny bottle of liquid.

"This is the remedy. I believe the Dark Witch tainted Diana, that's why normal vampire venom won't work," said Tyler, doubting himself for a moment. "I promise you, I will not hurt her." Looking down on the woman who had done so much for him over the last couple years, he knew he had to save her for Callie's sake.

"Wait," said Jason. For a moment, Tyler wasn't sure what the man was doing. Jason knelt down, keeping his eyes on Tyler whilst his hands were searching for something under Diana's bed. Rising to his feet, Tyler saw the distinct glisten of a metal gun barrel.

"I will kill you, if you do anything wrong," Jason put simply, checking the barrel to see if a wooden bullet was loaded. Tyler couldn't help but gulp. He unscrewed the lid and drank the contents of the bottle, wiping his mouth with his arm, before moving to Diana's bedside. The gentle beeping of machines was constant in the background.

Tyler approached Diana's neck, erecting his fangs, and Jason couldn't help himself. Jason moved, pressing his gun to Tyler's head. Tyler felt the cold steel of the gun, remnants of Wild Rose beginning to sting his head. Leaning down, knowing it was now or never, Tyler bit Diana's neck, inserting his venom into her blood, hoping Cara's remedy would work. Feeling every muscle and the warm sensation of blood on his fangs, Tyler pulled back, two puncture holes in Diana's neck. The hospital room remained calm—that was until the soft beeping of machines started speeding up. Jason was about to speak when suddenly Diana woke up screaming, alarming the hospital corridor and shattering the cold silence of her room.

"Diana," said Jason stunned. Tyler took a step back, letting Jason attend to a distressed Diana. Nurses came rushing down the hall towards the room.

"Don't let them come in," said Jason tersely. Tyler nodded, leaving the room to talk to the two nurses that had come scurrying along.

"Di, calm down, it's me," said Jason coolly, focussing his attention solely on Diana. She frantically looked around the hospital room, sweating a river as she twisted her head around, having no idea where she was.

"Jason," she said hoarsely. Her eyes looking everywhere but Jason's face.

"Diana," said Jason sternly. He held her head still, forcing her to look at him.

"Why does my neck ache?" Diana asked. She moved her hand around the two puncture holes, painting her hand in blood from the minor wound.

"It's dealt with," said Tyler, closing the door behind him. Jason looked behind to see the two nurses walking away.

"Tyler," Diana gulped.

"We need to have a chat," said Jason, his eyes snake-like. They were haunting, but Diana had seen them many times before. Besides, she didn't need to explain herself to Jason.

"If I told you, you would have had her killed. She is my daughter, and I am her mother. You lost Amy, what would you do, Jason, if you were about to lose Aiden?" This question resonated with Jason. He grabbed his chest, feeling his heart skip a beat at the mention of his dead wife. "Besides, you've already met my daughter," said Diana.

"I have?"

"Yes, the day we went to London. She was at your door talking to Aiden beforehand."

"We don't have time for this," Tyler interrupted. "The Dark Witch has Aiden and Callie."

It wasn't long before Diana was out of bed. Tyler had dealt with the nurses at the front desk, using his Silvertongue to discharge Diana in record timing, who had made a miraculous recovery in their eyes. Jason remained, helping Diana dress herself as they started to plan what they were going to do. Leaving the hospital, something took hold of Tyler as he took a deep breath. He was able to smell the desirable scent.

"I know where they are," said Tyler.

"How?" Jason asked.

"I can smell Aiden."

The three hunters all had to work together to restrain a frantic Aiden, who was trying his best to escape from their grasp. Tobias and Neil were on the side watching him carelessly.

"Perfect," Daria murmured. She flicked her hand, freezing Aiden. He was unable to move a muscle; the three hunters presented Aiden to Daria like a trophy, his body frozen from Daria's spell.

"After tonight, the world will be cleansed, and it will enter a new era," Daria whispered into his ear. She caressed Aiden's cheek with the back of her finger, looking him up and down. Still unable to move, Aiden cursed at Daria, looking directly into her mutilated face. Pulling her hand away, Daria pulled a knife from its sheath before teasing it around Aiden's sweaty neck.

"Stop!" a voice roared over the church grounds.

Jason, Diana and Tyler stormed in as Daria held the knife to Aiden's neck.

"Dad!" Aiden shouted, recognising his father's voice. "It's Daria," he followed.

Daria turned Aiden around so he was facing his dad, Diana and Tyler at the entrance to the church. Aiden felt the cold steel of the knife against his throat, but he couldn't help but feel bewildered. *What's Tyler doing with my dad? How is he alive?* Aiden was sure that even in a life-and-death situation, Jason would have killed Tyler, knowing he was a vampire. Did this mean he knew the truth? Whatever Tyler had told Jason to get him here had worked, and Aiden was relieved to see them.

"Hello, Daria," said Jason incredulously, just as shocked as Diana when they both saw Neil and the disfigured Daria.

"Hello, Jason and Diana. Have to say I am quite disappointed in your children."

"Well, they are kids, what do you expect," said Jason struggling to look at Daria's face, knowing now was not the time to ask questions.

"Where's my daughter?" Diana snapped.

"Oh what… this wretched creature?" Daria kicked the body that lay in front of her feet. The body fell from the edge of the podium and hit the ground with a thud. Diana let out a heartbreaking scream, the body of her daughter still and pale, her clothes drenched in her own blood.

"I'm going to kill you!" Diana screeched. She held a crossbow loaded with an arrow stun grenade. Aiming at the wall behind Daria, she fired the arrow. The church broke out in irregular flashing visuals and an ear-splitting tune which made Daria release Aiden to cover her ears. Tyler ran, grabbing Aiden, bringing him back to where he stood with Jason and Diana, Aiden now free from Daria's spell.

"You okay?" Tyler asked, handing Aiden a knife.

"Let's kill 'em," Aiden replied. Recovering from the flash grenade, Daria and the other hunters turned to face the hunters and Tyler.

"You can't run, Aiden. I will have your blood by the end of the night," said Daria, pointing a finger at Aiden.

"Come and get me," said Aiden tauntingly.

"Get them!" Daria shouted. Two hunters appeared from behind the pillars attacking Diana. Tobias ran for Aiden, Neil for Jason, and Tyler made quick work of the third hunter. Jumping off the man, fangs baring, Tyler gorged himself on the blood of the hunter, enjoying the moment where he would not feel guilty for killing this person. Tumbling forwards over the dead body on all fours at the bottom of the podium, Tyler roared at Daria, his face smeared with blood.

"Why didn't you kill me?" Tyler asked facing Daria.

"Killing you would have been mercy compared to what the Stone of Life would have done."

"You should have killed me when you had the chance then," said Tyler venomously.

"Evidently," said a hostile Daria.

Tyler pounced at Daria, but she hit him with a jolt of magic from her staff as if he were a baseball and she were the batsman. Tyler was sent flying through the air, crashing into a wall.

Aiden and Tobias were watching each other carefully as they threw punches. Aiden had successfully dodged more than he landed, his cheeks grazed and jaw sore. Tobias grinned, his face still perfect despite Aiden's attempts to break it.

"Come on, Dyer," teased Tobias as he threw another punch. This time aiming for Aiden's head, yet Aiden saw this move coming. Dropping to the floor, Aiden swung his legs around in a pivot, kicking Tobias to the floor. He groaned as Aiden climbed on top of him, punching him relentlessly, bruising the prince of Oakdale School's perfect face. But before he could land another punch, Aiden was tackled off by another person. Rolling to his feet, Aiden saw it was Neil. Jason came running when he saw Aiden in trouble.

"Stay where you are," Daria roared from the end of the church. A black electrical beam exited her fingers, roaring towards Jason.

"Dad!" Aiden shouted, but before the electrical beam hit the hunter, Jason was tackled aside by Tyler. Sighing with relief as Jason and Tyler slid across the floor of the church, Aiden was dazed when he was hit by Neil. Neil punched and kicked Aiden from side to side. Aiden kept his hands up, protecting his head, trying to evade any head shots, his sides sore from the kicks.

"Come on, have I not taught you anything?" Neil mocked. Aiden was waiting for the right moment. He ignored Neil's comment. Neil delivered a final kick as Aiden backtracked falling to his feet, groaning.

Now is the time, Aiden thought. He looked at Neil, quickly analysing his body composure and ran at him. Neil threw three quick punches, but Aiden avoided them easily. On the last punch, Aiden grabbed Neil's arm and used his strength to help hoist him onto his back. Aiden grappled his arms around Neil's neck; he locked his legs around his body and began choking him. The movement was something Neil didn't predict.

"I did learn something," Aiden hissed into Neil's ear, tightening his grip.

"That's for my daughter!" Aiden heard Diana shout, and he watched her force a wooden stake into Tobias's chest, killing him instantly before Neil slammed Aiden into the walls behind him.

Aiden refused to let go, and the adrenaline pulsing through his body helped reduce the pain Neil had inflicted. The way the two were acting looked like Aiden was riding a rampant bull.

Neil started to slow down, his body was screaming for oxygen. Aiden tightened his grip around the man's neck as Neil fell to one knee on the church grounds.

"No!" an echoing voice screeched through the hollow church. Daria looked at Aiden and Neil; she was watching her beloved hunter being choked to death by the boy she despised. She raised her staff in the air, chanting, aiming at Aiden, but Tyler ran, tackling Aiden from Neil's back as a luminous green glow filled the dark church.

A male scream filled the empty grounds.

Aiden was dazed. His head had hit the floorboards from where Tyler had tackled him off Neil's back. Aiden looked up just as Tyler pulled him to his feet. Neil was flapping his arms wildly in the air, his face burning brightly in a mystical green colour. Neil ran from the church screaming, his face burnt and disfigured from the lightning blast. His screams howled through the night as Jason and Diana watched the damaged hunter disappear into the darkness of the forest.

"Aiden," Tyler shouted, drawing his attention away from Neil. "Now." Tyler was right. This was the moment they were waiting for – a moment when Daria would be easy to take down. Jason and Diana were still preoccupied with fighting the rogue hunters.

"Let's do this," said Aiden maliciously. The time had come to avenge his mother.

"We have to destroy the stone," Tyler shouted, readying himself, Aiden nodding in return.

The two boys set off for Daria, and she glared at them both. Tyler pounced and Aiden ran at her.

Daria swung her staff around her head, hitting Tyler with yet another bolt of magic, throwing him against another wall. Aiden avoided the staff. If he got hit with that, who knew what would happen to him.

Aiden tackled Daria by the side, missing her staff once again. Tyler appeared, quickly recovering from the bolt of magic, tackling Daria's upper body. The two boys worked in sync, taking Daria down to the floor and away from the Stone of Life. Her staff flew from her hands and rolled across the podium. Aiden quickly rose to his feet, leaping forwards for her staff. The Stone of Life descended from the air, hovering centimeters from the ground.

Aiden grabbed Daria's staff and turned back round to face her, the staff held high above his head.

Daria moved slowly as Aiden inched closer to the Stone of Life, readying himself to slam the staff down, hoping this would destroy the stone.

"You… you the son of Jason Dyer, would destroy the Stone of Life, destroying the only artefact in the world that can rid the world of vampires," Daria spat.

"The VHA needs to learn a few things about vampires," Aiden replied, readying himself. He heard the distant fighting stop and knew his father was listening. "Some vampires are *not* monsters."

"Don't be stupid," Daria said scornfully.

"Too late," said Aiden. He hammered down the staff from above, slamming it against the Stone of Life. The orb at the end of Daria's staff shattered the stone instantly. Mayhemic magic filled the room, absorbing energy into the staff. Daria screamed before a strong wind erupted from the stones, filling the church ground.

Tyler punched his hands into the floorboards, resisting the strong winds. Jason and Diana held on to a church pillar, their bodies flapping in the air like flags as the gale force winds rolled the dead bodies of Tobias and the other three hunters over the grounds.

Aiden stood on the church podium, still holding the staff against the Stone of Life. Eventually, the winds which erupted from the stone threw Aiden back against the wall.

The powerful winds subsided, and Aiden fell to the floor hitting his head, watching Daria.

"What have you done!" Daria cursed. She ran towards the shattered stone. Aiden watched her, lying on his side, silent from the shock of energy. Daria cursed, looking towards Aiden, but he couldn't hear. A loud ringing noise echoed through his ears. Slowly, Daria's hands started to turn black. The dark marks spread like ink up her arms and across her entire body. Daria held the shattered stone in her hands, but not for much longer. A feeble wind blew through the church. Her arms disintegrated into a dust with the rest of her body slowly following. Her cursed face turned black as she attempted to scream. But nothing exited her mouth. A final breeze blew her body away, and she dissolved into the air. Her black clothing fell to the floor in a heap.

Daria, the Dark Witch, was dead.

Aiden's eyes started to tear up. He was happy. He had avenged his mum, and the Dark Witch was dead, but his heart was still broken – the girl he loved was dead. Her body must have still been lying on the floor in a heap.

Before Aiden shut his eyes, he saw a stunning girl run up to him, her top bloody and her hair a mess, but still she was beautiful to him. In the second before Aiden fainted, he heard the voice he thought he'd never hear again. It was Callie. She screamed his name, and then he blacked out.

28
A New Day

Callie sat there patiently, day in and day out. Jason had stayed for the first few hours, but after a persuasive Diana explained that her daughter would not hurt Aiden, Jason reluctantly left. Checking on him hourly, he began to relax as Jason witnessed how Callie watched Aiden intently, not blinking or moving a muscle. It reminded him of how Amy would watch him recover after a mission.

Diana continued to visit but refused to explain herself to Jason who wanted to understand her reasoning for transforming Callie into a vampire. All she said was, "If the day comes when you lose your son, which I hope it doesn't, come to me then and see what you will do."

Tyler was a recurring guest in Jason's house. Diana and Jason had to leave to clear the church, burning the bodies of the rogue vampire hunters. Neil was the sole survivor but couldn't be found after he escaped, though Tyler was doubtful that he would survive his injuries.

Finally sitting down that night with Diana, Tyler divulged everything to Jason. Jason remained still when he learnt Aiden was the Perfect Blood, but before Tyler could explain any more, Jason raised his hand, signalling him to stop. He needn't know more. He left the table and attended to his son, waiting for him to wake up.

Aiden was unconscious for the third day, when a soft humming broke through. He had heard this tune before… briefly in a lesson once, when she thought no one was listening. The soft melody made Aiden want to stay asleep a while longer, but his body refused, forcing him to wake up.

Aiden opened his eyes. Squinting from the brightness of the room, he turned his head and saw her. Callie, her head cradled in her arm beside Aiden, her eyes shut, as she held his hand. Aiden felt her soft skin against his and didn't want to move as he knew this would be a moment in which he would want to return to in the future. But Callie stopped, and Aiden couldn't help but think she knew he was awake.

"Morning," Aiden whispered hoarsely. Callie looked towards Aiden, overjoyed he was finally awake.

"Hey," she whispered back, looking like she might cry. Aiden rubbed his eyes, still adjusting to the brightness of the room. Callie moved, allowing him to sit up.

"You're alive?" said Aiden, looking into her beautiful forest-like eyes.

"Once the stone was destroyed, my heart regenerated as the spell was incomplete," said Callie.

Aiden couldn't help but smile. The supernatural world was full of curiosity. Placing his forehead against hers, happy to know she was alive, it took a moment for Aiden to realise where he was. In the corner of his eye, he saw the familiar weapons wall, a wooden stake taking centre stage amongst the other weapons, the white walls laced with maps and diagrams Aiden had studied months ago.

"We are in my dad's basement," he choked, feeling his heart skip a beat. "You need to leave." The fear of his father seeing Callie down in the basement caused a sudden rise in adrenaline.

"No, I don't. Jason knows."

"What?" snapped Aiden, finally on the verge of the breakdown that he had been withholding for the last few months. He turned to Callie, who remained calm. She looked at Aiden with adoration, and in that moment, Aiden knew he couldn't waste any more time. He grabbed Callie by her waist and pulled her into his warm body. He pressed his lips against hers dreading the thought of wasting another moment. Butterflies exploded in their stomachs. Callie wrapped her arms around Aiden's neck, her not wanting another day to go by without feeling him against her. Withdrawing, the two chuckled, looking at one another. Aiden wanted to be alone with her for a few minutes, but he heard Callie whisper, "He's awake."

Heavy footsteps broke the silence, and Diana walked into the basement, followed by Tyler, who looked like he had been giggling, Aiden knowing he had heard everything.

"Your father knows everything, Aiden," said Diana.

"That's right," said Jason, appearing behind Diana. Aiden looked at his father, leaning against the walls, bearing the same cold expression. Aiden didn't know what to do. His two vampire best friends were in his dad's basement, the basement which his father used to hunt their kind.

"What do you remember from that night?" said Diana, stepping forwards to readjust a drip.

"Uhm…" Aiden struggled to remember. He rubbed his head when all the memories came flooding back – Daria, the Stone of Life, destroying the stone and Daria's death.

"Everything, I think. How long was I out for?"

"Three days," said Callie.

While he digested the fact that he had been out for three days, Callie pulled the sheets from behind Aiden. Blotches of blood covering the whiteness of the sheet.

"What are you doing with them?" Aiden queried.

"Burning them so no vampire can find you," said Jason abruptly.

"This is for you as well," said Tyler, tossing a metal ring towards Aiden.

"What's this?" Aiden studied the stainless steel ring.

"Cara grew sick of making you bracelets. She found a witch and made a concealment ring for you. It will hinder your scent, and only you can put it on and take it off."

"Finally," said Aiden, himself having grown tired of the constant losing of bracelets.

An uncomfortable silence followed. Aiden looked down at his new ring, knowing that any moment he would have to look at his father and know how disappointed his father must be in him. That was hard to think about, especially after so many months of Jason being proud of Aiden with his VHA training.

"So, you know what I am then, Dad?" said Aiden, guilty as if he had committed a crime. He turned to look at his father.

"I do." Jason and Aiden looked at one another. Callie wanted to hug Aiden whilst Tyler and Diana exchanged timid looks at one another, yet there was no guilt in Aiden's stomach, and he felt stronger than before. "There's no point in telling me anything." Jason remained calm and collected. "When I return to the VHA, the Master Healers and the I-VHA will want to know how it came to be the ex-leader of the VHA was a dangerous witch. They will want to know how she was able to sneak under our radar without any of us knowing. To do so, they will use The Spell on me," said Jason.

"What's *The Spell?*" Aiden asked.

"It's a truth spell. I will tell them everything – what happened and how it came to be. So I need Tyler to Silvertongue my mind and to erase you three from the night and to change what happened. Then I won't lie as I won't know what happened," said Jason.

Aiden did not speak, he felt a little upset knowing he would not have the chance to explain to his father how he met Tyler and Callie, but he knew, after being in the VHA, it was safer this way.

"Aiden, I'm not going to lie. I am disappointed. You are friends with creatures I have hunted my entire life. Creatures which I've protected you from."

Callie and Tyler looked at one another as the basement room remained unpleasant. Aiden was upset but not surprised at what his father had said. He wasn't going to let it get him down after all he had endured. He would have almost been disappointed in his father if he hadn't said any of this.

"Dad," said Aiden, looking straight into his father's eyes, injecting confidence into his voice, "I don't care if you are proud of me or not. What I have been through in the last few months since arriving in Oakdale will astound you. I have been attacked several times, I spoke with Shun Yun Li face-to-face—"

Jason's eyes widened hearing what his son had said.

"And we defeated the Dark Witch. So be proud of me or not, but I am proud myself and I need to believe in myself more. You will accept it. Acceptance is everything because no matter what, I will always be your son."

Callie smirked, Tyler nodded in Aiden's direction and Jason stood still. Even Diana nodded in approval of Aiden's speech.

Pulling on some clothes, feeling good in what he had said, Aiden knew that for this brief moment before Tyler removed Jason's memory, he could be himself, holding Callie's hand in front of his father. Tyler moved behind Jason, breathing in and out, preparing himself.

"Okay. What is it you want me to do?" Tyler asked, knowing what he should say but slightly worried in messing it up.

"Erase all of you from the night. Make sure I know it was Daria that attacked the VHA and that Diana woke up from her coma without your venom. Remove Diana killing Tobias in my mind as well as Neil being there. They were killed in the explosion, and the other hunters were brainwashed."

"Why don't you just tell the truth?" Callie queried.

"Because if I did, the VHA would become insecure. I can sell Daria as the Dark Witch, but selling hunters who willingly choose to follow her will be hard; it will create a divide in the VHA," Jason answered.

"What about Aiden?" Diana piped up. Jason became still. He was looking at Diana who already knew what he should be doing. Jason heaved a great sigh, swallowing his pride and continued.

"Implement a new memory into my mind, I found Aiden stealing information from the VHA, I had a meeting with Daria informing her what Aiden had done. She expelled him, and Aiden can never return to the VHA." Diana nodded with approval, and Aiden felt a distinct tension in Callie's grip.

"Dad," said Aiden compassionately, knowing how hard it was for his father to have said that. Aiden, the first Dyer to not be a part of the VHA since its creation.

"It's okay, son. Just be safe for me. If you need me again, you know what to do," said Jason.

"Let's just hope we never have to make you remember," said Callie.

Tyler began his Silvertongue on Jason, repeating everything Jason had asked him to change. After Tyler had reconstructed Jason's memory, he put Jason to sleep.

"What's gonna happen now?" Callie asked her mother. Diana turned to embrace her daughter, as Tyler helped Aiden lift his father from the chair and take him to his bed, though Tyler's strength did most of the work.

"Now we wait," said Diana. "When he wakes, he will know everything that Tyler had told him, and we continue with our normal lives like normal."

"A new day has dawned over the VHA." Jason stood in front of the VHA the next day. He had a new memory. The hunters sat in silence, all eyes focussed on Jason. "As some of you may know, Daria was the Dark Witch. She betrayed our trust and killed our own." Diana and Hayden sat behind Jason. The two Master Healers were on the other side, with the seven I-VHA hunters in the middle. "Some of you are wondering whether I will become the next leader, but I will not. Diana, Hayden and I, including the I-VHA, will be going through a crucial process to find the next leader. The future candidates will lead the VHA into a new era. An era which will change the world."

Diana exhaled feeling relaxed, knowing that Tyler's Silvertongue had worked on Jason. All Jason knew was that vampires were the enemy, and no one could tell him differ. They had to be eradicated for the good of humankind… unless Tyler's Silvertongue said otherwise.

"Well, that was a pretty entertaining weekend," said Aiden.

"Tell me about it, I died and came back to life… again," Callie joked. The three friends sat under the night sky, the stars glistening like diamonds as Tyler's fire pit crackled in the middle. Aiden and Callie had wrapped themselves in one of Cara's luxury covers, Tyler watching the beginning of his dreaded third wheel status until Lydia returned. The logs crackled under the intense heat of the fire, the embers whipping and dancing in the breeze of the evening.

"Out of all the things we have been worrying about for the past few months, its actually quite nice to worry about homework and whether or not Mr Burton will give us a detention," said Aiden, looking directly at Tyler.

"What do we do with this then?" said Callie. The orange embers vibrated in the fire pit as Callie pulled the wooden box which contained the Scrolls of Decimation from underneath a blanket. She balanced the box on the edge of the fire pit, all three of them knowing the contents.

"How did you get that?" Aiden questioned, feeling a sudden fear rise in his stomach.

"I took it from the church when we rushed you back to your house," said Tyler. The hardened box emitted a foul stench as it balanced on the fire. Without asking, knowing he was the only one able to destroy the contents, Aiden leant forwards and tipped the box into the fire.

"Why did you do that?" Callie asked. The box began to shrivel and crack as a potent smell of burnt flesh filled the air. Aiden regretted the choice he had made, fighting the feeling to be sick.

"Because at the end of the day, I am the only one who can destroy it. If it fell into the wrong hands, who knows what could happen," said Aiden once the smell has lifted from the surrounding air.

The evening progressed without any further talk regarding the box or the Dark Witch. Aiden took a moment and looked at his friends; he was happy. Happy that he and Jason had moved to Oakdale. It had definitely been the best move they had made, and Aiden knew that he was going nowhere.

Oakdale was now his home.

Acknowledgements

I would like to say thank you to my editor, who not only made my book what it is today, but helped me become a better writer. Thank you to Ines, my typesetter, who delicately designed my page layout. A thanks to my proofreader and, finally, thank you to my book cover designer, Franzi, who not only brought my book to life but gave me the perfect shade of red. To everyone who helped me, words cannot describe how grateful I am, so thank you.

Author

B. T. Annett is a young adult fantasy author. Born and raised in West London, Annett has a love of travel and new adventures. He began writing his debut novel, *The Perfect Blood* in 2012 when he was just fourteen, and in 2019, he earned a bachelor in sports science.

If you would like to get in contact with B. T. Annett, go to www.btannett.com and sign up for his emailing list to keep up-to-date with news regarding The Perfect Blood Series.

Printed in Great Britain
by Amazon